Some Must Watch

Some Must Watch

Inspired the Classic Film *The Spiral Staircase*

Ethel Lina White

W F HOWES LTD

This large print edition published in 2015 by
W F Howes Ltd
Unit 4, Rearsby Business Park, Gaddesby Lane,
Rearsby, Leicester LE7 4YH

1 3 5 7 9 10 8 6 4 2

First published in the United Kingdom in 2012
by Arcturus Publishing Limited

A CIP catalogue record for this book is available
from the British Library

ISBN 978 1 47128 681 0

Typeset by Palimpsest Book Production Limited,
Falkirk, Stirlingshire

Printed and bound in Great Britain
by TJ International Ltd, Padstow, Cornwall

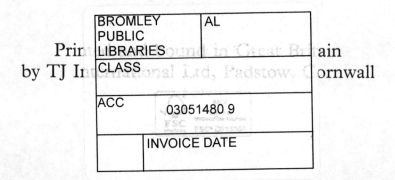

CHAPTER 1

THE TREE

Helen realized that she had walked too far just as daylight was beginning to fade.

As she looked around her, she was struck by the desolation of the country. During her long walk, she had met no one, and had passed no cottage. The high-banked lanes, which blocked her view, were little better than steep mudslides. On either side of her rose the hills – barren sepia mounds, blurred by a fine spit of rain.

Over all hung a heavy sense of expectancy, as though the valley awaited some disaster. In the distance – too far away to be even a threat – rumbled faint, lumpy sounds of thunder.

Fortunately Helen was a realist, used to facing hard economic facts, and not prone to self-pity. Of soaring spirit, yet possessed of sound common sense, she believed that those thinly-veiled pitfalls over hell – heaviness of body and darkness of spirit – could be explained away by liver or atmospherics.

Small and pale as a slip of crescent moon, she was only redeemed from insignificance by her bush of light-red springy hair. But, in spite of her unostentatious appearance, she throbbed with a passion for life, expressed in an expectancy of the future, which made her welcome each fresh day, and shred its interest from every hour and minute.

As a child, she pestered strangers to tell her the time, not from a mere dull wish to know whether it were early or late, but from a specialized curiosity to see their watches. This habit persisted when she had to earn her own living, under the roofs of fortunate people who possessed houses of their own.

Her one dread was being out of work. She could estimate, therefore, the scores of replies which had probably been received as a result of the advertisement for a lady-help at Professor Warren's country house; and, as soon as she arrived at the Summit, she realized that its very loneliness had helped to remove her from the ranks of the unemployed.

It was tucked away in a corner, somewhere at the union of three counties, on the border-line between England and Wales. The nearest town was twenty-two miles away – the nearest village, twelve. No maid would stay at such a forsaken pocket – a pocket with a hole in it – through which dribbled a chronic shrinkage of domestic labour.

Mrs Oates, who, with her husband, helped to fill the breach, summed up the situation to Helen, when they met, by appointment, at the Ladies Waiting Room, at Hereford.

'I told Miss Warren as she'd *have* to get a lady. No one else would put up with it.'

Helen agreed that ladies were a drug in the market. She had enjoyed some months of enforced leisure, and was only too grateful for the security of any home, after weeks of stringent economy – since 'starvation' is a word not found in a lady's vocabulary. Apart from the essential loneliness of the locality, it was an excellent post, for she had not only a nice room and good food, but she took her meals with the family.

The last fact counted, with her, for more than a gesture of consideration, since it gave her the chance to study her employers. She was lucky in being able to project herself into their lives, for she could rarely afford a seat at the Pictures, and had to extract her entertainment from the raw material of life.

The Warren family possessed some of the elements of drama. The Professor, who was a widower, and his sister and housekeeper – Miss Warren – were middle-aged to elderly. Helen classified them as definite types, academic, frigid, and well-bred, but otherwise devoid of the vital human interest.

Their step-mother, however, old Lady Warren – the invalid in the blue room – was of richer mould. Blood and mud had been used in her mixture, and the whole was churned up, thrice daily, by a dose of evil temper. She was the terror of the household; only yesterday, she had flung a basin of gruel at her nurse's head.

It had been her natural and ladylike protest against this substitute for the rare steak, which she preferred, but was unable to chew. As her aim was excellent, it had achieved the desired result; that morning Oates had driven the departing nurse into the town, and was coming back, in the evening, with a fresh target.

Helen, who had not yet been brought into contact with the old lady, rather admired her spirit. The household was waiting for her to die, but she still called the tune. Every morning, Death knocked politely on the door of the blue room; and Lady Warren saluted him in her customary fashion, with a thumb to her nose.

Besides this low-comedy relief, Helen suspected the triangle situation, as represented by the Professor's son, his daughter-in-law, and the resident pupil, whom the Professor was coaching for the Indian Civil Service. The son – a clever, ugly youth – was violently and aggressively in love with his wife, Simone. She was an unusually attractive girl, with money of her own, and a wanton streak in her composition.

To put it mildly, she was an experimentalist with men. At present, she was plainly trying to make sentimental history with the pupil, Stephen Rice – a good-looking casual young sprig, rejected of Oxford. Helen liked him instinctively, and hoped he would continue to resist the lady.

Although her curiosity hovered around the Summit and its inmates, her duties were her chief interest. The reminder that she had a new job to hold down made her pull a face as she glanced at her watch.

4

Already the first shadows were beginning to stir, as prelude to the short interlude between the lights. Very soon it would be dark.

A long walk stretched between her and the Summit. She could see it, in the distance, blocked with solid assurance, against the background of shrouded hills. But, dividing them, yawned a bowl of empty country, which dipped down for about a mile, into a tree-lined hollow, before it climbed up a corresponding slope, to the young plantation on its crest.

In spite of her stoicism, Helen's heart sank faintly at the prospect of re-passing through that choked dell. Since she had come to the Summit, she had been struck by the density of the surrounding undergrowth. When she looked out of the windows, at twilight, the evergreen shrubs on the lawn seemed actually to move and advance closer to the walls, as though they were pioneers in a creeping invasion.

Feeling secure as in a fortress, she enjoyed the contrast between the witched garden and the solid house, cheerful with lights and voices. She was inside and safe. But now, she was outside, and nearly two miles away.

'Idiot,' she told herself, 'it's not late. It's only dark. *Scram.*'

As she was denied the employer's privilege of abuse, she got even by saying exactly what she liked to herself. She whipped up her courage by calling herself a choice collection of names, as she began to run cautiously, slipping on the slimy camber of the lane, since the rutted middle was too stony for safety.

She kept her eyes fixed on her goal, which seemed to be sinking gradually into the ground, as she dipped lower and lower. Just before she lost sight of it, a light gleamed out in the window of the blue room.

It seemed to her a signal, calling her back to a special duty. Every evening, at twilight, she had to go around the house, locking the doors and putting the shutters over the windows. Hitherto, she had derided the job as the limit of precaution; but, here, in the tenebrous solitude, it assumed an unpleasant significance.

There was a connection between it and a certain atmosphere of tension – excitement in the kitchen, whispers in the drawing-room – which emanated from a background of murder.

Murder. Helen shied instinctively at the word. Her mind was too healthy to regard crime other than fiction, which turned newspapers into the sensational kind of reading matter, which is sold on Railway Station bookstalls. It was impossible to believe that these tragedies happened to real people.

She forced herself to think of a safer subject.

'Suppose I won the Irish Sweep.'

But, as the lane dropped deeper, its steep banks shutting out the light, she discovered that she had a mind above mere supposititious wealth. Simple pleasures appealed to her more at that moment

– the safety of the kitchen at the Summit, with Mrs Oates and the ginger cat for company, and dripping-toast for tea.

She made another start.

'Suppose I won the Irish Sweep. *Someone's got to win.* Out of all the millions of people in the world, a few people are *marked* out to win fortunes. Staggering.'

Unfortunately, the thought introduced another equally stupendous.

'Yes. And out of all the millions of people who die in their beds, a few are marked out to be murdered.'

She switched off the current of her thoughts, for before her, crouched the black mouth of the hollow.

When she had crossed it, earlier in the afternoon, she had been chiefly concerned in picking out a fairly dry passage over the rich black mould formed by leaf-deposits. She had only marked it down as a sheltered spot in which to search for early primroses.

But the promise of spring was now only a mockery. As she advanced, the place seemed an area of desolation and decay, with wind-falls for crops. In this melancholy trough – choked with seasonal litter – sound was reduced to furtive rustles; light was shrunken to a dark miasma, through which trees loomed with the semblance of men.

Suddenly, murder ceased to be a special fiction of the Press. It became real – a menace and a monstrosity.

Helen could no longer control her thoughts, as she remembered what Mrs Oates had told her about the crimes. There were four of them – credibly the work of some maniac, whose chosen victims were girls.

The first two murders were committed in the town, which was too far away from the Summit for the inmates to worry. The third took place in a village, but still comfortably remote. The last girl was strangled in a lonely country-house, within a five-mile radius of Professor Warren's residence.

It was an uncomfortable reminder that the maniac was growing bolder with success. Each time, he penetrated closer into the privacy of his victim.

'The first time, it was just a street-murder,' thought Helen. 'Then, he hid in a garden. After that, he went inside a house. And then – right upstairs. You ought to feel safe there.'

Although she was determined not to yield to panic, and run, she ceased to pick her way between cart-ruts filled with water, but plunged recklessly into muddy patches, whose suction glugged at the soles of her shoes. She had reached the densest part of the grove, where the trees inter-grew in stunting overcrowding.

To her imagination, the place was suggestive of evil. Tattered leaves still hung to bare boughs, unpleasantly suggestive of rags of decaying flesh fluttering from a gibbet. A sluggish stream was clogged with dead leaves. Derelict litter of broken boots and rusty tins cropped out of a rank growth of docks and nettles, to mark a tramp's camping-place.

Again Helen thought of the murders.

'It's coming nearer – and nearer. Nearer to *us*.'

Suddenly, she wondered if she were being followed. As she stopped to listen, the hollow seemed to be murmurous with faint sounds – the whisper of shrivelled leaves, the snapping of twigs, the chuckles of dripping water.

It was possible to fancy anything. Although she knew that, if she ran, her imagination would gallop away with her, she rushed across the soft ground, collecting poultices of mud on the soles of her boots.

Her heart was pounding when the opposite lane reared itself in front of her, like the wall of a house. The steepness however proved deceptive, for, around the first bend, it doubled, like a crooked arm, to relieve the steepness of the gradient.

Once more, Helen's normal courage returned, for her watch told her that she had won her race against time. The precious new job was safe. Her legs ached as she toiled upwards, but she cheered herself by the reminders that a merry heart goes all the way – that the longest lane has a turning – that every step was bringing her nearer home.

Presently she reached the top of the rise, and entered the plantation, which was thinly planted with young firs and larches, and carpeted with fallen needles. At its thickest part, she could see through it, and, suddenly, she caught sight of the Summit.

It was no longer a distant silhouette, but was so close that she could distinguish the colour of the window-curtains in the blue room. The vegetable garden sloped down to the wall which bounded the plantation, and a coil of rising smoke, together with a cheerful whistle told her that the gardener was on the other side, making a bonfire.

At the sight of her goal, Helen slackened her pace. Now that it was over, her escapade seemed an adventure, so that she felt reluctant to return to dull routine. Very soon, she would be going round, locking up in readiness for Curfew. It sounded dull, for she had forgotten that, in the darkness of the hollow, she realized the significance of a barred bedroom window.

The rising wind spattered her face with rain, and increased her sense of rebellion against four walls and a roof. She told herself that it was blowing up for a dirty night, as she walked towards the front gate.

At its end, the plantation thinned down to a single avenue of trees, through which she could see the stone posts of the entrance to the Summit, and the laurels of the drive. As she watched, fresh lights glowed through the drawing-room windows.

It was the promise of tea – calling her home. She was on the point of breaking into a run, when her heart gave a sudden leap.

She was positive that the furthest tree had moved.

She stopped and looked at it more closely, only to conclude that her fancy had tricked her. It was lifeless and motionless, like the rest. Yet there was something about its shape – some slight distortion of the trunk – which filled her with vague distrust.

It was not a question of logic – she only knew that she did not want to pass that special tree.

As she lingered, in hesitation, her early training asserted itself. She began to earn her living, at the age of fourteen, by exercising the dogs of the wealthy. As these rich dogs were better-fed, and stronger than herself, they often tried to control a situation, so she was used to making quick decisions.

In this instance, her instinct dictated a short way home, which involved a diagonal cut across boggy ground, through a patch of briars, and over the garden wall.

She carried through her programme, in the minimum of time, and with little material damage, but complete loss of dignity. After a safe, but earthy, landing in the cabbage-bed, she walked around to the front door. With her latchkey in the lock, she turned, for a last look at the plantation, visible through the gates.

She was just in time to see the last tree split into two, as a man slipped from behind its trunk, and disappeared into the shadow.

CHAPTER 2

THE FIRST CRACKS

The surge of Helen's curiosity was stronger than any other emotion. It compelled her to rush down the drive, in an effort to investigate the mystery. But when she reached the gate she could see only lines of trunks, criss-crossing in confusing perspectives.

Forgetful of her duties, she stood gazing into the gloom of the plantation while a first star trembled through a rent in the tattered clouds.

'It *was* a man,' she thought triumphantly, 'so I was right. He was hiding.'

She knew that the incident admitted the simple explanation of a young man waiting for his sweetheart. Yet she rejected it, partly because she wanted a thrill, and partly because she did not believe it met the case. In her opinion, a lover would naturally pass the time by pacing his beat, or smoking a cigarette.

But the rigid pose, and the lengthy vigil, while the man stood in mimicry of a tree, suggested a tenacious purpose. It reminded her of the concentrated patience of a crocodile, lurking in the shadow of a river bank, to pounce on its prey.

'Well, whatever he was doing, I'm glad I didn't pass him,' she decided as she turned to go back to the house.

It was a tall grey stone building, of late Victorian architecture, and it looked strangely out of keeping with the savage landscape. Built with a flight of eleven stone steps leading up to the front door, and large windows, protected with green jalousies, it was typical of the residential quarter of a prosperous town. It should have been surrounded by an acre of well-kept garden, and situated in a private road, with lamp-posts and a pillar-box.

For all that, it offered a solidly resistant front to the solitude. Its state of excellent repair was evidence that no money was spared to keep it weather-proof. There was no blistered paint, no defective guttering. The whole was somehow suggestive of a house which, at a pinch, could be rendered secure as an armored car.

It glowed with electric-light, for Oates' principal duty was to work the generating plant. A single wire overhead was also a comfortable reassurance of its link with civilization.

Helen no longer felt any wish to linger outside. The evening mists were rising so that the evergreen shrubs, which clumped the lawn, appeared to quiver into life. Viewed through a veil of vapour, they looked black and grim, like mourners assisting at a funeral.

'If I don't hurry, they'll get between me and the

house, and head me off,' Helen told herself, still playing her favourite game of make-believe. She had some excuse for her childishness, since her sole relaxation had been a tramp through muddy blind lanes, instead of three hours at the Pictures.

She ran eagerly up the steps, and, after a guilty glance at her shoes, put in some vigorous foot-work on the huge iron scraper. Her latch-key was still in the lock, where she had left it, before her swoop down the drive. As she turned it, and heard the spring lock snap behind her, shutting her inside, she was aware of a definite sense of shelter.

The house seemed a solid hive of comfort, honey-combed with golden cells, each glowing with light and warmth. It buzzed with voices, it offered company, and protection.

In spite of her appreciation, the interior of the Summit would have appalled a modern decorator. The lobby was floored with black and ginger tiles, on which lay a black fur rug. Its furniture consisted of a chair with carved arms, a terra cotta drain-pipe, to hold umbrellas, and a small palm on a stand of peacock-blue porcelain.

Pushing open the swing-doors, Helen entered the hall, which was entirely carpeted with peacock-blue pile, and dark with massive mahogany. The strains of wireless struggled through the heavy curtain which muffled the drawing-room door, and the humid air was scented with potted prim-ulas, blended with orange-pekoe tea.

Although Helen's movements had been discreet, someone with keen hearing had heard the swing of the lobby doors. The velvet folds of the portière were pushed aside, and a voice cried out in petulant eagerness.

'Stephen, you – Oh, it's *you*.'

Helen was swift to notice the drop in young Mrs Warren's voice.

'So you were listening for him, my dear,' she deduced. 'And dressed up, like a mannequin.'

Her glance of respect was reserved for the black-and-white satin tea-frock, which gave the impression that Simone had been imported straight from the London Restaurant thé-dansant, together with the music. She also followed the conventions of fashion in such details as artificial lips and eyebrows superimposed on the original structure. Her glossy black hair was sleeked back into curls, resting on the nape of her neck, and her nails were polished vermilion.

But in spite of long slanting lines, painted over shaven arches, and a tiny bow of crimson constricting her natural mouth, she had not advanced far from the cave. Her eyes glowed with primitive fire, and her expression hinted at a passionate nature. She was either a beautiful savage, or the last word in modern civilization, demanding self-expression. The result was the same – a girl who would do exactly as she chose.

As she looked down, from her own superior height, at Helen's small, erect figure, the contrast between them was sharp. The girl was hatless, and wore a shabby tweed coat, which was furred with moisture. She brought back with her the outside elements, mud on her boots, the wind in her cheeks, and glittering drops on her mop of ginger hair.

'Do you know where Mr Rice is?' demanded Simone.

'He went out of the gate, just before me,' replied Helen, who was a born opportunist, and always managed to be present at the important entrances and exits. 'And I heard him saying something about "wishing good-bye".'

Simone's face clouded at the reminder that the pupil was going home on the morrow. She turned sharply, when her husband peered over her shoulder, like an inquisitive bird. He was tall, with a jagged crest of red hair, and horn-rimmed glasses.

'The tea's growing stewed,' he said, in a high-pitched voice. 'We're not going to wait any longer for Rice.'

'I am,' Simone told him.

'But the tea-cake's getting cold.'

'I adore cold muffin.'

'Well – won't you pour out for me?'

'Sorry, darling. One of the things my mother never taught me.'

'I see.' Newton shrugged as he turned away. 'I hope the noble Rice will appreciate your sacrifice.'

Simone pretended not to hear, as she spoke to Helen, who had also feigned deafness.

'When you see Mr Rice, tell him we're waiting tea for him.'

Helen realized that the entertainment was over, or rather, that the scene had been ruthlessly cut, just when she was looking forward to reprisals from Simone.

She walked rather reluctantly upstairs, until she reached the first landing, where she paused, to listen, outside the blue room. It always challenged her curiosity, because of the formidable old invalid who lay within, invisible, but paragraphed, like some legendary character.

As she could hear the murmur of Miss Warren's voice – for the step-daughter was acting as deputy nurse – she decided to slip into her room, to put it ready for the night.

The Summit was a three-storeyed house, with two staircases and a semi-basement. A bathroom on each floor – and no water during a drought. The family – consisting of old Lady Warren, the Professor, and Miss Warren, slept on the first floor, while the spare rooms were on the second. The top attics housed the domestic staff – when any – and, at present, was only occupied by the Oates couple.

Newton now counted as a visitor, for he and his wife had the big red room, on the second floor, while his old room, which connected with the bedrooms of Lady Warren and the Professor, was turned into the nurse's sitting-room.

As Helen opened the door of Miss Warren's

room, a small incident occurred which was fraught with future significance. The handle slipped round in her grip, so that she had to exert pressure in order to turn the knob.

'A screw's loose,' she thought. 'Directly I've time I'll get the screwdriver and put it right.'

Anyone acquainted with Helen's characteristics would know that she always manufactured leisure for an unfamiliar job, even if she had to neglect some legitimate duty. It was the infusion of novelty into her dull routine which helped to keep undimmed her passionate zest for life.

Miss Warren's room was sombre and bare, with brown wallpaper, curtains, and cretonne. An old-gold cushion supplied the sole touch of colour. It was essentially the sanctum of a student, for books overflowed from the numerous shelves and cases, while the desk was littered with papers.

Helen was rather surprised to find that the shutters were fastened already, while the small green-shaded lamp over the bureau gleamed like a cat's eye.

As she returned to the landing, Miss Warren came out of the blue room. Like her brother, she was tall and of commanding figure, but there the resemblance ended. She appeared to Helen as an overbred and superior personality, with dim flickering features, and eyes the hue of rainwater.

In common with the Professor however, she seemed to resent the gaze of a stranger as an outrage on her privacy; yet, while her remote glance sent Helen away on a very long journey, the Professor decimated her out of existence.

'You're late, Miss Capel,' she remarked in her toneless voice.

'I'm sorry.' Helen looked anxious, as she wondered if her precious job were in peril. 'I understood, from Mrs Oates, that I was free till five. It's my first afternoon off since I came.'

'That is not what I meant. Of course, I am not reproaching you for any breach of duty. But it is too late for you to be returning from a walk.'

'Oh, thank you, Miss Warren. I *did* go farther than I intended. But it did not grow dark till the last mile.'

Miss Warren looked at Helen, who felt herself slipping away a thousand miles or so.

'A mile is a long way from home,' she said. 'It is not wise to go far, even by daylight. Surely you get sufficient exercise working about the house? Why don't you go into the garden to get fresh air?'

'Oh, but Miss Warren,' protested Helen, 'that is not the same as a good stretching walk, is it?'

'I understand.' Miss Warren smiled faintly. 'But I want you, in turn, to understand this. You are a young girl, and *I* am responsible for your safety.'

Even while the warning seemed grotesque on Miss Warren's lips, Helen thrilled to the intangible hint of danger. It seemed to be everywhere – floating in the air – inside the house, as well as outside in the dark tree-dripping valley.

'*Blanche.*'

A deep bass voice – like that of a man or an old woman, boomed faintly from the blue room. Instantly, the stately Miss Warren shrank, from a paralysing personality, to a schoolgirl hurrying to obey the summons of her mistress.

'Yes, Mother,' she called. 'I'm coming.'

She crossed the landing, in ungainly strides, and shut the door of the blue room behind her, to Helen's disappointment.

'I'm getting a strange contrast in my types,' she thought, as she slowly walked up the stairs, to the next landing. 'Mrs Newton is torrid, and Miss Warren frigid. Hot and cold water, by turns. I wonder what will happen in case of fusion?'

She liked to coin phrases, just as she enjoyed the reflection that she was brought into daily contact with two bachelors and a widower, thus reviving a lost art. Those derided Victorians, who looked upon every man as a potential husband, certainly extracted every ounce of interest from a dull genus.

Yet, while she respected the Professor's intellect, and genuinely looked forward to the visits of the young Welsh doctor, she resolved to go on buying Savings Certificates, for her old age. For she believed in God – but not in Jane Eyre.

She was on the point of entering her room, when she noticed that a light was shining through the glass transom of the bachelor's room. It drew her, as a magnet, to his door.

'Are you inside, Mr Rice?' she called.

'Come and see for yourself,' invited the pupil.

'I only wanted to know if the light was being wasted.'

'Well, it's not. Come in.'

Helen obeyed the invitation. She was used to two kinds of behaviour from men; they either overlooked her altogether, or paid her stressed attentions, in private.

Of the alternatives, she preferred to be insulted; she could always give back as good as she got, while she was braced by any kind of personal experience.

She liked Stephen Rice, because he treated her exactly as he treated other girls – with a casual frankness. He was smoking, as he pitched clothing into an open suitcase, and he made no apology for his state of undress, as his underwear satisfied his own standard of decency.

Although he did not appeal to Helen, who liked a man's face to betray some trace of intellect, or spirit, he was generally accepted as unusually handsome, on the evidence of heavy regular features, and thick waving hair, which grew rather too low on his brow.

'Like dogs?' he asked, shaking out a confusion of ties.

'Let me,' remarked Helen, taking them from him, with kind firmness. 'Of course, I like dogs. I've looked after them.'

'Then that's a bad mark to you. I loathe women who boss dogs. You see them showing off in Parks. Like the blasted centurion, who said come and he cometh. I always want to bite them, since the dogs are too gentlemanly to do their own job.'

'Yes, I know,' nodded Helen, who agreed, on principle, when it was possible. 'But my dogs used to boss *me*. They had a secret understanding to all pull at once, in different directions. The wonder is I didn't develop into a starfish.'

Stephen shouted with laughter.

'Good for them . . . Like to see something special in the way of dogs? I bought him, today, from a farmer.'

Helen looked around the untidy room.

'Where is he?' she asked. 'Under the bed?'

'Is that where you sleep? Inside the bed, you cuckoo.'

'Oo. Suppose he has fleas?'

'Suppose he hasn't? . . . Come, Otto.'

Stephen raised a corner of the eider-down, and an Alsatian peeped out.

'Bit shy,' explained Stephen. 'I say, what price old Miss Warren when she sees him? She won't allow a dog inside the house.'

'Why?' asked Helen.

'Afraid of them.'

'Oh, no, she *can't* be. It's the other way round. People are afraid of her, because she's so formidable.'

'That's only her make-up. She's a hollow funk. Put her in a jam, and she'd smash. She's got the wind up now, over this gorilla gent. By the way, are you afraid of him?'

22

'Of course not.' Helen laughed. 'Perhaps, I might be a bit if I was alone. But no one could feel nervous in a house full of people.'

'I don't agree. It all depends on the people. You'll always find a weak link. Miss Warren is one. *She'd* let you down.'

'But there's safety in numbers,' persisted Helen. 'He wouldn't dare to come here . . . D'you want any sewing done?'

'No, thank you, my dear. The godly Mrs Oates has kept me sewn up. In more sense than one, by the way . . . Now, there's a character, if you like. You can *bank* on her – if there's not a bottle about.'

'Why – does she drink?'

Stephen only laughed in reply.

'Look here, you'd better clear out,' he advised, 'before Miss Warren raises hell. This is the bachelor's room.'

'But I'm not a lady. I'm Staff,' explained Helen indignantly. 'And they're waiting tea for you.'

'You mean, Simone is waiting. Old Newton is wolfing down the tea-cake.' Stephen pulled on his coat. 'I'll take the pup down with me. Introduce him to the family, and make us two to one, in the muffin handicap.'

'Surely you don't call that large thing a pup,' cried Helen, as the Alsatian followed his master into the bathroom.

'He's quite young, really.' Stephen's voice was positively tender. 'I love dogs – and hate women. Reason. Remind me to tell you the story of my life.'

Helen felt slightly forlorn when his whistle died away in the distance. She knew she would miss the pupil. But a second glance around the untidy room reminded her that his absence would mean less work, so she resolved to leave all regret to Simone.

Her tea was calling her downstairs to the kitchen. Not stopping to clear away any litter, she hurried to her own room, and took off her coat and shoes. As the order for closed shutters only included the basement, ground-floor and first-floor, her own casement banged open to the wind.

In spite of her haste, she could not resist the luxury of lingering there, looking out over the valley, just to enjoy the sense of contrast. She could see only a spongy blackness. It seemed to stir and creep before the breath of the breeze. Not a gleam shone from any window of the sparsely sprinkled cottages.

'I wonder where I stood, looking across at the Summit,' she wondered. 'It seemed such a long way off, then. And now, I'm inside, safe.'

She was visited by no prescience to warn her that – since her return – there had been certain trivial incidents which were the first cracks in the walls of her fortress. Once they were started, nothing could stop the process of disintegration; and each future development would act as a wedge, to force the fissures into ever-widening breaches, letting in the night.

CHAPTER 3

A FIRESIDE STORY

Helen went down to the kitchen, by the back way – a spiral of steep steps, broken up into flights at each floor, by a small landing, where a door connected it with the main staircase. It was covered with the original linoleum – brown-and-biscuit, and small-patterned – like an old-fashioned tile, but still in excellent condition.

To Helen, this dingy back way down represented the essence of romance. It was a delicate filament connecting her with the glamour of the past, and revived memories of spacious and leisured days.

She had been brought up in a tiny mansion-flat, with no room to keep a maid, a hat-box, or a cat. The perambulator was housed in the bathroom, and the larder was thoughtfully built in the only spare recess, which happened to be next to the stove.

When Helen reached the basement-hall, she could hear the welcome rattle of china and see the glow of the kitchen fire through the frosted glass panels of the door. Mrs Oates was drinking tea from her saucer as she made herself another piece of toast.

She was a tall, strapping woman, broad-shouldered

and muscular, with an ugly, underhung face. She did not wear uniform, and her afternoon skirt was protected by an apron of red and black Welsh flannel.

'I heard you running down all them steep steps,' she said. 'You're free to use the front.'

'Yes, I know,' replied Helen. 'But back-stairs remind me of my granny's house. The servants and children were never allowed to go up the front way, because of wearing out the carpet.'

'Go on,' remarked Mrs Oates politely.

'Yes, indeed, and it was the same with the jam. Pots and pots of it, but the strawberry and raspberry were only for the elders. All the children had to eat was rhubarb, or ginger-and-marrow . . . How cruel we grown-ups were then.'

'Not *you*. You should say "them grown-ups".'

'"Them grown-ups,"' repeated Helen meekly, accepting the correction. 'I've come to invite myself to tea, as your husband is away.'

'And you're welcome.' Mrs Oates rose to get down fresh china from the Welsh dresser. 'I see as how you know the tricks of the trade. You want a brown pot to draw the flavour from the leaves. I'll get out the drawing-room cake for you.'

'Shop-cake? Not on your life. I want kitchen dough-cake . . . You don't know how all this appeals to me, Mrs Oates. I was thinking of this, about an hour ago, in very different circumstances.'

She looked around her with appreciative eyes. The kitchen was a huge room, with an uneven floor, and corners where shadows collected. There was no white enamel, no glass-fronted cabinet, no refrigerator; yet the shabby hearth-rug and broken basket-chairs looked homely and comfortable in the glow from the range.

'What an enormous cavern,' said Helen. 'It must make a lot of work for you and your husband.'

'Oh, it don't worry Oates.' Mrs Oates' voice was bitter. 'All the more places for him to muck up, and me to clean up after him.'

'It looks fine. All the same, Miss Warren would have a fit if she saw there were no shutters.'

As she spoke, Helen glanced at the small windows, set high up in the walls. They were on a level with the garden, and through the mud-speckled glass, she could see a faint stir of darkness, as the bushes moved in the wind.

'It's only just turned dark,' said Mrs Oates. 'They can wait till I've finished my tea.'

'But don't you feel nervous, down here all by yourself?'

'D'you mean *him*?' Mrs Oates' voice was scornful. '*No*, miss, I've seen too many work-shy men to be scared of anything in trousers. If he tried any of his funny business on me, I'd soon sock him in the jaw.'

'But there *is* a murderer,' Helen reminded her.

'He's not likely to trouble us. It's like the Irish Sweep; someone wins it, but it's never *you* and never *me*.'

They were consoling words and made Helen feel

safe and comfortable as she crunched her toast. The grandfather clock ticked pleasantly and the ginger cat purred on the best patch of rug.

Suddenly she felt in the mood for a thrill.

'I wish you would tell me about the murders,' she said.

Mrs Oates stared at her in surprise.

'Why, they was in all the newspapers,' she said. 'Can't you read?'

'I naturally keep up with all the important things,' Helen explained. 'But I've never been interested in crime. Only, when it's a local murder, it seems slack to know nothing about it.'

'That's right,' agreed Mrs Oates, as she relaxed to gossip. 'Well, the first girl was murdered in town. She did a dancing-turn, with no clothes on, at one of the Halls, but she was out of a job. She was in a public, and had one over the eight. They seen her go out of the bar, just before time. When the rest come out, she was lying in the gutter, dead. Her face was as black as that bit of coal.'

Helen shuddered. 'The second murder was committed in the town, too, wasn't it?' she asked.

'Yes. She was a housemaid, poor thing. It was her evening out, and when her master came out into the garden, to give the dog its run, he found her all doubled up, on the drive, choked, like the other. And no one heard a whisper, though it was quite close to the drawing-room windows. So she must have been took by surprise.'

'I know,' nodded Helen. 'There were shrubs on

28

the lawn, that looked like people. And suddenly, a shrub *leaped* on her.'

Mrs Oates stared at her, and then began to count on her fingers.

'Where was I? Let me see. One, two, three. Yes, the third was in a public-house, and it put everyone in a proper scare, because he'd come out into the country. The young lady in the bar had just popped into the kitchen, to swill a few glasses under the tap, and they found her there, two minutes after, choked with her own tea-cloth. There was people in the bar. But no one heard a sound. He must have crept in through the back-door, and jumped on her from behind.'

Helen listened with a sense of unreality. She told herself that these things had never really happened. And yet, they toned in too well with the damp darkness of the valley, where trees crept up to windows, until it was possible to imagine confused faces peering down into the kitchen. Suddenly she felt sated with secondary horrors.

'Don't tell me any more,' she implored.

But Mrs Oates was wound up to a finish.

'The last,' she said, 'was five miles from here, as the crow flies. A pure young girl, about your own age. She was a nursery-governess in some big family, but she was home for her holiday and she was going to a dance. She was up in her bedroom, drawing her beautiful party-frock over her head, when *he* finished the job for her. Twisted the lovely satin frock all round her neck, so as it ate right into her throat, and wrapped it all over her face, so that she never saw another mortal thing on earth. Looking at herself in the glass, she was, and that was her last sight, which shows these beauty competitions don't get you far.'

Helen did her best to resist the surge of her imagination, by picking on the weak spots in the tale.

'If she was looking at herself in the glass, she'd see him, too, and be warned. And if her dress was over her head, how could she see herself? Besides her arms would protect her throat.'

All the same, she could not help making a mental picture of the scene. Because her own possessions were so few, perhaps, she had a keen sense of property, and always exercised a proprietary right over her room, even if someone else paid the rent.

She imagined that the murdered governess occupied a bedroom much like her own at the Summit – brightly-lit and well-furnished. It was cluttered with girlish treasures, symbolic of the cross-roads – childish relics and womanhood's trophies of restaurant souvenirs. Hockey-sticks jostled with futuristic, long-bodied dolls; photographs of school-groups stood beside the latest boy. Powder, vanishing-cream – and the distorted satin shape on the carpet.

'How did he get in?' Helen asked, desperately anxious to prove that this horror could not be true.

'Quite easy,' Mrs Oates told her. 'He climbed up the front porch, just under her bedroom window.'

'But how could he tell she would be there alone?'

'Ah, but he's a luny, and they know everything. He's after girls. Believe me, or believe me not, if there was a girl anywhere about, he'd smell her out.'

Helen glanced apprehensively at the window. She could barely distinguish glistening twigs tossing amidst dim undergrowth.

'Have you locked the back-door?' she asked.

'I locked it hours ago. I always do when Oates is away.'

'Isn't he rather late getting back?'

'Nothing to make a song about.' Mrs Oates glanced at the clock, which told her its customary lie. 'The rain will turn them steep lanes to glue, and the car's that old, Oates says he has to get out and carry it up the hills.'

'Will he carry the new nurse too?'

Mrs Oates, however, resented Helen's attempt to introduce a lighter note.

'I'm not worrying about her,' she replied, with dignity. 'I could trust Oates alone with the very highest in the land.'

'I'm sure you could.' Helen glanced again at the greyness outside the window. 'Suppose we put the shutters up and make things look more cheerful?'

'What's the good of locking up?' grumbled Mrs Oates, as she rose reluctantly. 'If *he's* a mind to come in, he'll find a way . . . Still, it's got to be done.'

But Helen enjoyed the task of barring the windows.

31

It gave her a sense of victory over the invading night. When the short red curtains were drawn over the panes, the kitchen presented the picture of a delightful domestic interior.

'There's another window in the scullery,' remarked Mrs Oates, opening a door at the far end of the kitchen.

On the other side loomed the blackness of a coal-mine. Then Mrs Oates found the switch and snapped on the light, revealing a bare clean room, with blue-washed walls, a mangle, copper, and plate-racks.

'What a mercy this basement is wired,' said Helen.

'Most of it's as dark as a lover's lane,' Mrs Oates told her. 'There's only a light in the passage, and switches in the storeroom and pantry. Oates did say as how he'd finish the job properly, and that's as far as he'll ever get. He's only got one wife to work for him, poor man.'

'What a labyrinth,' cried Helen, as she opened the scullery door and gazed down the vista of the passage, dimly lit by one small electric-bulb, swinging from the ceiling, half-way down its length. The light revealed a section of stone-slabbed floor and hinted at darker recesses lost in obscurity.

On either side were closed doors, dingy with shabby brown paint. To Helen's imagination they looked grim and sepulchral as sealed tombs.

'Don't you always feel a closed door is mysterious?' she asked. 'You wonder what lies on the other side.'

'I'll make a guess,' said Mrs Oates. 'A side of bacon and a string of Spanish onions, and if you open the storeroom door, you'll find I'm not far out. Come along. That's all here.'

'No,' Helen declared. 'After your nice little bedtime tales, I shan't sleep until I've opened every door and satisfied myself that no one's hiding inside.'

'And what would a shrimp like you do if you found the murderer?'

'Go for him, before I'd time to think. When you feel angry, you can't feel frightened.'

In spite of Mrs Oates' laughter, Helen insisted on fetching a candle from the scullery and exploring the basement. Mrs Oates lagged behind her, as she made an exhaustive search of the pantry, store-room, larder, boot-closet, and the other offices.

At the end of the passage, she turned into a darker alley, where the coal-cellars and wood-house were located. She flashed her light over each recess, stooping behind dusty sacks and creeping into corners.

'What d'you expect to find?' asked Mrs Oates. 'A nice young man?'

Her grin faded, however, as Helen paused before a locked door.

'There's one place as you, nor no one else, will ever get into,' she said grimly. 'If the luny gets inside *there*, I'll say good luck to him.'

'Why?' asked Helen. 'What is it?'

'The wine-cellar – and the Professor keeps the key. It's the nearest you'll ever get to it.'

Helen, who was a total abstainer, through force of circumstances, realized that, since she had been at the Summit, no intoxicant had been served with the meals.

'Are they all teetotallers here?' she asked.

'There's nothing to hinder the Professor having his glass,' said Mrs Oates, 'seeing as he keeps the key. But Oates and the young gentlemen have got to go to the Bull for their drop of tiddley. And Mr Rice is the only one as has ever asked me if I have a mouth.'

'What a shame not to allow you beer, with all your heavy work,' sympathized Helen.

'I get beer-money,' admitted Mrs Oates. 'Miss Warren's got a bee in her bonnet about no drink served in the house. But she's like the Professor, no trouble so long as you leave her with her books. She's not mean – only you mustn't do a thing what's worth doing. That's her.'

That was exactly how Miss Warren had struck Helen – a grey studious negation.

Mrs Oates relieved her feelings by kicking the cellar door, before they turned away.

'I've promised myself one thing,' she said solemnly. 'It's this. If ever I come across the key of this cellar, there'll be a bottle short.'

'And the fairies will have drunk it, I suppose?' asked Helen. 'Come back to the fire. I've something thrilling to tell you.'

When they were back in the kitchen, however, Mrs Oates began to chuckle.

'You've something to tell me. Well, I've something to show you. Look at these.'

She opened one of the cupboards in the dresser, and pointed to a line of empty bottles.

'What Mr Rice calls "dead men." Many's the bottle of gin or stout he's brought back from the Bull.'

'He's kind,' admitted Helen. 'There's *something* about him. Pity he's such a rotter.'

'He's not as black as he's painted,' said Mrs Oates. 'He was sent down from his school in Oxford for mucking about with a girl. But he told me, one night, as he was more sinned against than sinning. He's not really partial to girls.'

'But he flirts with Mrs Newton.'

'Just his fun. When she says "A", he says "B". That's all.'

Helen laughed as she looked into the glowing heart of the fire. Unknown to her, fresh cracks had been started in the walls of her fortress. As she stroked the ginger cat, who responded with a startling rumble, her recent experience seemed very remote.

'I promised you a tale,' she said. 'Well – "believe me or believe me not" – when I was coming through the plantation, I met – the strangler.'

It was certain that she did not believe her own story, although she exaggerated the details, in order to impress Mrs Oates. It was such a thin-spun theme – a man hiding behind a tree, with no sequel to prove a dark motive.

She was not the only one to be incredulous. In a cottage half-way up the hill-side, a dark-eyed girl was looking at herself in a small mirror, spotted with damp. Her face was rosy from moist mountain air, and her expression was eager and rebellious.

Here was one who welcomed life with both hands. She perched a scarlet hand-knitted beret at a perilous angle on her short black hair, powdered her cheeks, and added unnecessary lip-stick to her moist red lips, humming as an accompaniment to her actions.

As she looked around the small room, with the low bulging white plaster ceiling and cracked walls, the limp muslin curtain before the shuttered window, her desire grew. She told herself that she was sick of confinement and the cheesy smell of indoors. She had stayed in, night after night, until she was fed up, and willing to chance any hypothetical criminal. She yearned for the cheery bar of the Bull, with a young man or two, a glass of cider, and the magic of the Wireless.

She buttoned up her red leather coat and put on Wellington boots, before her stealthy descent down the creaking stairs. When she slipped through the cottage door her heart beat faster, but only with excitement. She was as used to the narrow, pitchy lane, which dropped down precipitously to the valley, as a Londoner is to Piccadilly. Familiarity with loneliness had robbed it of any terror, just as immunity from attack had resulted in perfect nerve. Without fear or foreboding, she hurried down the stony hill-side, in sure-footed haste.

When she reached the plantation, she felt that she had nearly reached the goal of her desire. A bare mile of level ground separated her from the bar of the Bull. Civilization was represented by the Summit, which was so close to her that she could hear a broadcast of Jack Hylton's band.

Like most Welsh girls, she had a true ear and a musical voice. She took up the tune, jumbling the words, but singing with the passionate exaltation due to a revivalist hymn.

> 'Love is the sweetest thing –
> No bird upon the wi—ng'

The rain drove down upon her face, in steady slanting skeins, through the partial screen of the larches, and the hard ground under her feet was growing slimed, in spite of its carpet of spines.

Happy, healthy, and unwise, she hurried to meet the future. Careless of weather, and one with the elements, she sang her way through the wood – youth at its peak.

Her sight was excellent, so that she could distinguish the lane of single trees, where the plantation thinned towards its end. But her imagination was more blunted than Helen's, so that she did not notice that one of the trees was apparently rootless, for it shifted behind the trunks of its fellows.

Had she remarked it, she would have distrusted

the evidence of her eyes. Common sense told her that trees did not move from their stations. So she hurried on, and sang yet louder.

> 'I only pray that life may bring
> Love's sweet story to you.'

When she reached the last tree, it suddenly changed into a man. Its branches were clutching arms . . . But still she did not believe.

For she knew that these things do not happen.

CHAPTER 4

ANCIENT LIGHTS

'The tree moved,' declared Helen, finishing her story, in the safety of the kitchen. 'And – to my horror – I saw that it was a man. He was waiting there, like a tiger ready to spring on his prey.'

'Go on.' Mrs Oates was openly derisive. 'I've seen that tree, myself. Often seen him, I have, waiting for Ceridwen, when she used to work here. And was never the same tree twice.'

'Cerwiden?' repeated Helen.

'Yes. She lives in a cottage half-way up the hill. A pretty girl, but she would mix her cloths. Old Lady Warren couldn't abide her. She said as how her feet smelt, and when she dusted under her bed, her ladyship used to wait for her, with her stick, until she crawled out, so as to fetch her a clout on the head.'

Helen burst out laughing. Life might ignore her, but she remained acutely conscious and appreciative of the eternal comedy.

'The old darling gets better and better,' she declared. 'I wish you'd give me the job of dusting under her bed. She'd find me a bit too quick for her.'

'So was Cerwiden. She used to bait the old girl, shooting out when she wasn't expecting her . . . But she got her, in the end. She fetched her such a crack that her father came and took her away.'

'She certainly makes – What's that?'

Helen broke off to listen. Once again the sound was repeated – an insistent tapping on a window-pane. Although she could not locate it, it seemed to be not far away.

'Is someone knocking?' she asked.

Mrs Oates listened also.

'It must be the passage window,' Mrs Oates said. 'The catch is loose. Oates did talk of mending it.'

'That doesn't sound too safe,' objected Helen.

'Now, miss, don't worry. The shutter's put up. No one can get in.'

But, as the wind rose, the monotonous rattle and beat continued, at irregular intervals. It got on Helen's nerves, so that she could not settle down to her tea.

'It's a miserable night,' she said. 'If that tree was waiting for Cerwiden, I don't envy her.'

'He's caught her, by now,' chuckled Mrs Oates. 'She won't be noticing weather no more.'

'There it goes again . . . Have you a screwdriver?'

Helen's eyes lit up as she spoke, for she had a mania for small mechanical jobs.

'You see, Mrs Oates, this sound will irritate you,'

she explained. 'And then you'll spoil the dinner. And then we shall have indigestion. I'll see if I can't put it right.'

'What a one you are to look for work,' grumbled Mrs Oates, as she followed Helen through the scullery.

The smallish window was at the end of the passage, close to the scullery door. As Helen unbarred the shutter, a gust of wind struck it, like a blow, and dashed drops of rain against the streaming glass.

Together, the big woman and the small girl stood, peering out into the garden. They could see only a black huddle of shrubs and a gleam of thrashing boughs.

'Doesn't it look creepy?' said Helen. 'I wonder if I can fix this catch. Have you any small nails?'

'I'll see if I can find some. Oates is a terror for nails.'

Mrs Oates lumbered through the scullery, leaving Helen alone staring out into the wet garden. There were no bushes, on this side, to give the impression of a crawling greyness creeping towards the house; the night seemed to have become solid and definite – clear-cut chunks of threatening blackness.

It inspired a spirit of defiance in Helen.

'Come on – if you dare,' she cried aloud.

The answer to her challenge was immediate – a piercing scream from the kitchen.

Helen's heart leaped at the thin terror-stricken wail. There was only room for one thought in her mind. The maniac was lurking in hiding, and she had sent the poor unsuspecting Mrs Oates into his trap.

'He's got her,' she thought, as she caught up the bar and dashed into the kitchen.

Mrs Oates greeted her with another scream, but there was no sign of the source of her terror, although she was on the verge of hysteria.

'A mouse,' she yelled. 'It went over there.'

Helen stared at her in blank incredulity.

'You *can't* be frightened of a little mouse. It isn't done. Old stuff, you know.'

'But they make me crawl all over,' whimpered Mrs Oates.

'In that case, I suppose murder will have to be committed. A pity. Here, Ginger, Ginger.'

Helen called, in vain, to the cat, who continued to wash with an affectation of complete detachment. Mrs Oates apologized for him.

'He's a civil cat, but he can't abide mice. Oates would swat it.'

'If that's a hint, *I'm* not going to swat it. But I'll frighten it away.'

With her sensitized reaction to any situation, she was conscious of anti-climax, when she went down on her knees and began to beat the floor with her bar. Just whenever the drama seemed to be working up to a moment of tension, the crisis always eluded her and degenerated into farce.

Not until the night was over could she trace the repercussions of each trivial incident and realize

42

that the wave of fear which flooded the house, washed back to an insignificant source.

She could see her quarry – a small and rather attractive rodent – frisking in the distance, with the assurance of an old resident.

'Where's its hole?' she whispered.

'In that corner,' panted Mrs Oates. 'Oates did say as how he'd stop it up.'

Helen was driving the mouse homewards when she started at the sound of footsteps on the back-stairs.

'Who's that?' she cried.

'Not him,' laughed Mrs Oates. 'When he comes you'll not hear him on the way. He'll creep. That sounds like Mr Rice.'

As she spoke the door was pushed open, and Stephen Rice – carrying a suitcase – entered the kitchen. He stared at the sight of the demure Miss Capel on her knees, with her hair falling in a mane across her eyes.

'What's this?' he asked. 'Red Indians, or a crawling party? Count me in.'

'I'm chasing a mouse,' explained Helen.

'Great sport. I'll help.'

'No, I don't want to catch it.' Helen rose and placed the bar on the table. 'I think he's gone now.'

Stephen sat down and looked around him.

'I always feel at home, here,' he said. 'It's the one room I like in this horrible house. Mrs Oates and I hold our prayer-meetings here.'

'Where's your dog?' asked Helen.

'In my room. Miss Warren did not come to tea, unfortunately. So the row's postponed.'

'Why d'you have one at all?' asked Helen. 'You're leaving tomorrow. I expect Miss Warren would prefer not to know.'

'No.' Stephen stuck out his prominent chin. 'I'd rather come out in the open. Noble of me, when I know the heroic Newton will enlighten her darkness in any case.'

'He wouldn't tell?' cried Helen incredulously.

'Wouldn't he? To be frank, Otto was not a blazing success. The poor lad is not used to afternoon tea. Like his master, he's happier in the kitchen.'

'But Mrs Newton must have fallen for him,' insisted Helen, who argued along the familiar lines of 'love me, love my dog'.

'If she did, she controlled her passion.' Stephen opened his empty suitcase and turned to Mrs Oates. 'Where are the empties?' he asked. 'I thought I'd lift them now, and lug them over to the Bull tonight, to save that poor delicate husband of yours.'

'And I suppose you want to say "Good-bye" to your young lady there?'

Mrs Oates winked at Helen, who – enlightened by her previous gossip – understood the allusion to the daughter of the licensee of the Bull. Apparently, this young lady was not only the patron-saint of the bar, but the magnet that reassembled the sparse male population of the district. Mrs Oates took advantage of her privileged position to ask another more personal question.

'And what will your other lady say, if you spend your last night away?'

'My other – what?' demanded Stephen.

'Mrs Newton.'

'Mrs Newton Warren is a respectable married lady. She will naturally pass the evening in the company of her lawful husband, working out mathematical problems . . . Did you have a good tea?'

Helen did not hear the question, for she suddenly glimpsed an exciting possibility.

'Did Miss Warren have her tea up in the bedroom?' she asked.

'I suppose so,' replied Stephen.

'Then she's been up there for ages. I wonder if I might offer to relieve her?'

'If you do,' advised Stephen, 'see that she's supplied with cushions. Unless, of course, you're expert in dodging.'

'But does she always throw things at people?' asked Helen incredulously.

'It's the only way she knows of expressing her temperament.'

'Well, it doesn't matter. I think she sounds so *alive* for an old woman. I admire that.'

'You'll be disillusioned,' prophesied Stephen. 'She's a vile-tempered old cuss, with horrible manners. When I was presented to Her Majesty, she was eating an orange, and she spat out all the pips – to impress me.'

He broke off to laugh at a sudden recollection.

'All the same,' he said, 'I'd love to have seen her chuck the basin at that pie-faced nurse.'

'But, surely, that was an accident. She couldn't have known she was going to hit her.'

Mrs Oates looked up, with streaming eyes, from her task of peeling onions.

'Oh, no, miss,' she said. 'Lady Warren wouldn't miss. When she was younger, she spent all her time tramping over the fields, shooting rabbits and birds. They said she went to bed with her gun.'

'Then she's been here a long time?' asked Helen.

She believed that her curiosity was about to be given a real meal, for Mrs Oates' manner hinted at gossip.

Stephen rolled a cigarette – the cat purred on the rug – the mouse washed his face, in the safety of his hole. Inside, was firelight and tranquillity – outside, the rising storm.

A gust of wind smashed against the corner of the house, and spattered the unbarred shutter, before the passage window, with the remnants of its original fury. Slowly, as though pushed open by invisible fingers, the casement swung outwards over the garden. The house was open to the night.

It looked in, through the gap, and down the darkness of the passage. Its far end stretched away into shadows. Round the bend, was the warren of the offices – a honeycomb of cells, where a man could hide.

Inside the kitchen, Mrs Oates electrified her audience.

'They do say,' she said dramatically, 'as old Lady Warren shot her husband.'

'No,' gasped Stephen and Helen together.

'*Yes*,' declared Mrs Oates. 'It's an old wives' tale now, but my mother told me all about it. Old Sir Roger was just such a one as the Professor, quiet, and always shut up with his books. He made a lot of money with some invention. He built the Summit, so as to have no neighbours. And Lady Warren couldn't abide it. She was always jawing him about it, and they had one awful quarrel, in his study. She was overheard to threaten to shoot him for vermin. A few minutes later he was found shot dead, with her rook-rifle.'

'Looks pretty bad,' murmured Stephen.

'Yes, everyone thought she'd stand in the Dock,' agreed Mrs Oates. 'There was some nasty questions asked at the Inquest. She said as how it was an accident, and her clever lawyer got her off . . . But there was so much feeling about it that she went abroad – though she'd have gone, anyhow, as she fair hated the house.'

'Was it shut up afterwards?' asked Helen.

'No, the Professor left Oxford, and came here, and he's been just the same as his father before him – always staying in, and never going out. Old Lady Warren only came back when she said she was ill.'

'What's the matter with her?' asked Helen.

Mrs Oates pursed up her lips and shook her head.

47

'*Temper*,' she said firmly.

'Oh, but Mrs Oates, she must be ill, to have a nurse, and for the doctor to keep her in bed.'

'He reckons she's less trouble there. And she reckons she can give more trouble there. It's a fair game for her to drive the nurses away, so as to get fresh ones in to bully.'

'But Miss Warren told me that the Professor was anxious about her heart,' persisted Helen.

'Ah, but a man don't forget the mother that bore him,' declared Mrs Oates, lapsing into sentiment.

'But she's only his step-mother,' objected Stephen. 'She has no children. Still, she must be expected to croak, because the vultures are gathering. Simone told me that the old girl has made a Will, leaving her money to charities. She has a nasty perverted taste, and, apparently, likes Newton. Anyway, she makes him an allowance, which will cease at her death. That's why he's down here.'

'His pa sent for him,' explained Mrs Oates.

Helen thought of the Professor's glacial eye and Miss Warren's detached manner. It was impossible to believe that they were swayed by financial considerations.

'Hullo,' said Stephen suddenly, as he swung himself up on the table. 'What's this?'

He drew from under him a wooden bar, which Helen took from him, rather guiltily.

'Sorry,' she said. 'It belongs to the shutter in the passage. I'm glad you reminded me of it. I'll try and fix the window.'

After what she had heard, she felt eager to finish the job, and get upstairs, to the blue room, as quickly as possible. She made a make-shift fastening with some string and a peg, and then hurried back to the kitchen.

To her surprise, Stephen was peeling onions with Mrs Oates.

'She always makes me work,' he complained. 'It's her way of explaining a man in the kitchen, when Oates comes home . . . I say, isn't he very late? I bet you a fiver he's run off with the pretty new nurse.'

Mrs Oates snorted.

'If she's like the last, she'd have to hold his nose, to get him to kiss her . . . Are you really going to sit with Lady Warren, miss?'

'I am going to ask if I may,' replied Helen.

'Then, take my warning, and be on the watch out against her. It's my belief she's not as helpless as they make out, by a long way. I'm sure she can walk, same as me. She's got something up her sleeve. Besides, have you heard her voice, *when she forgets?*'

Helen suddenly remembered the bass bellow from the sick room. Here was a situation choked with mystery and drama. In her eagerness to be in the thick of it she almost ran to the door.

'I've tied up the window,' she said. 'Now, we're safely locked up, for the night.'

CHAPTER 5

THE BLUE ROOM

As Helen mounted the stairs to the blue room, she felt an odd stir of expectancy. It took her back to childish days, when she neglected her toys in favour of an invisible companion – Mr Poke.

Although she played by herself for hours, in a corner of the communal sitting-room, it was plain to her parents, that she was not indulging in a solitary game. She did everything with a partner.

And at twilight, when the firelight sent tall shadows flickering on the walls, she carried on an interminable conversation with her hero.

At first, her mother disliked the uncanny element in the society affected by her small daughter; but when she realized that Helen had discovered the best and cheapest of playfellows – imagination – she accepted the wonderful Mr Poke and used to ask questions about his prowess, to which there was no limit.

The staircase was lit by a pendant globe, which swung from a beam which spanned the central well. The first floor was between this light and the illumination from the hall, so that the landing was rather dark. Facing the flight of stairs, was an enormous ten-foot mirror, framed in tarnished gilt carving, and supported by a marble console table.

As Helen approached it, her reflection came to meet her, so that a small white face rose up from the dim depths of the glass, like a corpse emerging from deep lake-water, on the seventh day.

The thrill which ran through her veins, in response, seemed to her, an omen.

Miss Warren came to the door, in answer to her knock. Her pale face looked dragged and devitalized after hours of imprisonment with her step-mother.

'Has the new nurse come?' she asked.

'No.' Helen was aggressively cheerful. 'And we don't expect her for hours and hours. Mrs Oates says the rain has made the hills difficult for the car.'

'Quite,' agreed Miss Warren wearily. 'Please let me know directly she arrives. She must relieve me as soon as she has had something to eat.'

It was Helen's chance – and she took it.

'Might I sit with Lady Warren?' she asked.

Miss Warren hesitated before her reply. She knew that it would be against her brother's wish to entrust Lady Warren to an untrained stranger; but the girl seemed reliant and conscientious.

'Thank you, Miss Capel,' she replied. 'It would be kind. Lady Warren is asleep, so you will only have to sit very still, and watch her.'

She crossed the landing to her own room, and then turned to give further advice.

'If she wakes and wants something you can't find – or if you are in any difficulty, come, at once, to me.'

Helen promised, even while she was conscious that she would appeal to Miss Warren only as a last resource. She meant to cope with any situation on her own initiative, and she hoped that the need would arise.

The tide of her curiosity was running strongly when, at long last, she entered the blue room. It was a huge, handsome apartment, furnished with a massive mahogany suite, and sombre by reason of the prevailing dark blue colour of the walls, carpet and curtains. A dull red fire glowed in the steel grate. Although its closeness was mitigated with lavender-water, the atmosphere smelt faintly of rotten apples.

Lady Warren lay in the big bed. She wore a dark-purple silk quilted dressing-jacket, and her head was propped high with pillows. Her eyes were closed and she was breathing heavily.

The first glance told Helen that Stephen was right in his description. There was no sign of grand character in this bedridden old woman. The lines which scored her face, like an ancient map, were all plainly traced by bad temper and egotism. Her grey hair was cut short in a thick untidy shock and her nose was suspiciously red.

Stealing across the floor, Helen sat down in the low chair by the fire. She noticed that each coal was wrapped in white tissue paper, so that the scuttle appeared to be filled with snowballs. As she knew this transformation was a means to ensure quiet, she took the hint, and remained motionless, as though she were furniture.

Lady Warren's breathing continued with the volume and regularity of a steam-engine. Presently Helen began to suspect that it was a special performance for her benefit.

'She's not really asleep,' she thought. 'She's foxing.'

The breathing went on – but nothing happened. Yet Helen was aware of the quiver of her pulse which always heralded Mr Poke's approach.

Someone was watching her.

She had to turn her head round, in order to look at the bed. When she did so, Lady Warren's lids were tightly closed. With a joyous sense of playing a new game, Helen waited for a chance to catch her unawares.

Presently, after many feints and failures, she proved too quick for Lady Warren. Looking up unexpectedly, she caught her in the act of spying. Her lids were slit across by twin black crescents of extraordinary brightness, which peered out at her.

They shut immediately, only to open again, as the invalid realized that further subterfuge was vain.

'Come here,' she said, in a faint fluttering voice.

With a memory of Mrs Oates' warning, Helen advanced warily. She looked a small and insignificant person – a pale girl in a blue pinafore dress, which made her fade into her background.

'Come nearer,' commanded Lady Warren.

Helen obeyed, although her eyes wandered to the objects on the bed-table. She wondered which missile the invalid might choose to hurl at her head, and stretched out her hand for the biggest medicine bottle.

'Put that down,' snarled her ladyship faintly. 'That's *mine*.'

'Oh, I *am* sorry.' Helen spoke eagerly. 'I'm like that. *I* hate people to touch my things.'

Feeling that there was a link between them, she stood boldly by the bed, and smiled down at the invalid.

'You're very small,' remarked Lady Warren, at last breaking her silence. 'No style. Very unimpressive. I thought my grandson would have shown better taste when he chose a wife.'

As she listened, Helen realized that Simone had refused to enter the blue room, although Newton had urged her to do so.

'He showed excellent taste,' she said. 'His wife is marvellous. I'm not her.'

'Then – who are you?' asked Lady Warren.

'The help. Miss Capel.'

A ripple of some strong emotion passed over the old woman's face, leaving the black crescent eyes fixed and the lips hanging apart.

'She looks afraid,' thought Helen. 'But what's she afraid of? It – it must be *me*.'

Lady Warren's next words, however, gave the lie to this exciting possibility. Her voice strengthened.

'Go away,' she shouted, in the bass voice of a man.

Startled by the change, Helen turned and ran from the invalid, expecting every second, to feel the crash of a bottle on her head. But, before she reached the door, she was recalled by a shout.

'You little fool, come back.'

Quivering with expectation at this new turn, Helen crossed to the bed. The old lady began to talk in such a faint whine, that her words were almost inaudible.

'Get out of the house. Too many trees.'

'*Trees?*' repeated Helen, as her mind slipped back to the last tree in the plantation.

'Trees,' repeated Lady Warren. 'They stretch out their branches and knock at the window. They try to get in . . . When it's dark, they move. Creeping up to the house . . . Go away.'

As she listened, Helen felt a sense of kinship with the old woman. It was strange that she, too, had stood at the window, at twilight, and watched the invasion of the misted shrubs. Of course, it was all imagination; but that fact alone indicated a common touch of 'Mr Poke.'

In any case, she wanted to use the trees as a liaison between Lady Warren and herself. It was one of her small failings that, although she liked to succeed in her own line, she liked still better to make a success of someone else's job. She proceeded to try and make a conquest of Lady Warren.

'How strange,' she said. 'I've thought exactly the same as you.'

Unfortunately, Lady Warren resented her words as impertinence.

'I don't want to hear *your* thoughts,' Lady Warren whined. 'Don't dare to presume, because I'm help-less . . . What's your name?'

'Helen Capel,' was the dejected reply.

'How old are you?'

'Twenty-three.'

'Liar. Nineteen.'

Helen was startled by her acumen, as her employers had always accepted her official age.

'It's not exactly a lie,' she explained. 'I feel I'm entitled to put on my age, because I'm old in experience. I began to earn my own living when I was fourteen.'

Lady Warren showed no signs of being touched.

'Why?' she asked. 'Are you a love-child?'

'Certainly not,' replied Helen indignantly. 'My parents were married in church. But they couldn't provide for me. They were unlucky.'

'Dead?'

'Yes.'

'Then they're lucky.'

In spite of her subordinate position, Helen always found the necessary courage to protest when any vital principle of her Creed was assaulted.

'No,' Helen protested. 'Life is wonderful. I always wake up, just glad to be alive.'

Lady Warren grunted before she continued her catechism.

'Drink?' she asked.

'No.'

'Any men?'

'No chance – worse luck.'

Lady Warren did not join in her laugh. She stared at Helen so rigidly that the black slits of her eyes appeared to congeal. Some scheme was being spun amid the cobwebs of her mind.

The clock ticked away the silence and the fire fell in, with a sudden spurt of flame.

'Shall I put on more coal?' asked Helen, anxious to break the spell.

'No. Give me back my teeth.'

The request was so startling that Helen positively jumped. But the next second, she realized that Lady Warren was only referring to her denture, which was in an enamel cup, on the bed-table.

She looked away tactfully, while the august invalid fished them out of the disinfectant, with her fingers, and adjusted them in her gums.

'Helen,' she cooed, in a new dove-like voice, 'I want you to sleep with me, tonight.'

Helen looked at her, aghast, for the change in her was both grotesque and horrible. The denture forced her lips apart in a stiff artificial grin, which gave her an un-human resemblance to an old waxwork.

'You were afraid of me, without my teeth,' Lady Warren told her. 'But you won't be afraid now. I want to take care of you, tonight.'

Helen licked her lips nervously.

'But, my lady,' said Helen, 'the new nurse will sleep with you tonight.'

'I'd forgotten the new nurse. Another slut. Well, I'll be ready for *her* . . . But *you're* to sleep with me. You see, my dear, you're not safe.'

As she smiled, Helen was suddenly reminded of the grin of a crocodile.

'I *couldn't* pass a night alone with her,' she thought, even while she was conscious that her fear was only of her own creation. It was obviously absurd to be afraid of a bedridden old woman.

'I'm afraid I can do nothing without Miss Warren's instructions,' she said.

'My step-daughter's a fool. She doesn't know what's going on in this house. Trees always trying to get in . . . Come here, Helen.'

As Helen stooped over the bed, she felt her hand caught in a strong grip.

'I want you to get me something,' whispered Lady Warren. 'It's in the cupboard at the top of the wardrobe. Get on a chair.'

Helen, who was enjoying the rare flavour of an adventure, decided to humour her.

She climbed on to one of the heavy chairs and stood on her toes, in order to open the door of the cupboard.

She felt a little doubtful of the commission, as she groped with her hand, in the dark recess. It was evident that Lady Warren was using her as a tool, to procure forbidden fruit. With a memory of her inflamed nose, she suspected a hidden bottle of brandy.

'What is it?' she called.

'A little hard thing, wrapped in a silk scarf,' was the disarming reply.

As she spoke, Helen's fingers closed upon something which answered to the description.

'Is this it?' she asked, springing to the ground.

'Yes.' Lady Warren's voice was eager. 'Bring it to me.'

In the short journey to the bed, Helen was gripped with a sudden fear of the thing she held. Even under its mufflings, its shape was unmistakable. It was a revolver. She remembered Lady Warren's dead rabbits – and also a husband shot dead by accident.

'I wonder if it's loaded,' she thought fearfully. 'I can't even tell which is the dangerous end . . . I mustn't let her have it. Mrs Oates warned me.'

'Bring it to me,' commanded Lady Warren.

She made no attempt to disguise her excitement. Her fingers shook with eagerness, as she stretched out her hands.

Helen pretended not to hear. With affected carelessness, she laid down the revolver on a small table – at a safe distance from the invalid – before she advanced to the bed.

'Now, you mustn't get worked up,' she said soothingly. 'It is so bad for your heart.'

Fortunately Lady Warren's attention was distracted by her words.

'What does the doctor say about me?' she asked.

'He says your vitality is wonderful,' replied Helen.

'Then he's a fool. I'm a dead woman . . . But I'm not going to die till I'm ready.'

Her lids closed, so that her eyes were visible only as a narrow black rim. Her shrivelled face seemed to become a worn-out garment, and she spoke in the reedy voice of burnt-out forces.

'I've a job. Keep putting it off. Weak of me. But it is a job no one likes. Is it?'

Helen guessed immediately that she referred to her will.

'No,' she replied, 'Everyone puts it off.'

And then, because she could not resist her interest in the affairs of others, she added a bit of advice.

'But we all of us have to do it. It *must* be done.'

But Lady Warren was not listening. The eclipse was rapidly passing, for her eyes grew alert as they slanted across to the small bundle on the table.

'Bring it to me,' she said.

'No,' replied Helen. 'Better not.'

'Fool. What are you afraid of? It's only my spectacle case.'

'Yes, I know it is. I'm ever so sorry, my lady, but I'm only a machine. I have to obey Miss Warren's orders. And she told me I was only to sit and watch.'

It was plain that Lady Warren was not used to opposition. Her eyes blazed, and her fingers hooked to talons, as she clawed her throat.

'Go,' she gasped. 'Get – Miss – Warren.'

Helen rushed from the room – almost glad of the

attack, since the crisis of the revolver was postponed. As she reached the door, she looked back and saw that Lady Warren had collapsed upon her pillows.

A second later, the invalid raised her head. There was a stir amid the bedclothes, and two feet, in bed-socks, emerged from under the eider-down, as Lady Warren slipped out of bed.

CHAPTER 6

ILLUSION

Her heart beating fast with mingled exhilaration and fear, Helen hurried to Miss Warren's room. For the first time in her life, she was up against unknown possibilities. Unlike the other houses in which she had worked, the Summit provided a background.

It was true that Mrs Oates had heartlessly plucked the mystery from the last tree in the plantation, so that Helen was forced to accept him as the yokel lover of a rustic beauty; yet there remained material for macabre drama in the savage muffled landscape and the overhanging shadow of murder.

The old woman, too, with her overtures and her gleaming artificial smile, supplied a touch of real horror. She might be only a bed-ridden invalid, but the fact remained that she was under suspicion of having sent her husband prematurely to heaven or to hell.

Her sting might be drawn, but her desires were still lethal. Helen had proof of this in the incident of the revolver.

Her thoughts, however, slipped back to practical

62

subjects, when, as she turned the handle of Miss Warren's room, it once again slipped round in her grasp. 'I really must get at it the instant I have a chance,' she promised herself.

Miss Warren was sitting at her bureau, under the green light. Her eyes were fixed upon her book.

'Well?' she asked wearily, as Helen entered.

'I'm sorry to disturb you,' began Helen, 'but Lady War—'

Before she could finish her sentence, Miss Warren was out of her chair, and crossing the room with the ungainly gait of a giraffe.

In her element, Helen followed her to the blue room. Lady Warren was lying as she had left her, with closed eyes and puffing lips. The revolver, wrapped in the silk handkerchief, was still on the kidney table, and the width of the room remote from the bed.

Yet there was some change. Helen, who was observant, noticed the fact, at once, and, in her second survey, traced it to its cause. When she had gone to fetch Miss Warren, the bed-clothes were disordered. Now, the sheet was drawn down over the eider-down, as neatly as though it had been arranged by a hospital nurse.

'Miss Capel,' said Miss Warren, who was bending over the prostrate figure of her step-mother, 'fetch the oxygen-cylinder.'

Helen, who was always ready to experiment with unfamiliar properties, hurried to lug it across to the bed. She thoughtfully unscrewed the top, and managed to get a whiff of air, like a mountain breeze, before she surrendered it to Miss Warren.

Presently, Lady Warren revived under their joint ministrations. To Helen's awakening suspicions, it was an artistic performance, with calculated gradations of sighs, groans and fluttering lids.

Directly her eyes were open, she glared at Helen.

'Send her away,' she said weakly.

Miss Warren caught Helen's eye.

'Please go, Miss Capel. I'm sorry.'

Forgetful of her pose, Lady Warren turned on her stepdaughter, like some fish-wife.

'Idiot. Send her packing. Tonight.'

She closed her eyes again, and murmured, 'Doctor. I want the doctor.'

'He'll be here presently,' Miss Warren assured her.

'Why is he always late?' complained the invalid.

'Because he likes to see how you are, the last thing,' explained Miss Warren ungrammatically.

'It's because he's a slacker,' snarled Lady Warren. 'I must change my doctor . . . Blanche. That girl wasn't Newton's wife. Why doesn't she come to see me?'

'You are not strong enough for visitors.'

'That's not it. *I* know. She's *afraid* of me.'

The idea seemed to please Lady Warren, for her face puckered up in a smile. Helen, who was watching, from a safe distance, thought that she looked positively evil. In that moment, she could almost believe in the old story of a murdered husband.

Her eye fell on the nurse's small single-bed.

'I wouldn't be that nurse, for all the money in the world,' she shuddered.

Suddenly, Miss Warren became aware that she was still in the room, for she crossed over to her corner.

'I can manage by myself, Miss Capel.'

Her tone was so cold that Helen tried to justify herself.

'I hope you don't think I did anything to annoy her. She changed all of a sudden. Indeed, she took a fancy to me. Anyway, she kept asking me to sleep with her, tonight.'

Miss Warren's expression was incredulous, although her words were polite.

'I am sure that you were kind and tactful.'

Her glance towards the door was a hint of dismissal, and Helen turned to go; but her head was humming with confused suspicions which fought for utterance. Although experience had taught her that interference is usually resented, she felt that she must warn Miss Warren.

'I think there is something you ought to know,' she said, lowering her voice. 'Lady Warren asked me to get her something from the little cupboard above the wardrobe mirror.'

'Why do you consider that important?' asked Miss Warren.

'Because it was a revolver.'

Helen achieved her effect. Miss Warren looked directly at her, with a startled expression.

'Where is it now?' she asked.

'On that table.'

Miss Warren swooped down upon the small parcel with the avidity of some bird of prey. Her long white fingers loosened a fold of the silk wrapping. Then she held it out, so that Helen might see it.

It was a large spectacle case.

As she stared at it, Helen was swept off her feet by the tidal wave of an exciting possibility.

'That is not the same shape,' she declared. 'I felt the other. It had jutting-out bits.'

'What exactly are you hinting at?'

'I think that, when I went to fetch you, Lady Warren hid the revolver and put this in its place.'

'And are you aware that my mother has heart-disease, and has been unable to move, for months?'

All hope of conviction died, as Helen looked at Miss Warren's sceptical face. Its fluid lines seemed to have been suddenly arrested by a sharp frost.

'I'm sorry if I've made a mistake,' she faltered. 'Only, I thought I ought to keep nothing back.'

'I am sure you were trying to be helpful,' Miss Warren told her. 'But it only hinders to imagine stupid impossibilities.' She added, with a grim smile, 'I suppose, like all girls, you go to the Pictures.'

In the circumstances, her reproach was almost painful irony. She seemed to be divided from Helen, not only by space, but by time.

'She's pre-historic,' thought the girl. Her small

66

figure appeared actually shrunken as she went out of the blue room.

Besides being cheated out of the recognition, which was her due, she did not feel satisfied with Miss Warren's acceptance of the revolver incident.

'The customer is always right,' she reminded herself, as she walked down the stairs. 'But there's one comfort. Now that Lady Warren's soured on me, there will be no more talk about sleeping in her room.'

Luckily, in spite of her discouragement, her sense of duty remained unimpaired. As Oates was late, she decided to take on his job of laying the dinner-table.

At the sound of footsteps, the drawing-room door was opened, and Simone looked out – her eyes parched with longing. Instantly, her husband's head reared itself over her shoulder, like a serpent.

Simone showed no signs of discomfiture. She merely shrugged and smiled. 'So faithful,' she murmured, as she closed the door.

Braced by this glimpse of the clash of human passions, Helen went into the dining-room. For the first time, she felt a certain degree of sympathy with Simone.

'It would get on my nerves to be followed about, like that,' she thought.

It was evident that Newton's jealousy was working up to saturation-point; with Stephen's departure, he would probably become normal again. Meantime, he plainly meant to give his wife no opportunity of a final interview with the pupil.

In Helen's eyes, his obsession amounted almost to mania, as she considered the stolid indifference with which Stephen opposed Simone's passion. He did not run from her pursuit; he merely shoved her away. Even then, he was in the kitchen, helping Mrs Oates. He had been offered romance – and he chose onions.

The dining-room was the finest room in the Summit, with an elaborate ceiling of dark carved wood, and a massive fireplace and over-mantel, to correspond.

The great windows were screened with thick crimson curtains, while dark red paper covered the walls.

Helen crossed to the walnut sideboard, where the glass and silver was kept, and took a table-cloth from one of the drawers.

From years of practice, Helen could lay a table in her sleep. As she mechanically sorted out spoons and forks, her mind was busy in speculation. Although she was denied the privilege of argument with an employer, she was positive that, during her absence, there had been some monkey-work in the blue room.

'I'm sure Mrs Oates is right,' she thought. 'Lady Warren is not bed-ridden. She got up, and then she tried to cover her traces by tidying the bed. Well, she overdid it . . . . I'd like to talk it over with Dr Parry.'

Dr Parry was clever, young and unconventional. The first time he met Helen, he had shown a direct interest in her welfare, which she had accepted on a medical basis. He asked her personal questions, and seemed apprehensive of the influence of her surroundings on her youth.

What appealed to her most was his unprofessional gossip about his patient.

'Her heart's in a shocking state,' he told her. 'Still, hearts are sporting organs. She might climb Snowdon and be all right, and the next time she sneezed it might finish her off . . . But – she keeps me guessing. I sometimes wonder if she is so helpless. To my mind, she is an old surprise-packet.'

Helen remembered his words as she trotted to and fro, between the table and the sideboard. But her ears still burned whenever she recalled the irony of Miss Warren's voice.

'Well, I've warned her,' she thought. 'It's her pigeon. But I would like to know where that revolver is. You won't catch me in that room again, if I can help it.'

Although she tried to listen for the sound of the car, the fury of the storm prevented her from hearing the hum of the engine. It was not until she caught Mrs Oates' welcome to her husband, that she realized that the new nurse had come.

She rushed across the room and opened the door, but was too late to see her face, for she was in the act of following her guides through the entry to the kitchen stairs. Her back view, however, was impressive, for she was unusually tall.

Helen felt a burst of confidence.

'She's not a weak link, anyway,' she decided. 'She'd be an awkward customer for *him* to tackle.'

As she lingered in the hall, she remembered the loose handle of Miss Warren's door. She had watched where Oates kept his handful of tools, and discovered that he left them where he had used them. With this clue to guide her, she found the box stuck away in a corner of the boot-closet, in the hall.

As this was not a legitimate job, she crept up the stairs to the first-floor landing, and knelt before the door. She had hardly begun her investigations, when a sudden sound made her look up.

As she did so, she was the victim of an illusion. She was sure that the door across the landing, leading from the back-stairs, opened and shut again, giving her a glimpse of the face of a stranger.

It passed, like the dissolving memory of a dream, yet it left a horror in her mind, as though she had received a vision of elemental evil.

Even while she stared in stunned bewilderment, she realized that a door had actually opened and that the Professor was advancing towards her.

'It must have been the Professor,' she thought. 'It *must*. I believe it looked like him. Some trick of light or shadow altered his expression. It's so dark here.'

Even while she clung to this commonplace explanation, her reason rejected it. At the back of her mind remained a picture of the spiral of the back-stairs. The two staircases of the Summit offered special chances to anyone who wished to hide.

She reminded herself that no one could get in during the daytime. Besides, the house was so full of people that it would be impossible for anyone to escape notice. The intruder would have to know the habits and time-table of all the inmates.

Suddenly she remembered that Mrs Oates had commented on the supernormal cunning of a criminal maniac. *He would know.*

A shiver ran down her spine, as she wondered if she ought to tell the Professor of her experience. It was her duty, if any unauthorized person was secreted in the house. But, as she opened her lips, the memory of her recent encounter with Miss Warren made her afraid of appearing officious.

Although the Professor's eyes seemed to reduce her to the usual essential gases, the sight of his conventional dinner-clothes acted as a tonic. His shirt-front gleamed, his black tie was formal, his grey hair was brushed back from his intellectual brow.

Although he was rigid where his sister was fluid, he inspired her with – the same sense of unhuman companionship.

Suddenly aware that he might suspect her of spying through a bedroom keyhole, she broke into an explanation of the defective door-handle.

'Tell Oates to see to it, please,' he said, with an absent nod.

Toned by the incident, Helen resolved to test her nerve by a descent of the back-stairs. When

71

CHAPTER 7

THE NEW NURSE

When Helen entered the kitchen, she was greeted by the explosions of spluttering fat. Although the table was crowded with materials for dinner – in different stages of preparation – while vegetables bubbled on the range, Mrs Oates fried fish, juggled with her saucepans, and dried her husband's wet things over the boiler. In spite of the seeming confusion, she took these interludes in her stride, without loss of head, or temper.

Oates, in his grey woollen cardigan, was eating a huge meal in the corner, which his wife had cleared for him. He was a good-natured giant of a man, with the build of a prize-fighter.

At the sight of his small honest eyes, Helen's heart leaped in real welcome. Like his wife, he always appeared to her as a tower of strength.

'I'm so glad you've come back,' she told him. 'You're as good as three men about the house.'

Oates smiled sheepishly as he tried to return the compliment.

'Thank you for laying my table, miss,' he said.

'Is it still raining heavily?' went on Helen.

'Not near so much,' interposed Mrs Oates bitterly. 'Oates brought most of it in with him.'

Oates poured Worcester sauce over his fish, and changed the subject.

'Wait till you see what I've brought back with me,' he chuckled.

'You mean – the new nurse?' asked Helen.

'Yes, the little piece I picked up at the Nursing Home. By the look of her, she's as good as another man.'

'Is she nice?'

'As nasty a bit of work as ever I've come across. Talks with plums in her mouth, and kept me in my place . . . Well, if *she's* a lady, I'm Greta Garbo.'

'Where is she?' enquired Helen curiously.

'I put a meal for her in the sitting-room,' replied Mrs Oates.

'*My* room?'

Mrs Oates exchanged a smile with her husband. Helen's sense of ownership was a perpetual source of amusement to them, because of her small stature.

'Only for tonight,' she said soothingly. 'After her wet ride, I thought she'd rather not wait for the regular dinner.'

'I'll go and welcome her,' decided Helen, even while she knew that 'inspect' would be more appropriate.

Her own sanctum – a dingy semi-basement room, on the other side of the kitchen – was originally intended for the servants'-hall, in the days before the domestic drought. Its walls and ceiling had been washed butter-yellow, in an attempt to lighten the gloom, and it was shabbily furnished with the overflow of the rest of the house.

Because it had been assigned to Helen, she clung to it with jealous tenacity. Although she took her meals with the family, in recognition of the fact that her father had done nothing for his living, the corresponding fact that she, herself, was a worker, cut her off from the privilege of relaxing in the drawing-room.

As she entered her refuge, the nurse looked up from her tray. She was a tall broad-shouldered woman, and was still wearing her out-door nursing-uniform, of conventional navy-blue. Helen noticed that her features were large and reddened, and her eyebrows bushy and set close together.

She had nearly finished her meal and was already smoking, between mouthfuls.

'Are you Nurse Barker?' asked Helen.

'How do you do?' Nurse Barker spoke in a voice of heavy culture, as she laid down her cigarette. 'Are you one of the Miss Warrens?'

'No, I'm the help, Miss Capel. Have you every-thing you want?'

'Yes, thanks.' Nurse Barker began to smoke again. 'But I would like to ask a question. Why am I put in the kitchen?'

'It's not,' explained Helen. 'It's my own sitting-room.'

'Do you take your meals here, too?'

'No. I take them with the family.'

The sudden gleam in the older woman's deep-set eyes told Helen that she was jealous. Although it was a novelty to be an object of envy, her instinct advised her to smooth Nurse Barker's ruffled feelings.

'The nurse has her own private sitting-room, on the first floor, which is far superior to the basement,' she said. 'Your meals are served there. Of course, the same as us. Only, tonight, we thought you'd rather not wait, as you must be cold and tired.'

'I'm more.' Nurse Barker spoke in tones of tragic intensity. 'I'm *horrified*. This place is off the map. I never expected such a lonely spot.'

'You knew it was in the country.'

'I expected the usual country-house. They told me my patient was Lady Warren, which sounded all right.'

Helen wondered whether she ought to warn Nurse Barker of what was in store for her.

'I'm afraid you may find her a bit strong-willed,' she said. 'The last nurse was frightened of her.'

Nurse Barker swallowed a mouthful of smoke, in professional style.

'She won't frighten *me*,' Nurse Barker declared. 'She'll find it won't pay to try her tricks. I keep my patients in order. Influence of course. I believe in kindness. The iron hand in the velvet glove.'

'I don't think an iron hand sounds very kind,' remarked Helen. She looked up, with a sense of relief, as Mrs Oates entered. She had temporarily removed her greasy overall, and was looking forward to gratifying her social instinct.

'The dinner'll keep now, till it's time to dish-up,' she announced. 'I popped in to see if you would fancy a bit of pudding, Nurse. Plum-pudding, or a bit of gooseberry-pie.'

'Are the gooseberries bottled?' asked Nurse Barker.

'No, no, our new December crop, fresh-picked from the garden.'

'Then – neither, thanks,' said Nurse Barker.

'Well – a nice cup of tea?'

'No, thanks.' Nurse Barker's accent grew more refined as she asked a question. 'Is there any – stimulant?'

Mrs Oates' eyes gleamed, and she licked her lips.

'Plenty in the cellar,' she said. 'But the master keeps the key. I'll speak to him about it, if you like, Nurse.'

'No, thank you, I prefer to tell Miss Warren my own requirements . . . It is extraordinary that she has not come downstairs to interview me. Where is she?'

'Setting up with her ladyship. I wouldn't be in too great a hurry to go up *there*, Nurse. Once you're there, you've got to stay put.'

Nurse Barker pondered Mrs Oates' advice.

'I understood it was a single-handed case,' she said. 'But I've come straight off from duty. I only came to oblige Matron. I ought to have a good night's rest.'

She turned to Helen.

'Are you a good sleeper?' she asked.

'Ten to seven,' boasted Helen unwarily.

'Then a bad night won't hurt you. *You'll* have to sleep with Lady Warren tonight.'

Helen felt a pang of horror.

'Oh, no,' she cried. 'I *couldn't*.'

'And why not?'

'I – Well, it sounds absurd, but I'm afraid of her.'

Nurse Barker looked pleased at the admission.

'Nonsense. Afraid of a bed-ridden old woman? I never heard anything so fantastic. I'll arrange it with Miss Warren.'

Helen had a spasm of shrinking aversion as she thought of Lady Warren's artificial grin. She had something to smile about now. She alone knew where she had hidden her revolver.

Suddenly she wondered what would be the outcome, if the nurse insisted on her night in bed. As she looked around her, with troubled eyes, she thought of the young doctor. If she appealed to him, she was sure that he would not fail her.

'Well, we'll see what the doctor says about it,' she said.

'Is the doctor young?' asked Nurse Barker.

'Youngish,' replied Helen.

'Married?'

'No.'

Mrs Oates winked at Helen, as Nurse Barker

78

opened her bag and drew out a mirror and lip-stick. She coated her lips with a smear of greasy crimson.

'You understand,' she said, turning to Helen, '*I* interview the doctor. That is professional etiquette. You are not to talk to him about the patient.'

'But I don't talk to him about her,' remarked Helen.

'About what, then?' asked Nurse Barker jealously.

'Aha, what *don't* they talk about?' broke in Mrs Oates. 'Something saucy, you may depend. Miss Capel's a terror with the gentlemen.'

Although Helen knew that Mrs Oates only wanted to tease the nurse, the sheer novelty of the description made her feel gloriously triumphant, and capable – like her famous namesake – of launching ships.

'Mrs Oates is only pulling your leg,' she told Nurse Barker – responsive to the vague warning that she must not make an enemy. 'But the doctor's rather a darling. We're friends. That's all.'

Nurse Barker looked at Mrs Oates. 'What a curious house this is. I expected a staff of servants. *Why* are there none?'

'Funny thing,' she remarked, 'but as long as this place has been built there's been a trouble to get girls to stay here. Too lonely, for one thing. And then, it got an unlucky name with servants.'

'Unlucky?' prompted Nurse Barker, while Helen pricked up her ears for the answer.

'Yes. It's an old tale now, but right back in Sir Robert's time, one of the maids was found drowned in the well. Her sweetheart had jilted her, so it was supposed she'd threw herself down. It was the drinking-well, too.'

'Disgusting pollution,' murmured Nurse Barker.

'So it was. And then, on top of that, was the murder . . . Kitchen-maid it was, found dead in the house, with her throat slit from ear to ear. She was always hard on tramps and used to like to turn them from the door, and one was heard to threaten to do her in. They never caught him. But it got the house a bad smell.'

Helen clasped her hands tightly.

'Mrs Oates,' she asked, 'where, exactly, was she murdered?'

'In the dark passage, where the cellars are,' was the reply. 'I wouldn't tell you, just now, but Oates and I always call that bit, "Murder Lane".'

As she listened, it occurred to Helen that Lady Warren's rambling talk about trees breaking into the house was built on a solid foundation. When she was a young woman, she had been soaked to the marrow in this damp solitude. She had stood at her window staring out into the winter twilight, while the mist curled to shapes, and trees writhed into life.

One of the trees – a tramp, savage and red-eyed – had actually slipped inside. No wonder, now that she was old, she re-lived the scene in her memory.

'When did this happen?' she asked.

'Just before Sir Robert's death. Lady Warren wanted to give up the house, as they couldn't get no servants, and it was rows, all the time, till the accident.'

'And has the Professor servant-trouble, too?' enquired Nurse Barker.

'Not till now,' replied Mrs Oates. 'There's always been old and middle-aged bits, as wanted a quiet home. They've kept things going until these murders started the old trouble again.'

Nurse Barker licked her lips with gloomy relish.

'One of them was quite close to the Summit, wasn't it?' she asked.

'A few miles off.'

Nurse Barker laughed as she lit a fresh cigarette.

'Well, I needn't worry,' she said. 'I'm safe, as long as *she* is here.'

'Do you mean – Miss Capel?' asked Mrs Oates.

'Yes.'

Helen did not like being picked out for this special distinction. She felt sorry that she had stepped into the limelight, with the announcement of her alleged power to attract men.

'Why pick on me?' she protested.

'Because you are young and pretty.'

Helen laughed, with a sudden sense of fresh security.

'In that case,' she said, '*I'm* safe, too. No man would ever look at me, while the Professor's daughter-in-law was by. She is young, too, and oozes sex-appeal.'

Nurse Barker shook her head, with a smile full of dark meaning.

'No,' she insisted. '*She* is safe.'

'Why?' asked Helen.

In her turn, Nurse Barker put a question.

'Haven't you noticed it for yourself?'

Her hints were so vague and mysterious that they got under Helen's skin.

'I wish you would come out in the open,' she cried.

'I will, then,' said Nurse Barker. 'Haven't you noticed that the murderer always chooses girls who earn their own living? Very likely he's a shell-shock case, who came back from the War, to find a woman in his place. The country is crawling with women, like maggots, eating up all the jobs. And the men are starved out.'

'But I'm not doing man's work,' protested Helen.

'Yes, you are. Men are being employed in houses, now. There's a man, here. *Her* husband.' Nurse Barker nodded to indicate Mrs Oates. 'Instead of being at home, you're out, taking a wage. It's wages from somebody else. That's how a man looks at it.'

'Well – what about yourself?'

'A nurse's work has always been held sacred to women.'

Mrs Oates made an effort to relieve the tension, as she rose from her chair.

'Well, I'd better see what mess one man's made of the dinner. Upon my word, Nurse, to hear you talk, you might be a man yourself.'

'I can see through their eyes,' said Nurse Barker.

Helen, however, noticed that Mrs Oates had

scored a bull, for Nurse Barker bit her lips, as though she resented the remark. But she kept her eyes fixed upon the girl, who felt herself shrink under the relentless stare. Her common sense returned at the sound of Mrs Oates' loud laugh.

'Well, anyone what wants to get our little Miss Capel, will have to get past Oates and me first.'

Helen looked at her ugly face, her brawny arms. She thought of Oates with his stupendous strength. She had two worthy guardians, in case of need.

'I'd not afraid of getting preferential treatment,' she said.

As though she had some uncanny instinct, Nurse Barker seemed to know exactly how to raise up the spectre of fear.

'In any case,' she observed, 'you will have Lady Warren to keep you company. You are sleeping with her tonight.'

Helen heard the words with a horrible sense of finality. Lady Warren knew that Helen would have to come. Her smile was like that of a crocodile, waiting for prey which never failed it.

The old lady would be waiting for her.

CHAPTER 8

JEALOUSY

While Helen grappled with the problem of how to make the doctor understand her aversion to night-duty – so that he might back her up with the necessary authority – the triangle was working up to a definite situation. Had she known it, she would have been indifferent to any development of marital friction. For the first time in her life, she was removed from her comfortable seat in the theatre, and pushed on to the stage.

The more she thought of the prospect of sleeping in the blue room, the less she liked it. It was a case for compliance, or open rebellion, when she risked, not only dismissal, but a probable forfeiture of salary. She was positive that Miss Warren would side with the nurse, for her short spell as her deputy, had been both repugnant and inconvenient.

Nurse Barker's status in the household, as a trained professional woman, was far higher than the help's. If she declared an ultimatum, Helen must inevitably go to the wall. Moreover, in spite of his apparent interest in herself, she had an uneasy suspicion that – as a matter of etiquette – the doctor must support the nurse.

'If he fails me, I'll just have to grit my teeth and see it through,' she thought. 'But, first, I'll have a desperate dig at his higher nature.'

While there seemed to be no connection between her own grim drama of fear and the teacup tempest in the drawing-room, the repercussions of the trivial theme were to be of vital importance to her safety.

Yet the drawing-room and kitchen seemed a world apart. As Helen was grating nutmegs, Simone tossed her cigarette into the fire and rose, with a yawn. Instantly her husband's head shot up from behind the cover of his book.

'Where are you going?' he asked.

'To dress. Why?'

'Merely an opening gambit for conversation. Your unbroken silence is uncivilized.'

Simone's eyes flashed under her painted brows.

'You do nothing but ask questions,' she said. 'I'm not used to cross-examination – and I resent it. And another thing. I object to being followed.'

Newton stuck out his lower lip as he threw away his own cigarette.

'But your way happens to be my way, my dear,' Newton told her. 'I'm going up to dress, too.'

Simone spun round and faced him.

'Look here,' she said, 'I don't want to throw a scene here, because of the Professor. But I warn you once and for all, *I've had enough of it.*'

'And I warn you, too,' he told her, 'I've had enough of you and Rice.'

'Oh, don't be a fool, and start that Middle Ages stuff all over again. You've nothing on me. I'm free to do as I like. I can chuck you – and I will, too – if you persist in being impossible. I've my own money.'

'Perhaps, that's why I'm anxious to keep you,' said Newton. 'Don't forget, this family runs to brains.'

The anger faded from Simone's face and she looked at her husband with a flicker of real interest. Swayed by her senses and desires, she had deliberately stunted her own intellect. She despised cleverness in a woman, since she believed she needed only instinct, in order to explore every part of the territory – man.

Because it was an unfamiliar dimension, she respected a masculine brain. She married Newton, in spite of his ugly face, for the sake of the uncharted region behind his bulging forehead. Intensive spoiling had made her care only for the unattainable.

Her series of affairs with ardent undergraduates had made no impression on her, because they were too easy. Newton could have held her, had he persisted in his pose of indifference.

Unfortunately, his jealousy of Stephen Rice's good looks had dragged him down from his heights and into the arena. There was mutual dislike between them, on the score of an old episode which had sent Rice down from Oxford. For this reason, Stephen played Simone's game, whenever her husband was present, on purpose to annoy him.

At the drawing-room door, Simone turned and spoke to her husband.

'I'm going upstairs, *alone.*'

Newton stared at her, and then sullenly sank down again in his chair. A minute later, he threw down his book, and walked softly up the stairs, as far as the first landing, where he stood, listening.

Simone had reached the second floor, but she did not enter the red room. Instead, she scraped with her finger on the panel of Stephen's door.

'Steve,' she called.

Stephen was stretched on the bed, smoking, while the Alsatian lay beside him, his head on his master's chest. At the sound of Simone's knock, Stephen grimaced to him, as a sign to him to remain silent.

The dog showed the lining of his ears, while his eyes rolled, revealing their whites. Simone knocked louder and rattled the door-handle.

'Don't come in,' shouted Stephen. 'I'm dressing.'

'Then hurry. I want to see you.'

Simone sauntered back to the big red room, to find her husband already in possession.

'No luck?' he asked casually, as he took off his coat.

'I told you not to follow me,' she said.

'I didn't. I merely moved, in obedience to the

87

natural law. Even glaciers travel – although we don't see them do it.'

'If you travelled at their rate, I shouldn't complain.' Simone crossed to the wardrobe and took out the black velvet dinner gown, which she had worn since her arrival at the Summit.

Rejecting it in favour of a backless gown of pale-pink angel-skin, she drew it over her head.

'Excellent taste for a family dinner, in the wilds,' sneered Newton.

Simone looked at him defiantly.

'I'm not wearing it for the benefit of your family,' she told him.

She felt his eyes upon her, watching every process of making up her complexion.

'A touch of perfume behind the ears,' he advised. 'No man can resist it.'

'Thanks for the reminder.'

Simone finished her toilet – eyes brilliant with temper and her lips compressed. When she went out of the room, she deliberately flung the door wide open, so that her husband could hear her foot-steps cross the landing to the bachelor's room.

'Steve,' she called, 'I want to speak to you.'

'Oh – all right.'

The pupil appeared, looked both crumpled and sulky.

'Your hair's untidy,' said Simone, putting up her hands to part his heavy wave.

'Don't.' He shook his head impatiently. 'I detest fiddling.'

'But I like doing it.'

'Then keep on doing it, my dear.'

Stephen ceased to protest, for the reason that he heard footsteps behind him. He looked up at Newton with a malicious grin.

'You'll get the benefit of this, Warren,' he said. 'Your wife's practising on me.'

The veins swelled on Newton's temples as he watched his wife's bare arms clasped around Stephen's neck. With a laugh and a backward sweep of her hand, she rumpled his hair until it stood up in a mop.

'There – you're finished,' she declared.

Newton burst into a hoot of amusement at Stephen's discomfiture.

'He looks like Harpo,' he said. 'I hope my wife will continue to use you as her model, so long as she spares me that.'

Simone glanced at her husband's stubborn crest.

'Where's the difference?' she asked. 'Stephen, you've not admired my new dress.'

Although the young man had not even noticed her finery, he stressed his admiration for Newton's benefit.

'*Well*. I'm bowled over. Beautiful – and most revealing. I'll never mistake you for a nun again.'

Newton's mouth tightened and his glasses magnified the ugly gleam in his eyes. Stephen was self-conscious and truculent as Simone slowly revolved to display a back which had been pronounced perfect.

The scene appeared an ordinary exhibition of herd-instinct, complicated by a frustrate sense of ownership. Yet each released current of human passion was another tributary to swell the tidal-wave, which, later, would sweep Helen away, like a straw on flood-water.

Newton turned away, with an affected shrug.

'I'm afraid my wife's dresses are not the same novelty to me,' he said. 'Oh – by the way, Rice – what have you done with that dog?'

'He's in my bedroom,' snapped Stephen.

'In a bedroom? Really, that's going too far. It's hardly fair to the lady of the house. If you take my advice, you'll put him in the garage for the night.'

'I'll take nothing from you,' snarled Stephen.

'Not even my wife? Many thanks.'

Whistling in apparent unconcern, Newton strolled down the stairs, without a backward glance.

Stephen bristled with defensive instinct, although he knew that Newton's attitude was reasonable.

'Hanged if I'll park the pup in that draughty hole,' he stormed. 'He stays here – or I go with him.'

'For Heaven's sake, forget the dog,' exclaimed Simone. 'Tell me if you really like my dress.'

'What there is of it,' remarked Stephen, reverting to type, since Newton had gone. 'I'm keen on seeing how a boxer strips, when I've backed him; but I don't care about bare backs out of the ring.'

'You brute,' Simone cried. 'I put it on for you. I want you to remember our last night. And *me*.'

'Sorry, my dear,' said Stephen lightly. 'But I'm going to the Bull, after dinner.'

Simone's eyes blazed with sudden passion.

'You're going to see that tow-headed barmaid.'

'Whitey? Yes. But I'm going to see something else, too. Beer. Glorious beer.'

'Stay with me, instead . . . You're the only man I've ever had to ask before.'

Stephen stuck out his lip, like a spoiled child. He wanted an evening of masculine society – the freedom and alcoholic good company of the little country-inn. The landlord's flaxen-haired daughter was merely incidental to his pleasure, because she filled his mug.

He also wanted to get rid of Simone.

Had he known, he could have done so by a show of humility, or an avalanche of attentions. But when he turned away from her, he snapped yet another link of the chain which connected Helen with safety.

Almost running into his room, he slammed the door behind him, and threw himself on the bed.

'Women are the devil,' he told the Alsatian. 'Never get married, my lad.'

In an evil temper, Simone flounced down the stairs. On the landing, she met Mrs Oates who was showing Nurse Barker to her patient's room. At the sight of the ferocious looking woman, her expression slightly cleared, for her jealousy was so

inflamed that she would have resented an attractive nurse.

'Young Mrs Warren,' whispered Mrs Oates, as
she knocked at the door of the blue room.

Nurse Barker grunted, for she recognized the
type.

'Nymphomaniac,' she said.

'Oh, no, she's quite sane,' declared Mrs Oates.
'Just flighty.'

Miss Warren opened the door – a film of welcome
in her pale eyes.

'I'm glad you've come, nurse,' she said.

'Yes, I expect you're glad to pass on the job to
me,' observed Nurse Barker. 'Can I see the patient?'

She stalked after Miss Warren, into the blue
room, and stood beside the bed, where Lady
Warren lay in a shrunken heap, with closed clay-
coloured lids.

'I do hope she'll take a fancy to you,' hinted
Miss Warren nervously.

'Oh, we'll soon be friends,' said Nurse Barker
confidently. 'I've a way with old people. They want
kindness with firmness. They're just like children,
at the other end.'

Lady Warren suddenly opened an eye which was
not in the least child-like, unless it was that of an
infant shot out of an eternity of sin.

'Is that the new nurse?' she asked.

'Yes, Mother,' replied Miss Warren.

'Send her away.'

Miss Warren looked helplessly at the nurse.

'Oh dear,' she murmured, 'I'm afraid she's taken another dislike.'

'That's nothing,' said Nurse Barker. 'She's being a bit naughty, that's all. I'll soon win her over.'

'Send her away,' repeated Lady Warren. 'I want the girl back.'

Nurse Barker saw her chance of redeeming her unpopularity.

'You shall have her, tonight,' she promised.

Then she drew Miss Warren aside.

'Is there any brandy in the room?' she asked. 'I'm medically ordered to take a leetle stimulant.'

Miss Warren looked disturbed.

'I thought you understood this is a teetotal house,' she explained. 'As you know, you are paid a higher salary.'

'But it's not safe to have no brandy in a sick room,' insisted Nurse Barker.

'My mother depends on oxygen,' explained Miss Warren. 'It is her life . . . Still . . . Perhaps . . . I'll speak to the Professor.'

Driven before the towering form of Nurse Barker, she drifted across the landing, like a withered leaf in the eddy of an east wind.

The professor appeared at his bedroom door, in answer to his sister's tap. He greeted the nurse with stony courtesy, and listened to her request.

'Certainly you may have brandy, if you require it,' he said. 'I will go down, at once, to the cellar, and send a bottle up to your room.'

Helen, who was helping in the kitchen, glanced

curiously at Mrs Oates, when the Professor asked her for a candle.

'I shall want you to hold it,' he said. 'I'm going to the wine-cellar.'

Although the request amounted to mental cruelty, Mrs Oates hastened to obey. The electric pendant lit the passage only as far as the bend; around the corner it was quite dark. She walked ahead of the Professor, to guide him, and when she reached the door of the cellar, stood, holding her candle aloft, like a pilgrim who had reached his Mecca.

The key turned in the lock, and Mrs Oates and the Professor entered the sacred place. Fat lumps of greed swam in the woman's eyes as her master selected a bottle from a bin.

As she gazed at it thirstily, the Professor glanced at the thermometer which hung on the wall.

'That temperature cannot be right,' he said, thrusting the bottle into her hands. 'Hold this while I carry it to a better light.'

In a short time he returned from the passage, and relocked the cellar door. This time, he led the way back to the kitchen, while Mrs Oates walked respectfully in his rear. As she passed through the scullery, she ducked down for a second, beside the sink.

The Professor placed the bottle of brandy on the kitchen table and spoke to Helen.

'Please take this up to the blue room, immediately, after Mrs Oates has drawn the cork.'

When they were alone Helen sympathized with Mrs Oates.

'It's a shame. Why don't you keep back just a tablespoonful, to drink Lady Warren's health?'

'I wouldn't dare,' Mrs Oates told her. 'That nurse would know, and split on me. Besides, it would be sin to water down such lovely stuff.'

Helen admired the fortitude with which the woman thrust the bottle into her hands.

'Run off with it, quick,' she said, 'but be sure not drop it.'

Directly she was alone, the secret of her courage was revealed. Lumbering into the scullery, she groped for something she had hidden under the sink.

Opportunity had knocked at her door, and she had been swift in her response. When she returned to the kitchen, she smiled triumphantly at her spoil, before she hid it away among the empties in her cupboard.

It was a second bottle of brandy.

CHAPTER 9

THE OLD WOMAN REMEMBERS

When Helen carried the brandy up to the blue room, Nurse Barker opened the door, in answer to her tap. In her white overall – her dark-red face framed in its handkerchief headgear – she looked like a gigantic block of futuristic sculpture.

'Thank you,' she said. 'This will help me to get some sleep. I must have one good night, if I have to carry on this case, single-handed.'

There was a sinister glint in her deep-set eyes as she added, 'I have arranged for you to sleep here, tonight. Miss Warren was present, so she understands the agreement, and the old girl – Lady Warren—' she hastened to correct her slip – 'raised no objection.'

Helen thought it was wiser to let any protest come from an official quarter.

'Yes, Nurse,' she said. 'But I must hurry to dress.'

'Oh, *you* dress for dinner, do you?'

The woman's tone was so strained – her glance so spiked – that Helen was glad to get away.

'She's jealous,' she thought. 'And Miss Warren's

96

a coward. They're both weak links. I wonder what my special failing is.'

Like the majority of the human race, she was blind to her own faults, and would have protested vehemently against the charge of curiosity, although Mrs Oates already knew the origin of several trivial mishaps.

When she entered her bedroom, she recoiled with a violent start, at the sight of a black shape, which appeared to be swinging into her window.

Snapping on the light, she saw that she had been misled by the branches of a tall cedar, which was being lashed by the gale. Although it seemed so near, the tree was too far away for any athlete to leap from it into her room; but every gust swept the boughs towards the opening in an unpleasantly suggestive manner.

'That tree looks as if it was trying to force its way in,' thought Helen. 'I'll have to shut that window.'

When she fastened the casement, she noticed how the rain streamed down the glass, like a waterspout. The garden lay below, in sodden blackness amid the tormented landscape, over which the elements swept mightily.

She was glad to draw the curtains and gloat over the contrast of her splendid room. It contained the entire furniture of the bedroom of the first Lady Warren. When she had exchanged it for her dwelling in the family vault, it was still new and costly – so that time – combined with lack of use – had done little to dim its grandeur.

Miss Warren, on her return from Cambridge, had made a clean sweep of her mother's belongings to a spare room, in preference of stark and rigid utility; but Helen gladly accepted its superfluity of ornaments and its colour-scheme of terra-cotta and turquoise-blue, for the novelty of thick carpet and costly fabrics.

The original owner's photograph had the place of honour on the marble mantel-shelf. It was taken probably in the 'eighties, and represented an amiable lady, with a curled fringe, too little forehead, and too many chins.

Above her rose the mirror. Its base was heavily painted with bulrushes, water-lilies and storks.

As Helen thought of the ordeal which threatened her, she wished that Sir Robert had remained faithful to the dead.

'If *she'd* lived, she'd have been a dear old lady,' she thought. 'Still, I asked for it. You couldn't keep me out of that room.'

The need to win over Dr Parry became so urgent that she adopted Simone's tactics. As a rule, she wore a sleeveless white Summer frock, for dinner; but, tonight, she resolved to put on her only evening-dress, for the first time. It was a cheap little gown, bought in Oxford Street, during the sales. All the same, the artistic – if hackneyed – contrast of its pale-green colour with the flaming bush of her hair, made her smile at her reflection in the big swinging cheval-glass.

'Ought to fetch him,' she murmured, as she

hurried downstairs in sudden dread, lest he should have arrived in her absence.

She was still faced with her problem of making her opportunity to see him alone; for, of necessity, she was at the call of the household, owing to the elastic nature of her duties. But she had learned how to hide, in the commission of her work; and no S. O. S. could reach her when she was afflicted with temporary deafness.

'The lobby,' she decided. 'I'll take down a damp cloth, and wipe the dust from the palm.'

When she reached the landing, on the first floor, the door of the blue room was opened an inch, to reveal a section of white and the glint of Nurse Barker's eye. Directly she saw that she was observed, the woman shut the door again.

There was something so furtive about that secret examination that Helen felt uneasy.

'She was waiting for me,' she thought. 'There's something very queer about that woman. I wouldn't like to be alone with her, in the house. *She'd* let you down.'

As her instinct was always to explore the unfamiliar, she turned in the direction of the blue room. Nurse Barker saw that her ambush was discovered, and she opened the door.

'What d'you want?' she asked ungraciously.

'I want to warn you,' replied Helen.

She broke off, conscious that Nurse Barker was looking at her neck with hungry gloating eyes.

'How white your skin is,' she said.

'Red hair,' explained Helen shortly.

As a rule, she was sorry that she did not attract general attention; now, for the first time in her life, she shrank from admiration.

'Did you say you wanted to warn me?' asked Nurse Barker.

'Yes,' whispered Helen. 'Don't play Lady Warren too low.'

'What d'you mean?'

'She's hiding something.'

'What?'

'If you're as clever as she is, you'll find out,' replied Helen, turning away.

'Come back,' demanded Nurse Barker. 'You've either said too much, or not enough.'

Helen smiled as she shook her head.

'Ask Miss Warren,' she advised. 'I told her, and got nicely snubbed for my pains. But I felt I ought to put you on your guard.'

She started at the rumble of a deep bass voice from inside the blue room.

'Is that the girl?'

'Yes, my lady,' replied Nurse Barker. 'Do you want to see her?'

'Yes.'

'I'm sorry.' Helen spoke quickly. 'I can't stop now. I've got to help with the dinner.'

Nurse Barker's eyes glittered with a sense of power.

'Why are you so *afraid* of her?' she sneered.

'You'd be afraid, too, if you knew as much as I do,' hinted Helen.

Nurse Barker grasped her by the wrist, while her nostrils quivered.

'The dinner can wait,' she said. 'Miss Warren's instructions are that Lady Warren *must* be humoured. Come in.'

Helen entered the blue room with a sinking heart. Lady Warren lay in bed, propped up with pillows. She wore a fleecy white bed-jacket. Her shock of grey hair was neatly parted in the middle, and secured with pink bows.

It had obviously been Nurse Barker's first job to deck her patient out, like a sacrificial lamb. Helen knew that some grim sense of humour had made the old lady submit to the indignity. She was luring on the nurse to a sense of false security, only to make the subsequent disillusionment the harsher.

'Come here,' she said, in a hoarse whisper. 'I want to tell you something.'

Helen felt herself gripped and drawn downwards, so that Lady Warren's hot breath played on her bare neck.

'A girl was murdered in this house,' said Lady Warren.

'Yes, I know.' Helen spoke in a soothing tone. 'But why do you think about it? It happened so long ago.'

'How do you know?' rapped out Lady Warren.

'Mrs Oates told me.'

'Did she tell you that the girl was thrown down the well?'

Helen remembered that in Mrs Oates' version,

a more gory method was employed. The well figured in the suicide incident. It struck her that Mrs Oates had exaggerated the truth, in order to achieve the sensational interest of a murder.

'Perhaps it was an accident,' she said aloud.

Lady Warren lost her temper at the attempt to calm her.

'No,' she bellowed, 'it was murder. I saw it. Upstairs, from a window. It was nearly dark, and I thought it was only a tree in the garden. Then – the girl came, and it moved, and threw her in . . . I was too late. I couldn't find a rope . . . Listen.'

She drew down Helen's head almost on to the pillow.

'*You* are that girl,' she whispered.

Helen felt as though she were listening to a forecast of her own fate; but she caught Nurse Barker's eye in an attempt to delude her that she was humouring the invalid, in professional style.

'Am I?' she said lightly. 'Well, I'll have to be very careful.'

'You little fool,' panted the old woman. 'I'm warning you. Girls get murdered in this house. But you sleep with me. I'll take care of you.'

Suddenly Helen thought she might trap her to reveal the hiding-place of the revolver.

'How will you do it?' she asked.

'I'll shoot him.'

'Fine. But where's your gun?'

Lady Warren looked at Helen with a gleam of crocodile cunning in her eyes.

'I haven't a gun,' she whined. 'I had one once, but they took it away. I'm only a poor old woman. Nurse, she says I have a gun. Have I?'

'Of course not,' said Nurse Barker. 'Really, Miss Capel, you've no right to irritate the patient.'

'Then I'll go,' declared Helen thankfully. She added, in an undertone, 'You asked me a question, just now. You've had your answer. You know now what to look for.'

At the door, she was arrested by Lady Warren's bass bellow.

'Come back, tonight.'

'Very well, I will,' she promised.

To her surprise her nerves were quivering from the episode, as she went down into the hall.

'What's the matter with me?' she wondered. 'I believe I shall go goofy if the doctor doesn't get me out.'

She looked anxiously at the grandfather's clock. Dr Parry lived several miles away, so he always paid his last call at the Summit, in order to get back to his dinner.

He had never been so late before. A slight foreboding stole over Helen as she listened to the fury of the storm. When Miss Warren drifted by, like a woman in a dream, she appealed to her.

'The doctor's late, Miss Warren.'

Miss Warren looked at the clock. She was already dressed for dinner, in her usual mushroom lace gown.

'Perhaps he's not coming,' she said indifferently.

Helen gave a gasp of dismay. With the egotism of an employer, who never connected a young girl with an independent existence, Miss Warren believed that Helen's concern was on account of the family.

'My mother's condition is static,' she explained, 'although the end is inevitable. Dr Parry has given us instructions how to act, in case of sudden failure.'

'But why shouldn't he come tonight?' insisted Helen. 'He *always* comes.'

'The weather,' murmured Miss Warren.

A rush of wind crashing against the corner of the house illustrated her meaning with perfect timing. Helen's heart turned to water at the sound.

'He won't come,' she thought. 'I shall have to sleep in the blue room.'

CHAPTER 10

THE TELEPHONE

Helen had to sleep in the blue room. Everyone in the Summit had accepted the situation. Feeling that her ambush in the lobby would be a waste of time, since she was certain that Dr Parry would not come, she walked dejectedly towards the kitchen stairs.

She was intercepted by Newton, who slouched out of the morning-room.

'I hear you've made a conquest of my grandmother,' he said. 'Congratulations. How is it done?'

The interest in Newton's eyes invigorated Helen and made her feel mistress of a difficult situation.

'I haven't got to tell *you*,' she replied.

'You mean I'm her white-headed boy,' said Newton. 'That may be. But it doesn't take me far when financial interests are at stake. I can't live on sugar.'

Hitherto, Helen had been somewhat in awe of Newton, who completely ignored her as a social entity. She was there merely to do a job, and he supposed that she – like all the other girls – would go at the end of the month, if she lasted as long.

The novelty of his attention stimulated her confidence.

'Do you mean the will?' she asked boldly.

He nodded.

'Will she – or won't she?'

'We talked about it,' said Helen, inflated with her own importance. 'I advised her not to keep putting it off.'

Newton gave a shout of excitement.

'Aunt Blanche. Come here.'

Miss Warren was wafted by some terrestrial wind out of the drawing-room, in obedience to her nephew's call.

For some inexplicable reason, the shambling short-sighted youth seemed to sway the affection of his own womankind, even if he failed to hold his wife.

'What is it?' she asked.

'Epic news,' Newton told her. 'Miss Capel has worked faster in five minutes than the rest of us in five years. She's got Gran to talk about her will.'

'Not exactly that,' explained Helen. 'But she said she couldn't die, because she had a job to do – an unpleasant job, which everyone puts off.'

'Good enough,' nodded Newton. 'Well, Miss Capel, I only hope you will go on with the good work, if she's wakeful, tonight.'

Even Miss Warren seemed impressed by the fresh development, for she looked, more or less directly, at Helen.

'Extraordinary,' she murmured. 'You seem to have more influence over her than anyone else.'

Helen walked away, conscious that she had been betrayed by her impulse to play to the gallery. Now that the family had a direct personal interest in her relations with Lady Warren, she could only expect their opposition, if she appealed to them against the verdict of the blue room.

But she continued to hold her head high, as though sustained by popular support on her way to execution, even while she shrank from her first glimpse of the scaffold. In her last minute, she would be alone.

When she reached the kitchen, she was instantly aware that Mrs Oates was in no mood for gossip, while Oates kept out of his wife's way, in a significant manner. Regardless of Helen's finery, Mrs Oates pointed to a steaming basin, on the table.

'Just blanch these for the tipsy-cake,' she said. 'I'm behind with my dinner. And Oates keeps dodging under my feet, until I don't know if I'm up in the air, or down a coal-mine.'

In a chastened mood, Helen sat down and gingerly popped almonds out of their shrivelled brown skins. She had accepted the fact of the doctor's absence so completely that she ignored the sound of a bell ringing in the basement hall.

It was Mrs Oates who glanced at the indicator.

'Front door,' she snapped. 'That'll be the doctor.'

Helen sprang to her feet and rushed to the door.

'I'll let him in,' she cried.

'Thank you, miss,' said Oates gratefully. 'I haven't my trousers on.'

'Disgraceful,' laughed Helen, who knew he referred to the fact that he put on his best trousers and a linen jacket, in order to carry in the dinner.

Again hope soared, as she flew up the stairs and opened the front door, letting in a sheet of torrential rain, driven before the gale, as well as the doctor.

He was strongly-built, and inclined to be stocky, with short blunt clean-shaven features. Helen beamed her welcome, while he – in turn – looked at her with approval.

'Is this Gala Night?' he asked.

His gaze held none of the uncomfortable suction of the nurse's eyes, so that Helen rejoiced in her new evening frock. But Dr Parry was more concerned by the hollows in her neck than struck by the whiteness of her skin.

'Odd that you are not better developed,' he frowned, 'with all the housework you do.'

'I've not been doing any lately,' explained Helen.

'I see,' muttered Dr Parry, as he wondered why voluntary starvation, in the case of a slimming patient should fail to affect him, since the result was the same.

'Like milk?' he asked. 'But, of course, you don't.'

'Don't I? I'd be a peril, if I worked in a dairy.'

'You ought to drink a lot. I'll speak to Mrs Oates.'

The doctor drew off his leather motoring-coat and flung it on the chair.

'Dirty weather,' he said. 'It made me late. The roads are like broth. How is Lady Warren tonight?'

'Just the same; she wants me to sleep with her.'

'Well, if I know anything about you, you'll enjoy doing that,' grinned the doctor. 'Something new.'

'But I'm *dreading* it,' wailed Helen. 'I'm just hanging on you to tell them I'm not – not competent.'

'Jim-jams? Has the house got you, too? Are you finding it too lonely here?'

'Oh, no, it's not just nerves. I've got a *reason* for being afraid.'

Contrary to her former experience, Helen held the doctor's attention, while she told him the story of the revolver.

'It's a rum yarn,' he said. 'But I'd believe anything of that old surprise-packet. I'll see if I can find out where she's hidden it.'

'And you'll say I'm not to sleep with her?' insisted Helen.

But things were not so simple as that, for Dr Parry rubbed his chin doubtfully.

'I can't promise. I must see the nurse first. She may really need a good night, if she's come straight off duty . . . I'd better be going up.'

He swung open the doors leading to the hall. As they crossed it, he spoke to her in an undertone.

'Buck up, old lady. It won't be loaded. In any case, her eye will be out, after all these years.'

'She hit the nurse,' Helen reminded him.

'Sheer fluke. Remember she's an *old* woman. Don't bother to come up.'

'No, I'd better introduce you formally to the nurse,' insisted Helen, who was anxious not to infringe professional etiquette.

But the glare in Nurse Barker's eye, when she opened the door, in answer to Helen's knock, told her that she had blundered again.

'I've brought up Dr Parry,' said Helen.

Nurse Barker inclined her head in a stately bow.

'*How* long have you been here, doctor?' she asked.

'Oh, five minutes or so,' he replied.

'In future, doctor, will you, please, come straight to the bedroom?' asked the nurse. 'Lady Warren has been worried, because you were late.'

'Certainly, nurse, if it's like that,' said the doctor.

Helen turned away with a sinking heart. The woman seemed to dominate the young doctor with her will, even as she appeared to tower over him – an optical illusion, due to the white overall.

Simone – in all the glory of her sensational gown – swept past her in the hall. Even in the midst of her own problem, Helen noticed that she was literally drenched with emotion. Her eyes sparkled with tears, her lips trembled, her hands were clenched.

She was in the grip of frustrate desire, which converted her into a storm-centre of rage. She was angry with Newton – because he was an obstacle;

angry with Stephen – because he was unrespon-
sive; angry with herself – because she had lost her
grip.

And all these complex passions were slowly
merging on one person – whom she believed to
be the other woman in the case. She was obsessed
with the idea that Stephen was turning her down
for the sake of the flaxen-haired barmaid at the
Bull.

The help, in spite of her new frock, might
have been invisible, for she passed her without
the slightest notice. And when Helen reached the
kitchen, Mrs Oates also received her with silent
gloom.

It seemed as though the mental atmosphere of
the Summit was curdled with acidity.

'You won't have to hold back dinner much
longer,' said Helen in the hope of cheering Mrs
Oates. 'The doctor will soon be gone.'

'It's not that,' remarked Mrs Oates glumly.

'Then what's the matter?'

'Oates.'

'What's he done?'

'Nothing. But he's always here, night and day,
so that a woman can't never be alone. Don't you
never get married, miss.'

Helen stared at her. She had always admired
the good-nature with which Mrs Oates accepted
her husband's laziness and supplemented his
efforts. Although he did not pull his weight, she
always made a joke of it, while a rough, but real,

111

affection turned their partnership into very good company.

'It's for better, for worse,' said Helen tactfully, 'and I can understand Mr Oates grabbing you, because he could see you were a "better". Now, I can't see the man who'd marry Nurse Barker . . . I wonder if she drinks.'

'Eh?' asked Mrs Oates absently.

'Well,' shrugged Helen, 'she was probably right to insist on having the brandy, even if Miss Warren does say that the oxygen is Lady Warren's life.'

Mrs Oates only stared at Helen – her brow puckered as though she were grappling with a complicated sum in vulgar fractions. Presently, however, she finished her calculations, and gave her own jolly laugh.

'Well, you don't often see me under the weather, do you?' she asked. 'And, talking of husbands, the best is bad, but I've got the best . . . Now, my dear, just listen for the doctor. Directly he goes, I want to slip upstairs with a bit of pudding for Nurse.'

Helen vaguely resented the attention as treachery towards herself.

'Take her tipsy-cake, to go with her brandy,' she advised.

'Now, somebody's on her hind-legs.' Mrs Oates laughed. 'But she's got to go through the night on only a snack. She may look like a slab of stale fish, but a nurse's life is a hard one.'

Helen felt ashamed of her resentment, as she

waited on the kitchen stairs, which was her listening-in station. She was still puzzled by Mrs Oates' changes of mood, for she was not temperamental by nature.

For no explicable reason, she swayed to and fro, like a weather-cock. Whence came the mysterious wind which was blowing on her?

'There's something wrong about this house, tonight,' decided Helen.

Hearing Dr Parry's voice in the distance, she shouted to Mrs Oates, and dashed up into the hall. Directly he saw her, Dr Parry came to meet her. His face was red and he bristled with suppressed anger.

'Miss Capel,' he said, using the formal voice of a stranger, 'if there is any question of your sleeping with Lady Warren, tonight, understand, I will *not* sanction it.'

Helen realized, at once, that Nurse Barker had overreached herself with her high-handed methods. Although her heart sang at her release, experience had taught her the advantage of appealing to the fount of authority.

'Yes, doctor,' she said meekly. 'But if Nurse Barker goes to Miss Warren, she'll get her own way.'

'In that case,' he said, 'I'll go straight to the Professor. No woman shall bullyrag me. If there's any opposition to my orders, some other doctor can take the case. I only hang on, because my own mother – the dearest soul – had a tongue which would raise

113

a blister on a tortoise's back. For her sake, I've a bit of a weak spot for the old b – blessing.'

Helen drew back when they reached the Professor's study.

'Come in with me,' said the doctor.

In spite of her awe of the Professor, Helen obeyed eagerly. The curiosity which would have propelled her to visit any strange and savage beast in its lair, made her anxious to see her employer in his privacy.

She was struck by the resemblance to Miss Warren's room. Like hers, the furniture was merely incidental to the books and papers – supplemented in the case of the Professor, by files and shelves of volumes of reference. There was no trace of the comfort usually characteristic of a man's den – no shabby Varsity chair, no old slippers, or tobacco-jar.

The Professor sat at his American roll-top desk, his finger-tips pressed against his temples. When he looked up, his face appeared blanched and strained.

'Headache?' asked the doctor.

'So-so,' was the reply.

Helen bit her tongue to keep back her impulsive offer of aspirin, as she felt that professional advice should take preference.

'Take anything?' asked Dr Parry casually.

'Yes.'

'Good . . . The new nurse wants Miss Capel to take duty, tonight. I forbid it. Lady Warren's heart is in a bad way, and she is in too critical a condition to be left in the charge of an untrained girl. Will you see that this order stands?'

As he listened, the Professor kept his fingers pressed over his eyeballs.

'Certainly,' he agreed.

When they were outside, Helen turned to the doctor, her eyes limpid with gratitude.

'You don't know what this means to me,' she said. 'You—'

She broke off at the shrilling of the telephone-bell. As the instrument was in the hall, she rushed to answer it.

'Hold on, please,' she said, beckoning to Dr Parry. 'The call's for you. Someone's ringing up from the Bull. He asked if you were here.'

With her evergreen interest in the affairs of others, she tried to reconstruct the inaudible part of the conversation from listening to Dr Parry's end of the line.

'That you, Williams?' he asked. 'What's the trouble?'

His casual tone dulled to incredulity, as he heard, and then sharpened to a note of horror.

'*What?* . . . *Impossible* . . . What a horrible thing. I'll come at once.'

When he hung up, his expression testified to the fact that the telephone-message had proved a shock. While Helen waited for him to speak, Miss Warren came into the hall.

'Was that the telephone-bell?' she asked vaguely.

'Yes,' replied Dr Parry. 'Do you remember a girl – Ceridwen Owen – who used to work here? Well, she's dead. Her body has just been discovered inside a garden.'

CHAPTER 11

AN ARTICLE OF FAITH

As Helen heard the name, she remembered the gossip in the kitchen. Ceridwen was the pretty sluttish girl, who used to dust under Lady Warren's bed, and whose lovers waited for her, outside the house, with the patient fixity of trees. She believed she had actually seen one of them in the plantation, whose vigil had certainly proved in vain.

'Rum thing,' said Dr Parry. 'Williams says that when Captain Bean was coming home from market he lit a match to find the keyhole. That's how he chanced to see her – huddled up in a dark corner of his garden. He came, at once, hell-for-leather to the Bull, and asked Williams to ring my house. My housekeeper told them to try the Summit.'

'Very shocking,' observed Miss Warren. 'I suppose it was some seizure. Her colour was unusually high.'

'I'll soon find out,' announced Dr Parry. 'What beats me is this. The Captain's cottage is only the other side of the plantation. Why didn't he come over here, instead of running nearly a mile to the Bull?'

'He had quarrelled with my brother. The Professor

pointed out a scientific slip in one of his articles. And I believe there was trouble with Mrs Oates over some of his eggs.'

Dr Parry nodded with complete comprehension. Captain Bean was a morose and hot-tempered recluse, who would reject Einstein's Theory and the charge of supplying a bad egg with equal fury. He kept a small poultry-farm, did the work of his cottage, and wrote articles on the customs and religions of native tribes in unfrequented quarters of the Globe.

Dr Parry knew that his life of isolation tended to a lack of perspective, which would exaggerate a trifling grievance to the intensity of a feud; and he guessed that he would prefer to plough through torrential rain rather than ask a neighbour for the use of his telephone.

'I'll cut across the plantation,' he said. 'It will be quicker. I'll come back for my bike.'

The booming of the dinner-gong speeded his parting, but he left a sense of tragedy behind him. When the family was gathered around the table in the dining-room, the subject of Ceridwen cropped up with the soup.

Newton and his wife were not interested in the death of a domestic, but Stephen remembered her.

'Wasn't she the lass with the little dark come-hither eye and a wet red mouth?' he asked. 'The one Lady Warren coshed?'

'An animal type,' remarked Miss Warren. She hastened to add, in a perfunctory voice, 'Poor girl.'

'Why – poor?' asked Newton aggressively. 'We should all envy her. She has achieved annihilation.'

'"Healed of her wound of living, shall sleep sound,"' murmured his aunt, adapting the quotation.

'No!' declared Newton. 'No sleep. Too chancey a proposition. One might wake again. Rather – "I thank with brief thanksgiving whatever gods there be, that no life lives for ever, that dead men rise up never, that even the weariest river—"'

'Oh, dry up,' broke in Stephen. 'Even a river does that, when it's been in the sun.'

'But unfortunately, I am not drunk,' said Newton. 'No one could be, in this house.'

'There's always the Bull,' Stephen reminded him.

'And a devastating barmaid,' said Simone, with meaning in her voice.

'Oh, Newton knows Whitey all right.' Stephen grinned. 'But I've cut him out. I always do that, don't I, Warren?'

Helen was glad of any interruption, however uncomfortable. It had been distasteful to listen to a dreary Creed of Negation when every cell in her body rejoiced in life. What had hurt her even more, was the hint at a denial of the soul.

Her submerged sense of hostess made Miss Warren rouse herself from her dream. Although she was unconscious of Stephen's provocative grin, Simone's slanting glances of passion, and Newton's scowl, she was aware of some poisoned undertow. She changed the subject, after looking across at the Professor, who sat with his eyes covered by his hand.

'Is your head aching again, Sebastian?' she asked.

'I hardly slept last night,' he said.

'What are you taking, Chief?' enquired Newton.

'Quadronex.'

'Tricky stuff. Better be careful of your quantities.'

A sarcastic smile flickered round the Professor's dry lips.

'My dear Newton,' he said, 'when you were an infant you squalled so ceaselessly that I had to administer a nightly sedative, for the sake of my work. The fact that you survive is proof that I need no advice from my own son.'

Newton flushed as Stephen burst into a shout of laughter at his expense.

'Thank you for nothing, Chief,' he muttered. 'I hope you manage your own affairs better than you did mine.'

Helen bit her lip as she looked round the table. She reminded herself that these people were all her ethical superiors. They were better-educated than herself, and had money and leisure. The Warrens had intellect and culture, while Simone had travelled, and had knowledge of the world.

She always sat silent through a meal, since it would require moral courage for her to take any part in the general conversation. Miss Warren, however, usually made some attempt to include the help.

'Have you seen any good Pictures, lately?' she asked, choosing a subject likely to appeal to a girl who never read the *Times*.

'Only films of general interest,' replied Helen, whose recent visits to a Cinema had been confined to the free show at Australia House.

'I saw the *Sign of the Cross*, just before I left Oxford,' broke in Simone. 'I adore Nero.'

The Professor showed some signs of interest.

'*Sign of the Cross?*' he repeated. 'Have they revived that junk? And does the proletariat still wallow in an orgy of enthusiasm over that symbol of superstition?'

'Definitely,' replied Simone. 'The applause was absurd.'

'Amusing,' sneered the Professor. 'I remember seeing the Play – Wilson Barrett and Maud Jeffries took the leading parts – with a fellow-undergraduate. This youth was devoted to racing and completely unreligious. But he developed a sporting interest in the progress of the Cross. It appealed to him as a winner, and he roared and clapped, in its scene of ultimate triumph, while the tears rained down his face in his enthusiasm.'

The general laughter was more than Helen could bear. Suddenly, to her own intense surprise, she heard her own voice.

'I think that's – *terrible*,' she said shakily.

Everyone stared at her surprised. Her small face was red, and puckered up, as though she were about to cry.

'Surely a modern girl does not attribute any virtue to a mere symbol?' asked the Professor.

Helen felt herself shrivelled by his gaze, but she would not recant.

'I do,' she said. 'When I left the Convent, in Belgium, the nuns gave me a cross. It always hangs over my bed, and I wouldn't lose it, for anything.'

'Why not?' asked Newton.

'Because it stands for – for so much,' faltered Helen.

'*What* – exactly?'

Helen felt tongue-tied, under the battery of eyes.

'Everything,' she replied vaguely. 'And it protects me.'

'Archaic,' murmured the Professor, while his son continued his catechism.

'What does it protect you from?' he asked.

'From all evil.'

'Then as long as it hung over your bed I suppose you could open your door to the local murderer?' laughed Stephen.

'Of course not,' declared Helen, for she stood in no awe of the pupil. 'The Cross represents a Power which gave me life. But it gave me faculties to help me to look after that life for myself.'

'Why, she believes in Providence, too,' said Simone. 'She will tell us next she believes in Santa Claus.'

Hard-pressed, Helen looked around the table. She seemed ringed about with gleaming eyes and teeth, all laughing at her.

'I only know this,' she declared in a trembling voice, 'if I was like all of you I wouldn't want to be alive.'

To her surprise, support came from an unexpected quarter, for Stephen suddenly clapped his hands.

'Bravo,' he said. 'Miss Capel's got more spunk than the lot of us put together. She's taken us on, five to one, and she's only a flyweight. Hang it all, we ought to be ashamed of ourselves.'

'It is not a question of courage,' observed the Professor, 'but of muddled thinking and confused values, which is definitely hurtful. You, Miss Capel, are assuming man to be of Divine origin. In reality, he is so entirely a creature of appetites and instincts, that – given a knowledge of his key-interest – anyone could direct his destiny. There is no such thing as the guidance of Providence.'

Newton thrust his head forward, his eyes gleaming behind his spectacles.

'Rather interesting, Chief,' he said. 'I'd like to have a shot at developing a crime picture on those lines. No crude sliding-panels or clutching hands. Make one character do something which would set the rest into motion, so that each would do the natural and obvious thing.'

'You have some glimmering of my meaning,' approved his father. 'Man is but clay, animated by his natural lusts.'

Suddenly Helen forgot her subordinate position – forgot that she had a new job to hold down. She sprang to her feet and pushed back her chair.

'Please excuse me, Miss Warren,' she said, 'but I can't stay – and listen—'

'Oh, Miss Capel,' expostulated Newton, 'we were merely arguing. There was nothing personal intended.'

Before he could finish, Helen was out of the room and rushing down the kitchen stairs. She found Mrs Oates in the scullery, busy stacking dirty dishes.

'Oh, Mrs Oates,' she wailed, 'I've made such a fool of myself.'

'That's all right, my dear, so long as nobody makes a fool of you,' was the consoling reply. 'Now, I want Oates to help me with the washing-up. So, suppose, you take up the coffee for him?'

Helen's courage timed with her reviving curiosity. She wanted to see what effect her outburst had created on her audience.

'Oh, well, I suppose I'd better get it over,' she sighed.

But when she carried the coffee-tray into the drawing-room, she realized that the episode was already forgotten. The young people took their cups mechanically, as they heatedly debated the alleged attractions of a celebrated film-star. Miss Warren was cutting the pages of a new scientific journal, while the Professor had retired to his study.

Suddenly Mrs Oates appeared in the doorway.

'The nurse is downstairs and wants a word with the master,' she said.

'He cannot be disturbed,' Miss Warren told her.

'But it's important. It's her ladyship's life.'

Everyone looked up at the dramatic statement. The household had waited so long for the old terror upstairs to die that it had grown to accept her as immortal. Helen's thoughts flew to the unmade Will, and the vital importance of getting her signature before she struck her colours to death.

'Is she sinking?' asked Newton.

'No, sir,' replied Mrs Oates. 'But the nurse says as we are out of oxygen.'

CHAPTER 12

THE FIRST GAP

Newton broke the stunned silence.
'Who's responsible for such infernal carelessness?' he asked.

Miss Warren and Helen exchanged glances of mingled guilt and condemnation. While neither was exactly clear in her own conscience, each wanted to shift the responsibility on to the other.

As employer, Miss Warren was allowed the first thrust.

'Miss Capel, didn't you screw the cap on the cylinder, after use?' she asked.

'No, because you sent me out of the room.'

'But, surely you did so, before you went?'

'I couldn't, because you had the cylinder.'

Helen spoke with firmness, for the reason that she was not quite clear. Fortunately, Miss Warren was equally confused.

'Had I?' she murmured. 'Yes, I believe I was giving oxygen to Lady Warren. But I have a dim recollection of screwing on the cap.'

'What's the good of arguing?' broke in Newton. 'The thing is, to get in a second supply as soon as possible.'

'Yes, that is the essential point,' she said. 'I will speak to the Professor.'

Helen followed her into the study, to find that Nurse Barker had got there before them. Her heavy voice had lost some of its culture as she talked volubly to the Professor.

'It is unusual to come to a case and find such slackness,' she said. 'I'd like to know who's responsible.'

As she spoke, she fixed her deep-set eyes on Helen.

'*I am*,' replied Miss Warren quietly.

She appeared indifferent to Helen's look of gratitude, as she spoke to her brother.

'I suppose we must order another cylinder, at once.'

'Oh, there's no great hurry,' broke in Nurse Barker. 'She will go through the night quite well, on brandy. She—'

'Allow me to speak, please, Nurse.' The Professor raised his hand in protest. 'The doctor told me, this evening, that Lady Warren's condition is critical.'

'A green country doctor?' sneered Nurse Barker. 'She's not as bad as that. *I* know when a patient is going to die, and it's when I say she is.'

'The doctor's opinion stands,' said the Professor coldly. 'I will telephone for another cylinder to be rushed out, at once.'

'The Factory will be closed,' objected Miss Warren.

'And they'll never send it out to this wilderness, in such a storm,' added Nurse Barker.

'In that case, someone must fetch it.' The

127

Professor spoke decisively. 'Lady Warren's life shall not be risked for the sake of sparing someone a little trouble.'

Helen listened rather guiltily, for she feared that Dr Parry had stressed the gravity of the case for her sake.

'Does Lady Warren know that the doctor said I'm not to sleep in her room tonight?' she asked, anxious to have the matter clinched by the Professor's authority.

'Did he say that, too?' demanded Nurse Barker, a militant gleam in her eye.

The Professor pressed his brow with an impatient gesture, which made Helen realize that Nurse Barker – in rousing his antagonism – was proving her own unconscious ally.

'The doctor expects a crisis,' he explained, 'so, naturally, a trained nurse must be in attendance.'

'Why don't you have a second nurse?' asked Nurse Barker.

'We have not the accommodation,' replied Miss Warren.

'Yes, you have. *She*' – Nurse Barker nodded at Helen – 'can sleep in an attic. Besides, the bachelor's room will be empty, to-morrow.'

Helen stared at this revelation of a perceptive talent which eclipsed her own. In this brief time, the nurse – while, apparently not leaving her patient – had mapped the house.

'There is not enough work for two nurses,' said Miss Warren. 'The other nurses have all assured me

128

that Lady Warren sleeps nearly all through the night, so that their rest has not been unduly disturbed . . . Didn't the Matron tell you that the salary is proportionate to the demands?'

Nurse Barker grew suddenly meek.

'Yes, thank you,' she said, 'I'm quite satisfied with the conditions.'

The Professor turned to his sister.

'I will telephone myself,' he said, going into the hall, followed by Miss Warren. Left alone with Nurse Barker, Helen broke a heavy silence.

'I'm sorry. But you see, I'm not trained.'

'And I am.' Nurse Barker's voice was corrosive. 'To be "trained," means that I'm made of iron, and can eat leavings, and do without sleep, and work twenty-five hours to the day.'

'It's a shame. But it's not my fault.'

'Yes it is.' Nurse Barker pounced fiercely. 'You hung about to get at that doctor first, and you coached him what to say. Oh, you needn't think you can get the better of *me*. There's little I don't see, and what's left over I smell. We've not finished with this. If I turn the last trick – and I've something up my sleeve – you may yet sleep tonight in the blue room.'

Helen was not only scared by the uncanny penetration of the nurse, but she recognized the cruelty which made her hammer away at her fear of Lady Warren, like a torturer plucking at a nerve.

To break away from her company, she hurried into the hall, where the Professor was speaking into the telephone. He raised his hand, as a signal for her to remain. Presently he hung up the receiver and spoke to her.

'They can't make delivery until tomorrow, but they have promised to let my man have a cylinder tonight, from any time up to eleven. Miss Capel, please let Oates know he is to start, at once.'

Helen did not relish her job, when she found Oates stretched before the kitchen fire, enjoying his first pipe after his work. She admired all the more his self-control, and the obedience which he had learned in his Navy days.

He got up instantly, and began to lace up his boots.

'Just as I was looking forward to a nice lay-down on the bed,' he said. 'But that's life.'

'Shall I ask Mr Rice to go instead?'

'No, miss. Orders is orders, and the master said Oates. Besides, I wouldn't trust him with the car. No one but me knows how to ease my sweetheart up them hills.' He turned to his wife. 'Mind you lock up the back after me when I go out to the garage. Remember, you'll have to be double careful with *me* away.'

Helen felt a pang of dismay at the thought of losing Oates so soon. Merely to look at his gigantic frame and amiable face, made her feel safe.

It did not improve matters to realize that she was partly responsible for her own trouble.

'If I'd gritted my teeth, and said nothing to the doctor he wouldn't have been sent,' she thought.

'The Professor said we did things ourselves . . . But – did anyone *make* me do it?'

Suddenly she remembered how Nurse Barker had played upon her fears – and she shivered slightly.

'Oh, I do wish you weren't going,' she said to Oates.

'Same here, miss,' he replied. 'But you'll be all right, with two strong young gents, to say nothing of that nurse.'

'When will you be back?' asked Mrs Oates.

'It will be just as soon as I can make the grade.' He turned to Helen. 'Will you tell the master I'll sound the hooter and wait on the drive for a bit, in case he wants to speak to me.'

Helen delivered his message to the Professor, who had returned to his study. Although he repressed his irritation, she could see that he was fretted by the interruption.

'Thank you, Miss Capel,' he said. 'But Oates knows what to get, and where to go for it.'

Feeling that she wanted to speed his parting, although unseen, Helen went into the lobby, which was exposed to the full fury of the gale. As the wind shook the stout door with the impact of a mailed fist, and the rain gurgled down the pipes, she felt doubly sorry for Oates.

Presently she heard his hooter outside, and longed to open the door to wish him 'good-bye'. But she remembered how the wind had swayed the light when she let in the doctor.

131

The engine of the old crock burst into a series of spluttering explosions and deepened to a roar, before it gradually died away in the distance. With a pang of loneliness, Helen slipped through the swing doors.

She was just in time to witness a lively passage of arms between Miss Warren and Stephen Rice.

'Is it true,' demanded Miss Warren, 'that you have a dog in your bedroom?'

'Perfectly true,' replied Stephen flippantly.

'Take it out into the garage, at once.'

'Sorry. Can't be did.'

Miss Warren lost her habitual calm.

'Mr Rice,' she said, 'understand me, please. I *will not* have an animal in this house.'

'That's all right,' Stephen assured her. 'I'll push off to-night, and take my dog with me.'

'Where will you go?' asked Newton, who – lounging, with his hands in his pockets – was an appreciative spectator of the scene.

'Bull, of course. They'll put me up – and they'll be proud to have the pup.'

Simone gave a cry of protest.

'Don't be so childish, Steve. You can't go through this rain. You'd both be soaked.'

Stephen weakened as he gazed through the open door at the fire, leaping in the drawing-room grate.

'I'll stay if the pup stays,' he said. 'If he goes, I go, too.'

'I'll speak to the Professor,' cried Simone.

Her husband caught her by the arm.

'Don't worry the Chief,' he said. 'He's about all in.'

Simone wrenched herself away and rushed into the study. Unlike the rest of the household, she stood in no awe of the Professor. To her, he was merely an elderly gentleman to whom she paid a certain deference as her father-in-law.

In a few minutes, she appeared – her face radiant with triumph – to herald the Professor.

'I understand,' he said, speaking to Stephen, 'that there is some difficulty about a dog. As mistress of my house, Miss Warren's prejudices are law. But – as it is for one night only – she will relax her rule.'

He turned to his sister.

'You understand, Blanche?' he asked.

'Yes, Sebastian,' was the low reply.

She went upstairs, while the Professor returned to his study.

Suddenly Helen remembered her coffee. She never took any in the drawing-room, because the conventional cups were too small for her liking. Like a true pantry-mouse, she always re-boiled what was left in the pot, adding sufficient milk to make about a pint, which she drank in her own room.

At the end of the official day, it was etiquette not to disturb Mr and Mrs Oates, whose kitchen became their private property; so she always used her own saucepan and spirit stove.

Her room seemed a specially attractive refuge to-night, as, down in the basement, she seemed cut off from the worst of the storm. The light

133

glowed on her golden walls and ceiling, like artifical sunshine.

When she had settled down in her old basket-chair, she felt too comfortable to stir. Although the sound of stealthy footsteps, stealing down the back-stairs, followed by a succession of dull thuds, piqued her curiosity, for once it was submerged in laziness.

There were faces forming in the red heart of the fire; they peered at her, from between the coals, and she stared back at them. Her knees felt pleasantly warmed, and she was at peace with the world.

Presently she heard the footsteps again, ascending the back-stairs. This time, her nature reasserted itself in a surge of frantic curiosity. Leaping up, she was just in time to see the tail of Miss Warren's mushroom-lace gown whisking round the bend of the landing.

Mrs Oates did not look exactly pleasant when she opened the kitchen door in answer to Helen's knock.

'*You?*' she said. 'I expected to see Marlene Dietrich. What's the idea of getting me up, just when I was off my feet?'

'I only wanted to know what Miss Warren was doing down here?' asked Helen.

'And you got me up – just for *that?* As if the mistress wasn't free to go through her own kitchen without leave from *you.*'

'But it's the very first time I've seen her down here,' insisted Helen.

'And, please, how long have you been here? Since anny-domminy?' demanded Mrs Oates, as she slammed the door.

In a chastened mood, Helen returned to her own room and lit her spirit-lamp, in order to re-boil the coffee. She was watching the brown bubbles foam up in the saucepan, when she heard the front-door bell. Turning out the flame, she rushed upstairs, hoping to be first to let in the doctor.

She had a frantic fight to force the door open, for the wind seemed whirling in all directions; before she could throw it wide, Dr Parry slipped through the aperture, and slammed it behind him. Without a word, he fastened all the bolts, and put up the chain.

There was an urgency in his manner, and also in his silence, which excited her to a pitch of fearful expectation.

'Well?' she asked breathlessly. 'Why don't you say something?'

'It's a dirty night,' he said, taking off his dripping coat, while he looked at her with stern eyes.

'No, no,' she insisted. 'Tell me – have you found out the cause of that poor girl's death?'

'Yes,' was the grim reply. 'She was murdered.'

CHAPTER 13

MURDER

The news stunned Helen with such a shock of horror that she felt herself rock, while the house seemed to sway, with her, in the wind. When she was stationary again, she realized that the entire family had gathered in the hall, and was listening, with strained attention, to Dr Parry.

'She was strangled,' he said.

'When?' asked the Professor.

'Impossible to tell within an hour or so. But I should say, roughly, about five or six o'clock.'

'*Strangled*,' repeated Miss Warren. 'Is it – the same kind of murder as the others?'

'Definitely,' replied the doctor. 'Only more ferocious. Ceridwen was a strong girl, and she put up a fight, which enraged him.'

'Then' – Miss Warren's face wavered painfully – 'if she was murdered in Captain Bean's garden, the maniac was quite close to *us*.'

'Closer than that,' said the doctor. 'The murder was actually committed in the plantation.'

A gasp of horror sobbed from Miss Warren's lips, while Simone grasped Stephen's arm. Even in the midst of her own terrible excitement, Helen noticed that Mrs Newton was alive to the amatory possibilities of the situation, while her husband watched her with contracted eyes.

She felt herself slipping away on a back-wash of recent memories. While she stood, defenceless and stranded, staring at the stronghold of the Summit, across a bowl of empty country, she was even then in the company of Murder. All the time it was creeping nearer – unseen, unheard. She might even have passed close to It, while It hid in the undergrowth of the gulley.

But It had smelt her out – marked her down. It knew that she would have to come, and It waited for her, in the plantation, in evil mimicry of a tree.

'What a wonderful escape,' she thought.

Now that the danger was over, she could almost exult in the adventure, were it not for the reminder that the tree had not been cheated of its ultimate prey. The thought of poor Ceridwen, going lightheartedly to a horrible fate, made her feel faint.

When the mist had cleared from her eyes, it was a relief to notice that the Professor's face showed no sign of emotion. As he spoke in his habitual pedantic tones, she felt removed from a dark quivering landscape – split to reveal lightning glimpses of hell – and back in the comfortable interior of an English home.

'How do you establish your fact that this murder was committed in the plantation?' he asked.

'Because there were pine-needles in her clenched hands, and her clothing showed signs of having been dragged through a hedge . . . Of course, it is useless to try to follow the impulses of a distressed brain; but it seems rum to have taken such an unnecessary precaution. The body could easily have lain, undiscovered, in the plantation, for many hours.'

'And it might not,' remarked the Professor. 'You can depend on it, there was some basic idea behind the seeming absurdity.'

His son, who shared his dislike of their eccentric neighbour, gave a chuckle.

'Bean must have had a startling homecoming,' he said. 'A corpse propped up on his doorstep, to let him in.'

'He was a bit upset.' Dr Parry spoke coldly. 'It was a nasty shock for a man of his age. Sudden death is not really amusing – least of all, to the victim.'

His dark eyes flashed angrily over the stolid faces of the young men, and Simone's vermilion lips – parted eagerly, as though to sip sensation.

'I don't want to alarm you people,' he said. 'No, that's a lie. I *do* want to alarm you. Thoroughly. I want you all to realize that there is a criminal lunatic at large, who has tasted blood, and will probably lust for more. And he's somewhere near – quite close to you.'

'Will – Will he try to break in here?' quavered Miss Warren.

'Don't give him a chance. I take it for granted that the Professor will insist on everyone remaining in the house. It goes without saying that you will lock every door and window. Don't under-do your precautions – however ridiculous they may appear.'

'I have seen to all that. Ever since the – the governess,' Miss Warren told him.

'Good. It takes a clever woman to realize danger, and her responsibilities towards her juniors. You'll be all right. Oates, alone, could account for the chap, with one hand, if he should happen along.'

Again Helen was assailed by that odd pang of desolation as she listened to the Professor's explanation of Oates' absence. She felt strangely depressed, too, by the thought that Dr Parry would soon be gone.

His practical, cheerful personality seemed to reduce even murder to its proper proportions. It was an unnatural evil, which could be guarded against by natural means – which would prevail, since the defence was so much more powerful than the attack.

He presented an uncouth figure in contrast with the other men, who were all in immaculate evening-dress, but when he caught her eye and smiled at her, she knew, instinctively, that he could inspire both affection and trust.

Some bright elusive vision quivered before her eyes, filling her with happiness and hope. She felt she was on the verge of some discovery. But before she could collect her thoughts the doctor had turned to go.

'I must push off,' he said cheerfully. 'Professor.

I know you understand the importance of all the men staying in to-night to protect these two girls.'

His glance included Simone, who responded with an alluring smile.

'Peter,' she said, leaning her chin on the Professor's shoulder, 'you're not going to let the doctor go without offering him a drink.'

Before the doctor could refuse the unspoken invitation, Helen stepped into the breach.

'I've some coffee, downstairs,' she said. 'Shall I bring some up?'

'The very thing,' remarked the doctor. 'But may I come down and dry off a bit while I mop it up?'

Helen could not resist a feeling of triumph over Simone, as Dr Parry clattered after her, down the kitchen stairs. While Simone's man strained at his chain, she had hers coasting in her wake.

Her sitting-room looked even more cheerful and restful when Dr Parry sat opposite to her, gulping coffee from a huge breakfast cup.

'What are you beaming about?' he asked abruptly.

'I ought not to,' she said apologetically. 'This is all so terrible. But – it is *living*. And I've done so very little of *that*.'

'What *have* you done?' he asked.

'Housework. Sometimes, with children thrown in.'

'Yet you keep your tail up?'

'Of course. You never know what's just round the corner.'

Dr Parry frowned.

'Have you never heard that "Curiosity killed the

cat"?' he asked. 'I suppose, if you saw a smoking bomb, you'd feel bound to examine its fuse?'

'Not if I knew it was a bomb,' explained Helen. 'But I wouldn't know if it was, until I'd found out.'

'And *must* you find out?'

'Yes, you must – if you're *me*.'

'I give you up.' Dr Parry groaned. 'Haven't you enough wit to realize that there's a human tiger waiting to turn you into – what's left of Ceridwen. If you'd seen what I've just seen—'

'Oh, don't,' wailed Helen, her face suddenly pinched.

'But I want to frighten you. This sort of lunatic is usually normal in between his fits of mania. He might be living in this house with you, and you'd accept him, just as you accept young Rice or the Professor.'

Helen shuddered.

'Might it be a woman?' she asked.

'No, unless she was abnormally strong.'

'In any case, I should be bound to know.'

'No, that is the paralysing part of it,' insisted the doctor. 'Just imagine the horror of seeing a friendly face – like my own – suddenly change into an unfamiliar mask – with murder glaring out of its eyes?'

'Are you trying to tell me someone in this house committed all the murders?' Helen asked. 'Well, I'd take on anyone here, except Oates. *He* would be awful, if he turned inside out. A sort of King Kong.'

Dr Parry lost his temper.

141

'You're making a joke out of it,' he said. 'But what about a girl who was frightened of a poor old woman?'

Helen shrivelled, instantly, at the memory.

'I want to thank you for that,' she said. 'You were a real sport . . . She's different. There's something unnatural about her . . . But I think that everyone should do all the things they shouldn't do – and then, they won't.'

Dr Parry laughed as he rose reluctantly from the old creaking basket-chair.

'It takes a doctor to disentangle that,' he said. 'But I imagine you refer to moral inoculation.'

'Yes,' nodded Helen. 'Like being vaccinated against small-pox.'

'And would you like to have an injection of your own vaccine?' he asked. 'Get drunk? Sniff snow? Have a week-end in Brighton?'

'Oh *no*,' objected Helen. 'Of course, I didn't mean myself. I'm always out of things.'

As Dr Parry looked at her, the meaning in his eyes underlined his words.

'I think, before long, you'll find yourself very much in the picture. Perhaps Welshmen are more impetuous than Englishmen. In fact, I'm ready to bet that, within six months, you'll be Mrs Jones, or Hughes, or – Parry.'

Helen purposely reversed the order of the names, as she smiled back at him.

'Taken,' she told him. 'If I'm not Mrs Parry, or Jones, or the other, I'll collect off you.'

'Done,' said the doctor. 'You'll lose. But now that I've got outside your coffee I must go.'

'No, wait,' said Helen, arrested by a sudden memory. 'I want to tell you something first.'

In a few words she gave him a skeleton outline of her adventure with the tree. There was no need to colour any details, to get her effect this time; Dr Parry's eyes were fierce and his lips set in a rigid line, in his attempt to hide his concern.

'I take back that bit about the bomb,' he said. 'Thank Heaven, you've still got a scrap of precious sense of danger.'

'Then you don't think me a fool for running away?'

'I think it was probably the wisest thing you've done in your life.'

Helen became thoughtful.

'It's a pity I didn't really see him,' she remarked. 'I mean, when he turned to a man. Do you think it is a local person, as he was waiting in the plantation?'

Dr Parry shook his head.

'No. This is obviously the fifth murder in a series of connected crimes. As the first two were committed in town, it is probable that the criminal lives there. What the Police should do is to get acquainted with the time-table of some respected citizen, and find out if a handful of fringe is torn from his white silk scarf.'

'Do you mean there's a clue?' asked Helen.

'Yes. I found a hank of it inside Ceridwen's

mouth. She must have torn at it, with her teeth, when they were struggling. She didn't make it easy for him – or he for her . . . Come with me, to let me out, and see that every bolt is shot.'

Helen obeyed, although she hated to see him go into the streaming darkness. The dripping laurels of the drive, and the clipped evergreens on the lawn, shook in the gale, as though straining at their roots.

She banged the door, hearing the click of the spring lock with a definite sense of security. The hall seemed calm as a millpond after the howls of the wind. There was serenity in the soft glow of its lighting – comfort and warmth in the thick pile of the peacock-blue carpet.

As the hall was empty, Helen ran downstairs to her own room, where Dr Parry's presence still seemed to linger. But she had barely seated herself before the fire when Mrs Oates' head appeared around the door.

'I'm warning you,' she said, in a hoarse whisper. 'There's something *queer* about that new nurse.'

CHAPTER 14

SAFETY FIRST

Helen stared at Mrs Oates, with vague misgiving. There was something unfamiliar in the woman's appearance which eluded her. Her face, still flushed from the heat of the fire, wore its usual expression of good-natured surliness, so that Helen was puzzled to account for the change.

'The nurse?' she repeated. 'She's rather a brute – but what's queer about her?'

'*Things*,' Mrs Oates nodded mysteriously. 'I've noticed them, but taken no notice. They come back after, and then I wonder what they were.'

'What things?' insisted Helen.

'Little things,' was the vague reply. 'I'd like a word with Oates. He could tell me.'

As her voice thickened, Helen suddenly traced the difference in her to its source. Something had gone out of her face; her lips hung loosely, so that her jaw had lost its suggestion of a bulldog grip.

She felt vaguely uneasy. One of her special guards was gone – and the other had changed. She had no longer the comforting assurance of Mrs Oates' protection.

145

A thread of meaning, however, ran through Mrs Oates' talk, and Helen found her attention gripped.

'I want to see Oates,' declared the woman, 'and ask him just *where* he picked up that nurse. A baby could diddle Oates. If someone cut off his head, and stuck on a cabbage, he'd never notice the difference, and no more would you.'

'But I'm sure he told us he took her from the Nursing Home,' Helen reminded her.

'Yes – and how? I know Oates. He'd drive up, and then, because he hadn't me to hop out and ring the bell for him, he'd just sound the hooter, and wait for things to happen. The first body in a cloak and veil, what hopped inside the car, would be good enough for him.'

'Hum,' mused Helen. 'Still, even if she is an impostor, she couldn't have committed the murder, because she was driving with him, in the car, when it was committed.'

'What murder?' asked Mrs Oates.

Helen was human enough to relish the importance of announcing tragic news, which did not touch her personally. But Mrs Oates' reception of Ceridwen's death was disappointing. Instead of being thrilled with horror, she accepted it as though it were an item in the weekly schedule.

'You don't say,' she muttered. 'Well, you mark *my* words. There'll be another murder before we're one night older, if we're spared to live as long.'

'Aren't you a little ray of sunshine?' exclaimed Helen.

'Well, I don't trust that nurse. Folks said as how the looney must have had a woman, what used to talk to the girls, and take off their notice, so as he could spring.'

'You mean – a decoy?' asked Helen. 'I'll promise you this. If the nurse invites me to go for a little walk with her, in the garden, tonight, I won't go.'

'But she's not here for that,' said Mrs Oates. 'She's here to open the door to *him*.'

It was a most unpleasant idea, coming on the heels of Dr Parry's revelation. Helen awoke afresh to the loneliness of the storm-bound house. Even down in the basement, she could hear the fury of the gale, like a tidal-wave thudding against the shutters of the windows.

'I think I'll go upstairs and see what the others are doing,' she said, feeling that she needed a change of company.

The first person she met in the hall was Stephen Rice. He had opened the door of the closet where the coats were hung, and had just unhooked his ancient Burberry from its peg.

'You're never going out in this storm,' she cried.

'Hush. I'm stealing off to the Bull. I need the company of my fellow working men to get the taste of this nasty affair out of my mouth. I might even try the experiment of a glass of beer. I'm the sort of desperate chap who'd try anything once.'

'I believe there's one thing you wouldn't,' said Helen, who felt strung up to a reckless pitch.

'Meaning?'

'Running off with another man's wife.'

Stephen followed Helen's glance towards the drawing-room.

'You never said a truer thing,' he nodded. 'No women for me.' Then he held out his hand. 'Sister, can you spare me a dime?'

Helen couldn't believe that he was really borrowing money from her, until he explained.

'I want to settle my score at the Bull. Buying the pup cleaned me out.'

'Where is the pup?' asked Helen.

'Up in my room, asleep on the bed . . . Sister, what about that dime?'

'I haven't got it,' faltered Helen. 'I don't get paid until the end of my month.'

'Tough luck. Another country off the Gold Standard . . . Sorry I asked. Nothing for it, now, but to touch Simone. She's plenty of chink.'

As he spoke Simone sauntered across the hall.

'Where are you going?' she demanded.

'First of all, I'm going to you, my dear, to borrow some cash. Then, I'm going to the Bull, to hand over the said cash.'

Simone contracted her painted brows.

'You haven't got to invent any excuse for going to the Bull,' she told him. 'I know the special attraction.'

'Whitey?' groaned Stephen. 'For the love of Mike, stop harping on her. She's a nice little girl. We're friends, and that's all.'

He broke off, as Newton came out of the study.

'Will you all come into the study?' he said. 'The Chief has an announcement to make.'

The Professor was seated at his table, speaking in a low voice, to his sister. His face wore a look of exhaustion, which was not lost on Helen.

She noticed, too, the glass of water and the small bottle of white tablets which stood at his elbow.

'I have something to say,' he announced, 'which applies to everyone. No one is to leave this house to-night.'

Simone flashed a look of triumph at Stephen, who began to splutter.

'Oh, but, sir, I have an important appointment.'

'Then you will not keep it,' the Professor informed him.

'But I'm not a baby.'

'Prove it. If you are a man, you will realize that we are faced with a situation of actual danger and that it is the duty of every male member of this household to remain at home.'

Stephen continued to protest.

'I'd stay, like a shot, if there was any sense in it. But it's such bally rot. Of course, no woman should go out. But they are safe, at home. The chap wouldn't come inside the house.'

'Have you forgotten the girl who was murdered inside her bedroom?' broke in Miss Warren, in a dead voice.

'Her window was left open,' explained Stephen.

'But you heard what the doctor said?' insisted Miss Warren.

'And you've heard what *I've* said,' remarked the Professor sternly. 'I'm master of this house, and I will not have the safety of anyone here imperilled by disobedience.'

Helen felt his glance hover for one moment over her, and her heart throbbed with gratitude.

'There is another precaution I wish observed,' went on the Professor. '*No one* is to be admitted to this house, to-night. If anyone knocks, or rings, he – or she – will remain outside. I forbid the doors being unbolted, on any pretext whatsoever.'

This time objection came from Newton.

'That's rather drastic, Chief,' he said. 'Anyone might come; the Police, or someone with important news.'

The Professor took up a paper as though he were weary of the discussion.

'Those are my orders,' he said. 'I am only concerned, to-night, with the safety of those under my roof. But I warn you this. Anyone who goes outside the house – if only for a minute – *will not return*. The door will be locked on him, or her, and it will not be opened again.'

A host of disturbing possibilities flitted across Helen's mind. In particular, she had a vision of Dr Parry – on a special mission which concerned herself – standing outside in the rain.

'But, if we recognize the voice, will that alter things?' she asked timidly.

150

'Certainly not,' said the Professor. 'Voices can be imitated. I repeat. You are to open to no one, man, woman or child.'

'Oh, but, Professor, you *can't* mean a child?' cried Helen. 'If I heard a baby crying outside I'd just have to take it in.'

The Professor smiled bleakly.

'You'd probably find your baby waiting to grip your throat,' he told her. 'Surely you've heard child-impersonators over the Wireless, whose imitations are faultless?'

'He could squeal his head off for all the effect he'd make on me,' said Stephen brutally. 'I was done out of my chance of a fortune by an unexpected Blessed Event in my family . . . And I promise you this, too. I wouldn't cross the room for any woman alive.'

The look which Simone threw him was a challenge, which was intercepted by Newton. He gave a faint hoot of laughter.

'Ever heard of Shakespeare, Rice?' he asked caustically. 'Or of a quotation – "Methinks the lady doth protest too much"? We hear so much about your being a woman-hater, and see so little evidence.'

The Professor rapped the table, as though he would silence a noisy Session.

'That is all,' he said. 'Miss Capel, will you please pass on my orders immediately to Mrs Oates and Nurse Barker?'

'Yes, Professor,' said Helen.

Suddenly she was assailed by a fresh complication.

'What about Oates?' she asked.

'He will remain outside,' was the relentless reply. 'He can garage the car, and remain there, until the dawn.'

'But Lady Warren might want her oxygen?'

'Lady Warren must take her chance with the rest. I am committed to a policy of Safety First. Perhaps I understand the situation better than the rest of you . . . When I was in India, in my youth, I remember a tiger which prowled outside a cattle-enclosure. Again and again it broke through the defence, in spite of every precaution.'

He dropped his voice, as he added, 'There is a tiger, outside this house, *now*.'

As he spoke, there was the sound of loud knocking on the front door.

CHAPTER 15

SECRET INTELLIGENCE

The knocking ceased, and a bell was pealed which brought Helen instinctively to her feet.

'I'll answer the door,' she said.

She crossed the room before she realized the significance of her action. No one else had moved; but all were looking at her – their expressions passive, scornful, or amused, according to temperament.

The Professor nodded at his sister – a sardonic gleam in his eye.

'The weak link,' he observed, in an undertone.

The familiarity of the phrase brought home to Helen its special meaning, so that she coloured to the roots of her hair.

'I'm sorry,' she faltered, 'but it's second-nature for me to answer a bell.'

'You gave us a demonstration of that,' said the Professor acidly. 'I don't wish to be severe, but you must remember that forgetfulness, in this case, ranks with disobedience.'

The knocking was repeated, and again a bell pealed in the distance. Even although she was under observation, and on her guard, Helen found it an ordeal to stand by and do nothing.

'It's like watching milk boil over,' she thought, 'or seeing a child play with fire. Someone *ought* to do something. I'm sure it is all wrong.'

She noticed how the muscles of Miss Warren's face quivered at every blow, and her own nerves twitched in sympathy.

A third assault was made on the door. This time Stephen seemed conscious of the tension.

'Look here, sir, with due deference to you – and all that – isn't this going a bit too far? Cutting all the wires, I mean. That may be the postman, with an unstamped letter for me, to say my Cousin Fanny has passed out, and left me her heir.'

The Professor explained, with the dreary patience with which he enlightened a pupil's ignorance.

'I have just given an order, Rice. It would be reactionary conduct on my part to commit the same fault for which I've just rebuked Miss Capel. If once we begin to make exceptions to a precaution which is intended for the general safety, it ceases to have any value.'

'Yes, sir.' Stephen grimaced at a fourth, and louder assault on the knocker and bell. 'But it gets my goat not knowing who's outside.'

'Oh, my dear Rice, why didn't you say that in the beginning?' The Professor's smile flickered and went out. 'Of course, it is the Police.'

'Police?' echoed Newton. 'Why have they to come here?'

'A mere formality, since the Summit is in the radius of – of this affair. They will want to know if we can furnish them with any information. If they would accept a negative answer, and go, I would relax my rule in their favour.'

'But you can't keep them out, Sebastian,' cried Miss Warren.

'I have no intention of keeping them out. When they call tomorrow, they will be admitted. I'm master of my house, and I've wasted too much time already, to-night.'

Through his glasses, his eyes flashed hungrily over the papers on his desk.

Helen hoped fervently that Mrs Oates would answer the door, for the Police seemed a direct answer to prayer. She had a mental vision of a compact body of solid, uniformed men, bringing with them the protection of the Law.

Suddenly she thought that she might force the Professor's hand.

'But *I* could tell them something,' she said.

'Miss Capel,' he said, in measured tones, 'have you any clear, concise knowledge that will be of definite use to the Police? For instance – have you seen the criminal, so that you could describe him?'

'No,' replied Helen.

'Then, have you any idea as to who he is, or where he is?'

'No,' replied Helen, wishing she could sink into the floor.

'Well – have you any valuable theory?'

'No, but – but I think he hides behind trees.'

Simone led the suppressed laughter, in which even Miss Warren joined.

'Thank you, Miss Capel,' said the Professor. 'I think the Police can wait for your help, until to-morrow morning.'

Helen's heart sank. It seemed always 'to-morrow,' and she still dreaded the night which divided her from the dawn.

The Professor, however, seemed to have some pity for her confusion, for he spoke to her, in the voice of a considerate employer.

'Now, Miss Capel, will you be so kind as to tell Mrs Oates and Nurse Barker, my decision.'

'Indeed, I will,' Helen assured him.

'I suppose Gran doesn't know about the murder?' asked Newton.

'No,' replied Miss Warren, 'neither she nor the nurse can know. I'm the only person who has been upstairs, since Dr Parry brought us the news. And I should certainly not dream of alarming her.'

'She *must not* be told,' commanded the Professor.

The hall was silent when Helen passed through it. The Professor had worn down the patience of the Police, who happened to be in the singular person. After exposure to what was practically a water-spout, he drew his own conclusion from the barred windows, and decided to call by daylight. Apparently the fear of the maniac had spread from the cottages to the big houses of the neighbourhood.

156

When Helen reached the kitchen, to her surprise, she was unable to enter. At first, Mrs Oates did not answer her tap; but presently, a huge distorted shadow crossed the frosted glass of the door, and a key clicked in the lock.

Mrs Oates towered over her, with a confused red face and sleepy eyes.

'Must have lost myself,' she explained.

'But is it safe to go to sleep with the door locked?' asked Helen. 'Suppose your clothes caught on fire, and we couldn't get at you?'

'Yes, you could. Nearly all the locks here has the same key; only you can't turn them, because they're never used.'

'Naturally,' said Helen. 'You only lock your door in loose houses, and hotels. I've always taken pure situations, and I've never locked my door in my life.'

'Well, if I was you, I'd oil my key, and lock my door, to-night,' said Mrs Oates.

'How useful,' laughed Helen, 'if any other key would fit it.'

'But theirs would be rusty,' explained Mrs Oates.

When Helen delivered the Professor's message, she jerked her head defiantly.

'Thank his lordship for nothing. Doors are not my work, and never was.'

As she retreated inside the kitchen, Helen caught her sleeve.

'Please, Mrs Oates, don't lock the door,' she entreated. 'I'd hate to feel I couldn't reach you.

I'm such a fool, to-night. But I depend on you, more than anyone else in the house.'

'That's right.' Mrs Oates shot out her jaw in the old aggressive way. 'If anyone gets in, I'll knock his block off.'

With the comforting assurance ringing in her ears, Helen mounted the stairs, to the blue room, which had regained some of its former fascination. As though she had been listening for her step, the door slid open an inch, to reveal Nurse Barker.

'I've something to tell you,' Helen whispered. 'There's been another murder.'

Nurse Barker listened to every detail. She asked questions about Ceridwen's character, her duties about the house, her lovers. At the end of the story, she gave a short laugh.

'She's no loss. Her sort asks for it.'

'What d'you mean by "her sort"?' asked Helen.

'Oh, I know the type. You've not got to tell me . . . Sluttish. Little dark eyes, saying "Come into a dark corner," to every man. A slobbery red mouth, saying "Kiss me." A lump of lust.'

Helen stared as Nurse Barker reeled off the glib description, for she had not mentioned Ceridwen's personal appearance.

'Have you heard of Ceridwen before?' she asked.

'Of course not.'

'Then how did you know what she looked like?'

'Welsh.'

'But all Welsh girls are not like that.'

Nurse Barker merely changed the subject.

'As for the Professor's orders about the doors, they are not necessary. Answering doors is not part of a nurse's duty. And I should certainly not risk my life by going outside, in this storm. It is an insult to my intelligence.'

Helen felt more at her ease when Nurse Barker exalted her own importance. She became a definite type – which, although unpleasant – was only too common, in her experience. It did not pair with that mephitic shade raised by Mrs Oates – the midnight hag, who crept down the stairs, when the household was asleep, to let in Murder.

'Nurse!'

At the familiar bass voice, Nurse Barker turned to Helen.

'I want to go down to the kitchen, to see about certain things,' she said. 'Could you stay with her?'

'Certainly,' replied Helen.

'Not frightened now?' sneered Nurse Barker. 'When did you have a change of heart?'

'I was just silly before,' explained Helen. 'I'm a bit run down. But now we've got something *real* to fight, fancies must go to the wall.'

With her old confidence, she entered the blue room, expecting a welcome. But Lady Warren seemed to have forgotten her former interest.

'What was all that knocking?' she asked.

'You've very keen hearing,' said Helen, while she tried to think of some explanation.

'I can see – hear – smell – feel – taste,' snapped Lady Warren, 'and better than you. Can you tell

159

the difference between an underdone steak – and one that is rare?'

'No,' replied Helen.

The next question raised a more unpleasant issue.

'Could you aim at the whites of a man's eyes, *and* pot them? . . . What was that knocking?'

'It was the postman,' explained Helen, lying to meet the Professor's instructions. 'Oates has been sent out, for fresh oxygen, as you know, and I was somewhere else; so no one heard him, at first.'

'Disgraceful organization in *my* house,' stormed Lady Warren. 'You needn't stare. It's still *my* house. But I had servants in livery . . . Only they all left . . . Too many trees . . .'

The whimper in her voice was not assumed, and Helen knew that the past had gripped her again.

But even while she sympathized with this derelict of time, Lady Warren became several degrees more vital than herself; for she heard footsteps on the stairs which had been inaudible to Helen, and her eyes brightened in anticipation.

The door swung open, and the Professor entered the bedroom.

Helen was interested to notice how the sex-instinct triumphed, even on the threshold of the grave, for Lady Warren's reception of her step-son was very different from her treatment of any woman.

'So, at last, you condescend to visit me?' she exclaimed. 'You're late, to-night, Sebastian.'

'I'm sorry, madre,' apologized the Professor.

He stood – a tall, formal figure – at the foot of the bed – in the shadow of the blue canopy.

'Don't go,' he whispered to Helen. 'I'm not remaining long.'

'But the post was late, too,' remarked Lady Warren casually.

Helen's respect for the Professor's intelligence was increased by his immediate grasp of her subterfuge.

'He was delayed by the storm,' he explained.

'Why didn't he push the letters through the slit?'

'There was a registered letter.'

'Hum . . . I want a cigarette, Sebastian.'

'But your heart? Is it wise?'

'My heart's no worse than yesterday, and you didn't make a dirge about it then. Cigarette.'

The Professor opened his case. Helen watched the pair, as he leaned over the bed, a lighted match in his fingers. The flame lit up the hollow of his bony hand, and Lady Warren's face.

Helen could tell that she was an experienced smoker, by the way she savoured her smoke before blowing it out in rings.

'News,' she commanded.

In his dry voice, the Professor gave her a summary, which reminded Helen of the *Times* leading article chopped up into mincemeat.

'Politicians are all fools,' remarked Lady Warren. 'Any murders?'

'I must refer you to Mrs Oates. They are more

in her line than mine,' replied the Professor, turning away. 'If you will excuse me, madre, I must get back to my work.'

'Don't overdo it,' she advised. 'You look very old-fashioned about the eyes.'

'I've not slept well.' The Professor smiled bleakly. 'Were it not that I know it to be a popular fallacy, I should say I had not a single minute of sleep, during the night. But I must have lost consciousness, for minutes at a stretch, for there was a gap in the chimes of the clock.'

'Ah, you're a clever man, Sebastian. The fools of nurses pretend that they wake if one of my hairs falls out – but they sleep like pigs. I could roll about, on wheels, and they wouldn't stir. Blanche, too. She dropped off, in her chair, when it was growing dusk, but she'd never admit it.'

'Then you couldn't use *her* to establish an alibi,' said the Professor lightly.

Helen wondered why the speech affected her disagreeably. Whenever she was inside the blue room, its atmosphere seemed to generate poison-cells in her brain.

'Where's Newton?' asked the old lady.

'He'll be coming up to see you, soon.'

'He'd better. Tell him life is short, so he'd better not be late for the Grand Good Night.'

The Professor shook her formally by the hand and wished her a restful night. In obedience to his glance, Helen followed him outside the door.

'Impress on the nurse, when she returns, not to

162

let Lady Warren know about – what happened to-night.'

'Yes, I understand,' nodded Helen.

When she came back, Lady Warren was watching her intently, with black crescent eyes.

'Come here,' she said. 'Another murder has just been committed. Have they found the body?'

CHAPTER 16

THE SECOND GAP

As Helen listened, a herd of vague suspicions and fears galloped through her mind. Lady Warren spoke with the ring of authority. She was not guessing blindly; she knew something – but not enough.

It was this half-knowledge which terrified Helen. Had any of Dr Parry's audience told her about the murder she would naturally have heard, also, about the discovery of the body in Captain Bean's garden. Nurse Barker, alone, stood outside the circle of informed listeners. That fact did not necessarily assume the most sinister significance. To use the Professor's phrase, her alibi was established. When Ceridwen was being done to death, she was bumping, in the old car, towards the Summit, in Oates' company.

Yet – if she had told her patient – she must have possessed some horrible specialized knowledge of the movements, or intentions of the maniac – which stopped short with the commission of the murder.

As Lady Warren gripped her wrist, Helen realized that it was useless to lie.

'How do you know?' she asked.

The old woman did not reply. She gave a hoarse gasp.

'*Ah*! Then they've found her. That knocking was the Police. I knew it . . . Tell me *all*.'

'It was Ceridwen,' Helen said. 'You remember? She used to dust under your bed, and you objected to her feet. She was strangled in the plantation, about tea-time, and carried afterwards to Captain Bean's garden. He found her.'

'Any clue?'

'One. She tore out a handful of fringe from the murderer's white silk scarf.'

'That's all . . . Go away,' commanded Lady Warren.

She pulled up the sheet, and covered her face entirely, as though she were already dead.

On her guard against foxing, Helen sat by the fire, where she could watch the bed. Although one fear had swallowed up the other – like two large snakes snatching at the same prey – she had an instinctive dread of exposing her back to Lady Warren.

To steady her nerves, she made a mental inventory of the situation.

'There's the Warren family – four; Mrs Oates, Nurse Barker, Mr Rice and me. Eight of us. We ought to be more than a match for one man, even if he's as clever and cunning as the Professor says.'

Then her mind slipped back to a former situation, as nursery-governess in the house of a financier.

With her phonographic memory for phrases, she reproduced one of his remarks to his wife.

'We want a merger. Separate interests are destructive.'

Her face grew graver as she thought of heated passions rising to boiling-point, and the strangling complications of the triangle. Had she known of the actual situation in the drawing-room, she would have been still more worried.

Stephen was affected most adversely by the confinement. He was not only specially rebellious against closed windows, but he was nervous of Simone. Her ardent glances made him uncomfortable, as he remembered the Oxford episode, when he had been made the goat in another undergraduate amour.

He remembered that when the wretched girl had screamed, Newton had been first to come to her alleged rescue, and that he had always been censorious in his judgment, and his refusal to believe in Stephen's innocence. Even then, the seeds of jealousy had been sown, although Simone had only expressed vague admiration for a regular profile.

It had been perversity on his part which made him become the Professor's pupil, in order that his son might feel some sense of obligation – an impulse which he had repented, since the visit of the young couple to the Summit.

He stopped his ceaseless pacing of the carpet, to address Newton.

'With due respect, and all that sort of bilge, to

your worthy father, Warren, he doesn't get our angle. Our generation isn't afraid of any old thing – dead, alive, or on the go. It's being cooped up together, like rats in a drain, that *gets* me.'

'But I'm adoring it,' thrilled Simone. 'It's like a lot of married-couples being snow-bound, in one hut. When they come out, just watch how they'll pair off.'

She seemed lost to all sense of convention, as she stared at Stephen with concentrated eagerness, as though they were together on a desert island.

Completely unselfconscious, she never realized the presence of an audience. A spoilt brat, who'd been given the run of the toyshop to sack, she simply could not understand why her desire for any special plaything should not be instantly gratified.

'What are your plans, Stephen?' she asked.

'First of all,' he told her, 'I shall fail in my Exam.'

'Fine advertisement for the Chief,' remarked Newton.

'After that,' continued Stephen, 'I shall probably go to Canada, and fell timber.'

'Your dog will have to go into quarantine,' Newton reminded him spitefully.

'Then I'll stay in England, just to please *you*, Warren. And I'll come and have tea with Simone, every Sunday afternoon, when you're having your nap.'

Newton winced, and then glanced at the clock.

'I must go up to Gran. Any use asking you to come with me, Simone? Just to say "Good-night"?'

'None.'

Raising his high shoulders, Newton shambled from the room.

When he had gone, Stephen made an instinctive movement towards the door. Before he could reach it, however, Simone barred his way.

'No,' she cried. 'Don't go. Stay and talk . . . You were telling me your plans – and they're pathetic. Supposing you had money, what would you do?'

'Supposing?' Stephen laughed. 'I'd do the usual things. Sport. A spot of travel. A flutter at Monte.'

'Does it appeal?'

'You bet. A fat lot of good it is talking about it.'

'But *I* have money.'

'How nice for you,' he said.

'Yes. I can do anything. It makes me secure.'

'No woman should feel too secure.' Stephen strained desperately to keep the scene on a light level. 'It makes her despise Fate.'

Simone appeared not to hear him, as she came closer and laid her hands upon his shoulders.

'Steve,' she said, 'when you go away, to-morrow, I'm coming with you.'

'Oh, no, you're not, my dear,' he said quickly.

'Yes,' she insisted. 'I'm mad about you.'

Stephen licked his lips desperately.

'Look here,' he said, 'you're jumpy and all worked-up. You're delirious. You don't mean one word. To begin with – there's old Newton.'

'He can divorce me. I don't care. If he doesn't, I still

168

don't care. We'd have lots of fun – together.'

Stephen cast a hunted glance towards the door. Fright made him brutal.

'I don't care for you,' he said.

The repulse had only the effect of making her more ardent.

'I'll soon make you care for me,' she said confidently. 'You're just a silly boy with inhibitions.'

Exultantly, she raised her face to his, her lips expectant of his kiss. When he shook her off, the first shade of doubt crept into her eyes.

'There's another woman,' she said. '*That's* why.'

Desperation made him lie.

'Of course,' he told her. 'There always is.'

He was both startled and relieved by her reception of his news. Her face lost its look of immaculate and finished artifice, and crumpled up with elemental rage.

'I hate you,' she cried furiously. 'I hope you'll go to the dogs and die in the gutter.'

Rushing from the room, she banged the door behind her. Stephen took a deep breath and then thumped his chest.

'Thank the pigs,' he said piously.

But the incident left him worried. He wondered whether Simone contemplated some mean form of revenge. Assuring himself that it was no good meeting trouble halfway, as on the morrow he would be gone, for good, he tried to forget his problem in the excitement of a thrill-novel.

Presently he became aware that his attention was

no longer gripped. He kept raising his eyes from the pages, to listen. Above the howls of the gale rose a faint whine. It sounded like a dog in distress.

He bit his lip and frowned in perplexity. In spite of his objection, he realized that the Professor's precautions were probably sound, and he was prepared to obey them to the last letter. But, while the Professor had referred to 'man, woman, or child' he had forgotten to include any animal.

Stephen frowned as he realized that he was up against an acid test. If this were a trap, some unknown brain had detected his blind spot, and knew how to exploit it.

'It's Newton,' he thought. 'He's trying to lure me outside, so I'll be shut out. The fool thinks he's got to protect his wife from me.'

Again the faint howl was borne on the wind, bringing him to his feet. But again he sat down.

'Hang it,' he muttered aloud. 'I won't. They shan't get at me. It's not fair to risk the women.'

He took up his novel, and tried to concentrate on what he read. But the lines of print were a meaningless jumble of words, because he was awaiting – and dreading – a repetition of the cry.

At last, it came – pitiful and despairing, as though the creature were growing weaker. Unable to sit still, he stole out into the lobby and unbolted the front door. As he put his head outside, the wind seemed about to tear off his ears, but it also bore the barking of a dog.

While it might be a faithful animal imitation,

there was something familiar about the sound. Struck by a sudden suspicion, Stephen cautiously rebolted the door and hurried up to his room.

'Otto,' he called, as he threw open the door.

But no dog leaped to welcome him. The bed was tidy and the room had been hurriedly put in order.

'The dirty tykes,' he said. 'They've run him out. This settles it. I clear out, too.'

Swearing under his breath, he hurriedly changed into his old tweeds and laced on thick shoes. Bag in hand, he clumped down the back-stairs. No one saw him, when he crossed the hall; but, as he banged the front door behind him, Helen heard the slam.

Newton's visit to his grandmother had released her from her vigil, as the old lady had ordered her from the room. Although it was her usual bed-time, Helen decided to break her rule of early hours.

The whole household was upset; while boredom usually drove the family prematurely to their rooms, they all seemed restless tonight.

Mrs Oates, also, would be sitting up to let in her husband. Helen felt she had better share her vigil, in case she should drop off to sleep again, and miss his ring. She flew to the front door, just in time to recognize Stephen as he retreated through slanting sheets of rain.

As the light flashed out over the gravel drive, he turned and shouted to her defiantly:

'Lock up . . . I'm never coming back.'

Helen hastened to slam the door and re-fasten the bolts.

171

'*Well*,' she said. 'The young rip.'

She was laughing over the incident when Nurse Barker came up from the kitchen.

'What was that noise?' she asked suspiciously.

'Mr Rice has gone,' Helen told her.

'Where?'

'He didn't tell me, but I can make a pretty good guess. He's been terribly keen to go to the Bull, to pay up and say "Good-bye".'

Nurse Barker's deep-set eyes glinted angrily.

'He's disobeyed the Professor and risked our safety,' she stormed. 'It's criminal.'

'No, it's all right,' Helen assured her. 'I locked up after him, directly. And he's not coming back.'

Nurse Barker laughed bitterly.

'So it's all right, is it?' she asked. 'Don't you realize that now we have lost *our two best men*?'

CHAPTER 17

WHEN LADIES DISAGREE

As Helen stared at Nurse Barker, she was appalled by the revelation of her eyes. Anger had given way to a murky gleam of satisfaction, as though she realized the weakening of the defence.

Remembering that she was marked out for distinctive bait, the knowledge inspired the girl with defiance.

'We've still two men,' she said. 'And five women – all able-bodied and strong.'

'Are *you strong*?' asked Nurse Barker, sneering down at Helen, from her superior height.

'I'm young.'

'Yes, you're young. You may remember that – before you're much older. And – perhaps – you may regret your youth.'

Helen tossed back her red mane impatiently.

'I suppose the Professor ought to be told about Mr Rice,' she said.

'And, of course, *you* will tell him.'

'Why – me?' asked Helen.

'He's a *man*.'

'Look here, Nurse,' Helen said, in her mildest

voice, 'I think that bickering, just now, is silly. We all want to pull together. We don't want to keep harping on men. And I'm sure you don't want me to be the next victim. You're too good a sport.'

'I have no ill-feeling towards you,' Nurse Barker assured her in a muffled voice.

'Good,' said Helen. 'When you go up to Lady Warren, will you tell Mr Newton what's happened, and ask him to let his father know.'

Nurse Barker bowed her head, in stately assent, and began to mount the staircase. Helen stood in the hall, watching her flat-footed ascent, as the tall white figure gradually towered above her.

'You can wear high Spanish heels, when you're small,' she thought, looking down, with satisfaction, at her own feet. 'She walks just like a man.'

She noticed that, as Nurse Barker retreated, she appeared little more than a dim glimmer crossing the dimly lit landing, as though some ghostly shape were rising from its churchyard bed. The illusion reminded her of her own experience, before dinner, when she had been appalled by a momentary vision of evil.

'It *must* have been the Professor,' she assured herself. 'I fancied the rest.'

Suddenly she remembered an additional detail. The Professor had emerged from his bedroom, whereas she had another recollection of a door being opened and then shut immediately.

'Odd,' she thought. 'The Professor wouldn't

174

open his door, and then, slam it – and then open it again. There's no sense in that.'

Staring up at the landing, she noticed that the door of the Professor's bedroom was close beside that of the back staircase. Someone might have looked out from the one, just as the other was opening, with the meticulous timing of a lucky chance.

The notion was not only absurd, but so disquieting that Helen refused to admit it.

'No one could have got into the house,' she told herself. 'It was all locked up, when Ceridwen was strangled . . . But, supposing there was some secret way in, of course the murderer could have rushed from the plantation and been lurking on the back-stairs, when I saw him . . . Only, it was the Professor.'

In spite of the seeming impossibility of anyone entering the fortress, she began to wonder, if – for a minute or so – any chink had been left in the defence. At the back of her mind, something was worrying her . . . Something forgotten – or overlooked.

She had been unmethodical, all the evening, breaking off in the middle of a job to start another. For example, she had not even begun to screw up the handle of Miss Warren's bedroom door. Before she had discovered how to tackle the difficulty, she had been interrupted by the Professor, and left her tools lying on the landing.

'Anyone might think I was untidy,' she thought. 'I'll go up again and experiment a bit.'

As the resolution crossed her mind, it was swept aside by the spectacle of Newton, hurrying down the stairs. His sallow face was flushed with excitement, as he spoke to her.

'So the noble Rice has walked out on us?'

'Yes,' replied Helen. 'I was there when he went – and I locked him out.'

'Good . . . I suppose he was alone?'

'I only saw him on the drive. But it was very dark and confusing in the rain.'

'Quite.' Newton's eyes flickered behind his glasses. 'Do you mind waiting here, just for a minute?'

Helen knew what was in his mind as he galloped upstairs to the second floor, and she smiled over his groundless fear, even while she knew that she could have saved him his journey, at the expense of tact.

A minute later, he clattered down again, ostentatiously flourishing a clean handkerchief, to excuse his flight.

'My wife is a bit upset,' he remarked casually. 'Headache, and so on. Perhaps you'd see if you could do something for her, when you've time?'

'Certainly,' promised Helen.

Newton's smile was so unexpectedly boyish, that Helen understood the secret of his popularity with his women-kind.

'What a lot we Warrens expect for our money,' he said. 'I do hope you get a decent salary. You earn it . . . Now, we must tell the Chief about Rice.'

176

Once again, Helen was flattered at being asked to help him. Although her sympathies were with Stephen, she had infinitely more respect for Newton. All the men seemed to be inviting her cooperation, that night; instead of being in the background, she was constantly on the boards.

It was true that she was there, chiefly to feed the principals, and was not picked out by the limelight; but, in the circumstances, it seemed safer not to advertise. She even congratulated herself that Nurse Barker was not present, to witness her entrance into the study, since personal triumph was not worth more friction.

The Professor was lying back in his chair, with his eyes closed, as though in concentration. He did not open his lids, until Newton called his name. When he did so, Helen thought that his pupils looked curiously fixed and glassy.

Apparently, Newton shared her impression.

'Been mopping up the quadronex?' he asked.

The Professor's stare reproved the impertinence.

'As I'm the financial head of this house,' he observed, 'I have to conserve my strength, for the benefit of my – dependents. I must insure some sleep, tonight . . . Have you anything to tell me?'

His lips tightened as he listened to Newton's news.

'So Rice rebelled against my restrictions?' he said. 'That young man may develop into a good citizen, ultimately, but, at present, I fear he is a Goth.'

'I should call him a bad relapse,' remarked Newton.

'Still, he was a hefty barbarian,' his father reminded him. 'In his absence, Newton, you and I have more to do.'

'Which means myself, Chief. You're a bit past tackling a maniac.'

Helen guessed that the Professor was irritated by the remark.

'My brain remains at your service,' he said. 'Unfortunately, I was only able to pass on a section of it to my son.'

'Thanks, Chief, both for the compliment and your help. I am afraid a formula for poison-gas hardly meets the case. We need brute-force.'

The Professor smiled bleakly.

'My despised brain may yet prove the trump-card,' he said. 'Does Simone know that Rice has left?'

'Yes.' Newton bristled at the implication. 'What of it?'

'I leave that to you.'

'She's got a headache,' said Helen. 'Mr Warren has asked me to see to her.'

The Professor's eyes slanted slightly inwards, as though he were trying to peer inside the lighted recesses of his brain.

'An excellent idea,' he said. 'Remember my daughter-in-law is temperamental. You may have to influence her, but don't irritate her.'

He whispered to his son, who nodded, and passed

178

on the instruction. 'Miss Capel, it might be wiser not to leave her alone.'

Helen felt rather important as she went up to the red room, although she was slightly doubtful of the success of her mission. As she paused outside the door, she could hear the sounds of strangled sobbing. No notice was taken of her knock, so she entered, uninvited – to find Simone stretched, face downwards, on the bed.

'Oh, your lovely dress,' she cried. 'You'll ruin it.'

Simone raised her head, showing a tear-streaked face.

'I hate it,' she snarled.

'Then take it off. Anyway, you'll feel freer in a wrapper.'

It was second nature to Simone, to be waited on, so she made no protest as Helen peeled the sheath-like gown over her head.

The younger girl took rather a long time in her selection of a substitute, from the wardrobe. The sight of so many beautiful garments aroused her wistful envy.

'What lover-ly things you have,' she said; as she returned to the bed, carrying a wisp of georgette and lace, which was less substantial than the discarded gown.

'What's the good of them?' asked Simone bitterly. 'There's no man to see them.'

'There's your husband,' Helen reminded her.

'I said "*man*".'

'Shall I get you some aspirin for your head?' asked Helen, who was determined to keep Simone's ailments on a strictly physical basis.

'No,' replied Simone. 'I feel foul. But it's not that. I'm so terribly unhappy.'

'But you've everything,' cried Helen.

'Everything. And nothing I want . . . My whole life has been one of sacrifice. Whenever I want something, it's taken from me.'

She coiled herself into a sitting posture, as a prelude to confidence. While her make-up was ruined, the tempest had swept harmlessly over her plastic coiffure, for her hair gleamed like unflawed black enamel.

'Has Stephen Rice ever flirted with *you?*' she asked.

'No,' replied Helen. 'And, if he did, I shouldn't tell you. Affairs should be kept private.'

'But, my good woman, how can they be? One goes out – balls, restaurants, and so on. And there's always the inevitable man.'

'I wasn't thinking of you,' said Helen. 'I was naturally speaking for myself.'

'*You?* Have you a lover?'

'Of course,' replied Helen recklessly, as she remembered Dr Parry's prophecy. 'I'm sorry, but I'm more interested in myself than you. Of course, I know that you have your photograph in the papers and that people talk about you. But to me, you're a type. I see lots like you, everywhere.'

Simone stared incredulously at Helen, whom she had only vaguely noticed as someone small, who wore a pinafore and shook a perpetual duster. Although she was staggered to realize that the nonentity was actually claiming individuality, she could not keep off her special subject.

'What do you think of Stephen?' she asked.

'I like him,' replied Helen; 'but I think he's a rotter. He shouldn't have left us in the jam.'

'*Left* us?' echoed Simone, springing up from her reclining posture.

'Yes, he's gone for good. Didn't you know?'

Helen was rather startled by the effect of her news on Simone. She sat, as though stunned, her fingers pressed tightly over her lips.

'Where did he go?' she asked in a low voice.

Helen determined to make a thorough job of Simone's disillusionment.

'To the Bull,' she replied.

'To that woman, you mean.'

'If you mean the landlord's daughter,' Helen said, 'he was talking about her in the kitchen. He said he couldn't go away without wishing her "Good--bye".'

The next second, she realized her blunder, as Simone burst into a storm of tears.

'He's gone,' she cried. 'That woman has him . . . I want him so. You don't understand. It's burning me up . . . I must *do* something.'

'Oh, don't yearn over him,' entreated Helen. 'He's not worth it. You're only making yourself cheap.'

'Shut up. And get out of my room.'

'I don't want to be where I'm not wanted,' Helen said stoutly. 'But I've orders not to leave you.'

Her speech roused Simone to white fury.

'So that's it?' she cried. 'You were sent to spy on me? That was clever of them. Oh, *thank* them from me. But why didn't I think of it for myself?'

'What do you mean?' asked Helen nervously.

'You'll see. Oh, you'll see.'

Helen watched in silent dismay, as Simone whirled around the room, snatching at garments and dressing in frantic haste. She realized that the situation had passed from her control. She could no more arrest the inevitable catastrophe than subdue a runaway engine.

She cried out in protest, however, as Simone dragged on her fur coat. 'Where are you going?' she demanded.

'Out of this house. I won't stay to be watched and insulted.' Simone snatched up a handful of jewellery, thrust it inside her bag, and turned to Helen. 'I'm going to my lover. Tell the Professor I shan't be back – tonight.'

'No, you shan't go,' declared Helen, trying to grip Simone's wrists. 'He doesn't want you.'

The struggle was short and desperate, but Simone was the stronger, besides being entirely reckless. Careless of consequences, she pushed Helen away with such force that the girl was thrown to the floor.

Although Helen was not hurt, she wasted a little

time in assuring herself that such was actually the case. While she was rubbing her aching head, she heard the click of a key in the lock, and realized that she was a prisoner.

CHAPTER 18

THE DEFENCE WEAKENS

The sound brought Helen to her feet and sent her rushing to the door, even while she knew that she was too late. She tugged at the handle and battered on the panels, to relieve her feelings, rather than with any hope of release.

It was a humiliating situation, and indignation was her strongest emotion. She had been thrown about, as though she were a dummy, in a film. Worst of all, she had failed again in a position of trust. The thought quickened her sense of responsibility and made her rack her brain for some method of arousing the household – only to be forced back on the hopeless expedient of ringing the bell.

Even as she pressed the button, she knew that no one would come. The bell rang down in the basement-hall, where Mrs Oates would only hear it as a soothing accompaniment to her snores. Were she roused, she would ignore it, on principle.

Bells were none of her business. She did so much during her working-hours, that she was forced, in self-defence, to guard her precious leisure. Helen remembered how she would point, either to her husband or the girl, and sing 'The bells of Hell go ting-a-ling-a-ling, for *you*, but not for me,' whenever she noticed an unanswered tinkle.

It was soon obvious that she did not intend to relax her rule on this occasion. Helen stopped prodding the button, and resigned herself to an indefinite wait.

At first, she had plenty of occupation, for she was able to satisfy her curiosity over Simone's wardrobe and toilet-aids; but she could not bring her usual interest to her investigations. Every silk stocking and pot of rouge reminded her of Simone. She was out in the storm – lashed on by a spluttering match of desire, which she had magnified to a torch of passion.

Helen reconstructed her – a luxury-product, spoiled neurotic and useless. From her cradle, every wish had been gratified and every whim forestalled. She had been shielded under a glass-case, lest life should blow too roughly upon her.

And, even then, the horror might be closing over her – the glass shattered, leaving her defenceless, to face reality. Instead of protecting arms, she would see hands stretched out, in menace. She would cry for help, and – for the first time in her life – she would cry in vain.

That was the vision which kept flashing across Helen's mind, as she thought of Simone's peril. Although she had done her best, she still felt a sense of guilt. In order to prepare her story for the defence, she began to reconstruct the incident.

As she did so, she was again visited by a disquieting memory. This time, it was an auditory illusion. She was positive that she had heard the key click in the lock at the same time as she listened to the sound of Simone's frantic flight down the stairs.

'Someone else locked me in,' she whispered. 'Who? And why?'

She could only conjecture that Nurse Barker had been on the landing, probably attracted up there by the noise of the scuffle. If she had grasped the situation, her jealousy might have urged her to imprison Helen, in order to stamp her as an incompetent.

Suddenly Helen received a belated inspiration. Mrs Oates had told her that all the doors in the Summit were fitted with the same lock. In that case, Newton's dressing-room key should fit the bedroom keyhole.

She had some difficulty in wrenching it out, for it was rusted from desuetude. From her recent investigations, she knew where to find Newton's hair-oil; but before she began her lubrications, she decided to match it with the lock.

As she grasped the handle of the bedroom door, it slipped round in her fingers, and swung open. Her lips, too, fell apart, as she stared out at the deserted landing.

'*Well*,' she gasped.

Faced with the prospect of a violent drop in favour, she ran downstairs, to raise the alarm. While she had established the fact that she was the victim of a practical joke – or trick – it was impossible to prove it to her employers.

She decided that it would be wiser to accept any blame, and remain silent, only to find that no explanation was required. When she blurted out the news of Simone's flight, the Warren family was united in a solid front, to save the situation.

As the Professor, Miss Warren and Newton looked at each other, the likeness between them, became plain. The muscles of their thin over-bred faces worked convulsively as the steel jaws of a trap, betraying the violence of their emotion, and the force of their self-control.

Although Newton's high voice broke in an occasional squeak, his manner remained as temperate as though the subject of discussion was the weather.

'You say, Miss Capel, that she went to the Bull, to join Rice,' asked the Professor.

'Yes,' said Helen, avoiding looking at Newton. 'I fought with her, but—'

'Yes, yes . . . The question is – who will go after her, Newton. You or I?'

'I'm going,' replied Newton.

'No, darling,' urged Miss Warren. 'You're the younger man. Your father will have more authority. Your place is here.'

'You're in no danger,' Newton told her. 'But she's running a horrible risk.'

The Professor laid his hand on his son's shoulder, to steady him, and Helen noticed that his thin knotted fingers trembled slightly.

'I understand your feelings, Newton,' he said. 'But I think the chances are against your – maniac being outside in this storm. If he's not back in his home, he will be sheltering in some barn. I am sure Simone will reach the Bull safely.'

'What a happy prospect.' Newton bit his lip. 'All the more reason for her husband to be there.'

'Perhaps you're right. But before you go we'd better discuss our line of procedure. We want to avoid a scandal.'

'I don't want to divorce Simone.' Newton's voice cracked. 'I only want to get her away from that – from Rice.'

'Personally, I think she is in no danger from Rice,' remarked the Professor. 'He is very definitely not an amatory type.'

'He locked that poor girl in his room at Oxford,' declared Newton heatedly.

'You forget, Newton, that I've been an undergraduate in my time. Such episodes can be staged. I've always kept an open mind on that charge. Wash out Rice. The question is – how to account for Simone running through the rain, to a small public-house?'

'A brain-storm, caused by nerves,' suggested Miss Warren. 'The murder would explain her condition.'

The Professor nodded approval.

'I'm afraid you'll both have to put up at the Bull, for the night,' he said. 'They have no conveyance, and Simone could not return through the storm.'

'Couldn't you come back, Newton, when you've

explained everything and made all arrangements for Simone?' asked Miss Warren.

Newton laughed as he thoughtfully buttoned his waterproof.

'Excellent. I could leave her in Rice's care . . . Don't worry Aunt. Expect us back tomorrow morning.'

Helen was assailed by a fresh pang of loneliness when the chain was re-fastened, after the exodus. As Newton went out of the house – his head thrust forward as though he were butting the storm – the partially-opened door revealed a section of chaos, interlaced with veins of slanting rain, spinning round in the shaft of electric-light.

After that glimpse of a watery confusion, the atmosphere of the hall appeared stagnant, and clogged with femininity. All the virility had been drained out of it with the departure of the men. It was true that the Professor remained, but he seemed exhausted by the excessive burden of responsibility.

'Mr Rice will have to come back tomorrow to fetch his dog,' said Miss Warren.

Helen's face brightened.

'Shall we free it, to roam the house?'

Miss Warren's face betrayed indecision.

'I fear and dislike all dogs,' she said. 'Still – the creature might be a protection.'

'I'm used to dogs,' Helen told her. 'May I feed him and then bring him down, with me?'

'It has been fed, by Mrs Oates, before I took it

out to the garage.' Miss Warren's gaze challenged her brother. 'Perhaps, Sebastian, you will bring it in?'

Helen pricked up her ears as the secret of the strange noises upon the back-stairs was explained. Mrs Oates' reticence was but another proof of her loyalty to her employers.

The Professor was looking at his sister, a faint smile touching his lips.

'Typical, my dear Blanche,' he murmured. 'Is the door of the garage unlocked?'

'Locked. I have the key upstairs.'

As they waited for Miss Warren's return, Helen tried to conquer her dread of the Professor. Like a kitten, which pats a suspicious object, and then springs sideways, she could not resist an attempt to explore his mind.

'I admire Miss Warren's strength of character,' she said. 'Of course she can't help being afraid of dogs.' She hastened to bring out the classic excuse of analogy. 'Lord Roberts was frightened of cats.'

'But my sister is not afraid in your sense of the word,' explained the Professor. 'That is to say, she is not afraid of being bitten or worried by a dog. But she realizes the danger of bacteriological infection which lurks in the parasites of animals.'

Helen did her best to reciprocate his intelligence.

'I know,' Helen said. 'There are millions of germs everywhere. Enough to kill all the people in the world. But – I understood that there were good germs to fight the bad germs.'

The Professor's faint smile did not conceal his scorn.

'Even as your good angels strive with devils?' he enquired. 'There may be some sort of combat, but, in the Animal Kingdom, the Ultimate Good does not prevail, as in your fairy-tale Creed.'

Although she felt choked with nervousness, Helen continued the argument.

'If the destructive germ were the more powerful,' she said, 'we should all of us be dead.'

'We soon shall be dead. Longevity is only comparative, while many die young. Think of infant mortality, which is Nature's method of dealing with surplus population. Unfortunately, medical science has interfered with her good intentions, to a certain extent. Still, death wins.'

Helen felt too overawed by the sardonic gleam in the scientist's eye, to dare to argue further. She knew herself outclassed, even while her heart protested against his dreary materialistic outlook.

'What is Miss Warren's special subject?' she asked timidly.

'She ranges. Her plane of vision is, consequently, different from your own. You see with eyes, but she sees through a microscope. Terrors, which are lost to you, are revealed to her.'

Helen rather liked the way the Professor was trying to gloss over his sister's imperfections. She believed that, even as shadows on the sea betray the presence of rocks, so trifles indicate character.

Whatever his theological disbelief, the Professor was staunch.

'How interesting,' she said politely.

'My sister is of too sensitized nature to mix with the outside world,' went on the Professor, 'yet her nerve is of iron. She did valuable work, during the War, at the Front, which took daily toll of her reserves. Yet she never showed any sign of strain, and emerged with a fine record. That is one of the reasons why she insists on a teetotal household – so great is her horror of any kind of bestiality.'

'I think that was fine,' said Helen.

'It was. Especially, as you have already remarked, she suffers from a deficient pituitary gland.'

Helen did not understand his allusion, so she gazed with new respect at Miss Warren, when she came down the staircase. In silence she handed her brother a key, and then walked into the library.

'Bolt the door after me, please,' said the Professor, 'and remain here to let me in again.'

It was dreary waiting in the hall which was now so empty and silent. No sound of youthful voices, or strains of wireless floated from the drawing-room.

'Thank goodness, I'll soon have the dog,' Helen thought.

Even that consolation was denied her. When – a little later – heralded by his knock, the Professor was blown inside the lobby, he was alone.

'Rice has made good his threat,' he told her. 'I found the padlock on the garage door forced and the dog gone.'

Stripping off his dripping coat, he walked into his study.

Feeling doubly forlorn, Helen ventured to invade Mrs Oates' privacy. She knocked several times on the kitchen door without attracting any attention, although the light was shining through the frosted-glass panels.

She was on the point of turning away when she was startled by an unfamiliar thick voice.

'Come in, my dear.'

In spite of the genial invitation, Helen entered the kitchen with a sinking heart – not knowing what she feared.

Mrs Oates sat slumped back in her chair, like a sack of potatoes, a stupid smile on her red face.

In spite of her inexperience, Helen guessed that the ultimate disaster had befallen her. Her second guard had failed her. Mrs Oates was drunk.

CHAPTER 19

ONE OVER THE EIGHT

As Helen looked at Mrs Oates, she felt in the grip of a bad dream. Everything had changed in the course of a few hours. It was impossible to believe that the kitchen was the same cheery place, where she had drunk her tea.

It was not only comfortless and untidy, but actually darker, for no leaping fire helped to illuminate it. Crumbs and egg-shells were strewn on the bare table. Even the ginger cat had deserted his rug for the peace of the empty drawing-room.

But the change in Mrs Oates was the worst feature of the transformation. An ugly woman at her best, she had lost the redeeming quality of her expression. The loyalty had been soaked from her eyes and the characteristic lines of her face had melted together in an idiotic grin. When Helen gave her the latest bulletin of news, she received it with such indifference that the girl wondered whether she had actually grasped the fact of the wholesale desertion.

'Women can't get drunk decently,' she thought.

It struck her that, in this special accomplishment,

men remained supreme. Women equalled their records in other fields, but, while a man, in his cups, could be amusing – or even brilliant – a drunken woman only relapsed into bestiality.

Yet, although she was disgusted by Mrs Oates' gross red face, she realized that she was only partially intoxicated. Since the catastrophe was not complete, it might be possible to appeal to her sense of trust, and to pull her round again.

'Have you been drinking my health?' she asked.

Mrs Oates registered exaggerated innocence.

'Funny, ain't you? Beer – money I get – I'll allow you that. But never a drop of tiddley.'

'Odd,' sniffed Helen. 'I thought I could smell brandy.'

'Must be that nurse, spilling her breath. She's been poking down here.'

Helen decided to try guile.

'Bad luck,' she sighed. 'I could do with a spot myself. Just to buck me up, after all the upset.'

She watched the conflict in Mrs Oates' inflamed face, as native kindliness struggled with greed and caution. In the end, generosity prevailed.

'And so you shall, you poor little squirt,' she declared.

Ducking down her head, she dived under her skirt, and drew out a bottle of brandy, which she placed triumphantly on the table.

'Help yourself,' she said hospitably. 'Plenty more where that comes from.'

'Where did you find it?' asked Helen.

'In the cellar, when the master went to look at the thermommomm—'.

As Mrs Oates continued to wrestle with the word, with a flicker of her old bulldog tenacity, Helen stretched out her hand for the bottle.

'You've drunk nearly half already,' she said. 'Hadn't you better save some for tomorrow?'

'No,' declared. Mrs Oates solemnly. 'I can't taste nips. I must have swallows. I always finish a bottle.'

'But you'll get drunk, and then Miss Warren will sack you.'

'No, she won't. I done this before. The master only says she must put temptation out of my way and not give me another chance.'

Helen listened with the dismay of a card-player who has mistaken a small pip for a trump. A valuable trick – fear of the consequences – was lost to her.

It was obvious that Mrs Oates was callous with regard to the future. The Warren family balanced an occasional lapse against the value of her services.

'Still, put a little by for a rainy day,' she urged, as Mrs Oates' fingers closed around the bottle.

'For Oates to find? Not blooming likely. He'll know I've had one over the eight, and he's always out to block me. *No*, I'm going to hide it in the only safe place.'

'What rotten luck your husband had to go off,' wailed Helen tactlessly. 'Why should it happen tonight, of all nights?'

Mrs Oates began to laugh shrilly.

'I done that,' she crowed. 'I took up the pudding to the bedroom when I knew the nurse was busy with her ladyship, washing down the decks. I just gave the cap of the cylinder a twist as I was setting down the plate.'

'What made you think of it?' gasped Helen.

'*You*. You said it was her life. But if it hadn't worked I'd have thought up some other way to get rid of Oates.'

The nightmare oppression increased as Helen sat opposite Mrs Oates and watched her drain her glass. There seemed to be a conspiracy against her; yet when she traced back effect to cause, she could find no evidence of human malice.

There was nothing extraordinary in the fact that Mrs Oates should have a failing, and it was natural that her husband should try to check her; it therefore followed – also naturally – that she should sharpen her wits to get him out of her way.

The same logic characterized the events which had been responsible for the clearance of the young people. Stephen Rice was devoted to his dog and resented its banishment, while Simone had behaved in the normal manner of a spoiled neurotic girl, whose desires had been thwarted. The Professor, too, could not have done otherwise, when he authorized Newton to follow his wife.

Of course, there had been unlucky trifles which had been the levers which set the machinery in motion; but the responsibility for them was divided equally among the members of the household.

It was unfortunate that Stephen should have brought home a dog, in the first place, and doubly unfortunate when it clashed with Miss Warren's prejudice against all animals. The Professor's lapse was also lamentable, although he could hardly credit Mrs Oates with the audacity of committing a theft under his nose.

Helen had to admit that she, too, had lent a hand in weaving this extraordinary tissue of consequences. She had influenced Dr Parry to exaggerate the gravity of Lady Warren's condition, while her unlucky remark about the oxygen had been the origin of Mrs Oates' brain-wave.

Yet, even as she marshalled her arguments she grew afraid. Something was advancing towards her – some vast slow movement of affairs, which she was powerless to deflect from its course.

Blind chance alone could not be responsible for this string of apparent accidents. Natural things were happening – but with unnatural complicity. The process was altogether too smooth and too regular; they timed too perfectly, as though some brain were directing their operations.

The sight of Mrs Oates slowly dissolving from a shrewd woman into a sot, stung Helen to desperate action.

'Give me that,' she cried, seizing the bottle. 'You ought to be ashamed of yourself.'

She realized her mistake when Mrs Oates turned on her, in a fury.

'Lay off that,' she shouted.

Helen tried to turn her action into a joke as she dodged around the kitchen, pursued by Mrs Oates.

'Don't be so silly,' she urged, still hugging the bottle. 'Try and pull yourself together.'

Red-eyed and panting, Mrs Oates pent her into a corner, snatched the bottle from her, and then slapped her cheek.

As the girl reeled back under the force of the blow, Mrs Oates gripped her shoulders and practically hurled her out of the kitchen.

'Good riddance to bad rubbish,' she muttered as she slammed the door. 'You keep out of here.'

Helen was glad to escape, for she realized the need to enlist fresh help. Too timid to appeal to the Professor, she went into the library. Miss Warren, who was hunched together, poring over a book, did not welcome the interruption.

'I hope, Miss Capel, you've not disturbed me for a trifle,' she said.

'No,' Helen told her, 'it's important. Mrs Oates is drunk.'

Miss Warren clicked with disgust, and then glanced at the clock.

'There's nothing to worry about,' she said calmly. 'She will sleep it off tonight. Tomorrow she will do her work as usual.'

'But she had not quite passed out,' persisted Helen. 'If you were to speak to her now you might stop her.'

'I am certainly not going to argue with a semi-intoxicated woman,' said Miss Warren. 'And my brother's work is far too important to be inter-rupted. If you are wise you will not interfere . . . This has happened before.'

Miss Warren took up her book again, to indicate that the interview was over.

Feeling utterly miserable, Helen wandered into the hall. At the sight of the telephone, however, her courage revived. It reminded her that while she had been feeling lonely as though marooned on a desert island, the Summit was still linked with civilization.

'I'll ring up the Bull,' she decided. 'We ought to find out if Simone is safe. And then I'll ring up Dr Parry.'

She was conscious of sharp suspense as she took the receiver from the hook. In this gale telephone-poles must be crashing down all over the country. So many disasters had piled themselves up, that she quite expected to find that she was cut off.

To her joy, however, she heard the buzz of connection, and an operator's voice at the Exchange enquiring the number. After a short interval, another voice, speaking with a strong Welsh accent, informed her that he was Mr Williams, landlord of the Bull.

In answer to her enquiries he told her that Mr and Mrs Newton Warren had arrived at the Inn, and were staying the night. He added that Mr Rice had left, with his dog, immediately after their arrival, presumably to make room for the lady.

'Where did he go?' asked Helen.

'To the parsonage. He said he knew Parson would put him up, seeing as he's partial to dogs.'

Feeling that she had family news to offer as her excuse, if she were surprised at the telephone, Helen looked up Dr Parry's number in the directory. Presently she heard his voice at the other end of the wire. It sounded tired, and not exactly enthusiastic.

'Don't tell me the old lady has thrown an attack. Have a heart. I'm only just started on my meal.'

'I want some advice,' Helen told him. 'There's no one else to ask but you.'

But at the end of her story she had not succeeded in convincing even herself of the gravity of the position. Everything sounded petty and stressed; and she was sure that Dr Parry shared her view.

'Bit of a landslide,' he said, 'but there's nothing you can do. Don't tackle Mrs Oates again.'

'But I *do* want to get her sober,' pleaded Helen. 'It's so lonely with no one.'

'Are you afraid?'

'N-no,' replied Helen.

'Because, if you are, I'll come over at once.'

As he expected, the offer braced Helen to a refusal. He was hungry, wet, and dog-tired; although he was susceptible, at that moment a fire and his pipe appealed to him more than the brightest eyes.

'I know that watch-tower of a house can't be too cheerful in a gale,' he said. 'But say your prayers and it won't come down. Of course, you've had a nasty shock, this evening, and you naturally feel lonely with those people walking out on you. Still, there's quite a respectable number left. Lock up, and you've nothing to fear.'

'Yes,' agreed Helen, starting at a violent crash outside one of the shuttered windows.

'If you went to bed now, and locked your door, could you sleep in this gale?' asked Dr Parry.

'I don't think so. My room's high up, and it's rocking like a cradle.'

'Then keep up the fire in your sitting-room, and make up a shakedown there. You'll hardly hear the storm. Before you know it, it'll be tomorrow morning.'

'And things look so different in the morning,' said Helen.

It was easy to be brave with Dr Parry's cheerful voice ringing in her ears.

'Remember this,' he said. 'If you feel afraid, ring me up and I'll come over.'

With the promise to cheer her, Helen rang off. But as she looked around the hall her confidence died. The house seemed to sway with the gale, and the night to be full of sounds. A great voice roared down the chimney, until she felt she was on the verge of catching actual words.

Feeling that any reception was better than loneliness, Helen went down to the kitchen again. To her relief, Mrs Oates beamed a welcome. Her colour had grown a trifle more congested, while the brandy in the bottle had sunk.

'I mustn't irritate her,' thought Helen, as she

sat down and patted Mrs Oates familiarly on the knee.

'We're friends, old thing,' she said. 'Aren't we?'

'Yes,' nodded Mrs Oates. 'Oates said "Look after little Miss." Them were his last words, before he was called away. Look after little Miss.'

'Oh, don't talk as if he was dead,' cried Helen,

Stroking Mrs Oates' hand the while, she began to talk persuasively.

'But how can you look after me if you're drunk?'

'I'm not drunk,' objected Mrs Oates. 'I can toe the line. And I can cosh anyone as dared to lay a finger on little Miss.'

Rising, with only the slightest stagger, she walked across the room, sparring at shadow adversaries with such vigour that Helen felt comforted.

'If I can only keep her like this,' she thought, 'she's as good as any man.'

Mrs Oates stopped, blowing like a porpoise, to receive Helen's applause.

'I've been setting here,' she said, 'thinking. And thinking. I'm worrying about that nurse. Why does she speak with her mouth all choked up with bread-crumbs? What's the answer to that?'

'I don't know,' replied Helen.

'I do,' Mrs Oates told her. 'She's putting on a voice. Depend on it she's got another one of her own, same as the old lady upstairs. And she's putting on a walk. She's reminding herself not to tramp as if she was squashing beetles. Now, what do you make of that?'

'What do *you*?' asked Helen uncomfortably.

'*Ah*. May be she's not a woman – same as you and me. Maybe, she—'

As Mrs Oates broke off to stare, Helen turned and saw Nurse Barker standing at the open door.

CHAPTER 20

A LADY'S TOILET

Helen shrank back, aghast, before Nurse Barker's stare. She had never before seen hatred – unmasked and relentless – glaring from human eyes.

It was only too obvious that Mrs Oates' words had been overheard; yet Helen made a feeble attempt to explain them away.

'We were just talking of Lady Warren,' she said. 'Isn't she an extraordinary woman?'

Nurse Barker brushed aside the subterfuge. In ominous silence she stalked over to the kitchen range and seized the kettle.

'No hot water,' she said.

'I'm so sorry but the fire's gone out.' Helen apologized for Mrs Oates. 'If you can wait a few minutes, I'll boil up some on my spirit-stove.'

'I need no help,' said Nurse Barker. 'I can do my own jobs. *And* finish them.'

The words were harmless, but she infused into them a hint of grim and settled purpose. With the same ominous significance she looked first at the bottle on the table, and then at Mrs Oates, who sagged in her easy-chair, like a sack of meal.

'Brandy,' she remarked. 'In a teetotal house.'

Instantly Mrs Oates raised her glass defiantly.

'Good health, Nurse,' she said thickly. 'May all your chickens come home to roost.'

Nurse Barker gave a short laugh.

'I see,' she said. 'I shall soon have *you* on my hands. Well I shall know how to deal with you.'

Before Mrs Oates could retaliate, she had gone from the room.

'Well,' gasped Mrs Oates, sniffing vigorously, 'wot a nasty smell. She'd better try no tricks on me, nor call me out of my name, or I'll give her a thick ear . . . I won't be bullied by *that*.'

'"That"?' echoed Helen.

'Well, who's to say if it's a woman, or a man?'

Again Helen was gripped with the nightmare horror of the situation, as Mrs Oates sunk her voice to a hoarse whisper. She had drained her glass again, in greedy gulps. It was only too clear that her guardian was slipping away from her, leaving her to solve the enigma of the nurse.

It was true that she had still the moral support of the Professor and his sister; but they were too negligible to help. They seemed to retreat always to their distant horizons – aloof and invulnerable as shadows.

As a child, she had the reputation of never crying; but at this crisis she suddenly broke down.

'Oh, don't,' she cried piteously. 'I can't stand much more.'

As she began to cry, Mrs Oates looked at her with puzzled eyes.

'What's the matter, dearie?' she asked.

'I'm terrified,' confessed Helen. 'You keep on drinking. Soon, you'll be a log, and then you'll be in her power. You're asking for it. I'll do my best, of course – but she'd make three of me, and leave scrapings. And upstairs they won't believe a word I say, until it's too late.'

Helen spoke wildly, but her exaggeration had the desired effect of sobering Mrs Oates. In her turn she daubed lurid colours on her picture of the future.

'It's you she's after,' she said. 'She wants to do me in, to get at you. Well, we'll show her.'

Gulping with emotion, she pushed the bottle of brandy across the table.

'Put it somewhere where I can't reach it.'

Helen took a rapid survey of the kitchen, while Mrs Oates watched her with painful interest. She had repented her noble resolution before the girl started to climb up on to the tall dresser. She had to pull herself up to the second shelf, before she was able to hoist the bottle on to the top ledge; but directly it was out of Mrs Oates' reach, she felt a sudden glow of confidence.

Scrambling from her perilous perch she began to make a bargain.

'You've been wonderful,' she said. 'If only you'll go on playing the game, I promise you shall finish that bottle, tomorrow evening, in my sitting-room. I'll keep Oates out, and I'll stand any racket.'

'Swear,' said Mrs Oates.

Helen went through the ritual of crossing her throat.

'Now, I'm going to make some strong coffee, to pull you round,' she said.

'Cawfee,' groaned Mrs Oates. 'If ever you get a man who lifts his elbow, Heaven help the poor bloke.'

Helen actually whistled when she was in her sitting-room, for lighting the spirit-stove revived memories of Dr Parry. Since he had gone she had experienced such a whirl of emotions that she had no time to think of him. But as she passed the episode in retrospect it glowed with the dawn of happiness.

She remembered his eyes when he prophesied her marriage, and his recent promise to come to her aid if she were in need of him. At that moment she re-lived her previous experience, when she had stood looking at the refuge of the Summit, across the division of a dark spread of country.

She felt that, now, she was gazing down the length of a pitchy tunnel, to a golden glory, which shone at its end. But, between her and the dawn of a new day coiled the black serpent of the night.

The water boiled over and she made the coffee, filling a cup with strong dark fluid, which she carried to Mrs Oates.

'Here you are,' she said, 'Black as night and hot as hell.'

'Hell,' repeated Mrs Oates, as she held her nose and swallowed it in a draught.

'Mrs Oates,' asked Helen suddenly, 'is Dr Parry engaged?'

'Not yet, but may be soon,' replied Mrs Oates. 'I'm always asking him when he's going to get married and he always says he is waiting for a young lady as he can pick up and pitch over the moon.'

Although Mrs Oates' remark was under suspicion of being inspired by her audience, Helen smiled, and felt she must spread a little of her own happiness.

'I'll take some coffee up to the nurse,' she said. 'I'm afraid we hurt her feelings just now.'

When she reached the blue room, she knocked several times, but Nurse Barker did not appear.

After a slight hesitation, Helen cautiously opened the door an inch, and peeped into the room.

It was in semi-darkness, for the electric light had been switched off; only a faint bluish light from a shaded lamp, and the fitful glow from the fire illumined the gloom. Stealing over the thick carpet, she could make out the outline of Lady Warren's fleecy jacket between the bed-hangings of ultramarine. Apparently the old lady was asleep, for her snores whined up and down the scale.

Afraid of waking her, Helen could not warn Nurse Barker of her approach. The light shining through the partially-opened door of the dressing room told her that the nurse was inside.

Creeping closer, Helen took her unawares. She

was apparently busy with her toilet, for she stood before the glass intently examining her reflection. As she rubbed a finger over her chin, Helen caught the gleam of some small glittering object in her doubled-up fist.

She started violently as Helen scraped on the panel of the door, and looked at the girl suspiciously.

'Well,' she said bitterly. 'This is the one place where I thought I might expect some privacy.'

'Yes, the arrangements are abominable,' agreed Helen. 'I thought you might like some coffee.'

'Thanks.'

Nurse Barker began to sip with studied refinement which reminded Helen of a stage performance she had witnessed.

'But the man I saw gave a more natural female-impersonation,' she thought. She was so fascinated that she tried to find some excuse for lingering.

'As you saw, Mrs Oates has been drinking,' she said. 'Can you tell me of anything that will put her right?'

'Try an egg in Worcester sauce, and a hair of the dog that bit her,' advised Nurse Barker. 'What time do you go to bed?'

'About ten. But I'm not going to bed tonight.'

'Why?'

'Well, someone must sit up to let Oates in.'

Suddenly Nurse Barker pounced on the girl.

'So you've forgotten the Professor's order already? He said you were to admit *no one*.'

Helen looked the picture of guilt as she remembered Dr Parry's promise. If he came, she did not intend to keep him outside.

'I did forget,' she confessed. 'Please don't tell the Professor or Miss Warren.'

'I'll make no promises,' declared Nurse Barker. 'If you are not watched constantly, you will imperil the safety of everyone under this roof . . . It's bad enough having you here, at all – to draw him on us. For he's after *you*.'

At the reminder, Helen felt a tightening of her scalp.

'Why do you keep on trying to frighten me?' she asked.

'Because you forget.' Nurse Barker laid down her empty cup and approached Helen. 'There's another thing I've been saving up to tell you,' she added. 'I'm not satisfied about that Welsh doctor.'

'Dr Parry?' asked Helen incredulously.

'Yes, he's a queer, excitable type – unbalanced and neurotic. He might be a homicidal maniac.'

'Oh, don't be a fool,' Helen said.

'You know nothing about him,' went on Nurse Barker. 'These crimes are committed by some man who inspires the confidence of his victims, and who can move quickly from place to place . . . Well, think of the way he rushes all over the country on his motor-bike – here, one minute – a mile away, the next. And everyone trusts the doctor.'

'Of course they do,' declared Helen hotly. 'I do, for one. I'd trust Dr Parry with my life. He's a darling. He's promised to come to the Summit, in this awful storm, if I feel nervous.'

Nurse Barker took a cigarette from her case and stuck it – unlighted – in the corner of her mouth.

'You needn't trouble to send for him,' she sneered. 'He may come without waiting for an invitation.'

Helen turned towards the door.

'I won't disturb you any longer,' she said. 'Besides – I think you're goofy.'

Nurse Barker gripped her arm.

'You're afraid of me,' she said.

'I'm not.'

'What do you think of me?'

'I think you are very reliant – and clever.'

'A fool?'

'Oh, anything but that.'

'Then,' said Nurse Barker, 'perhaps you will listen to me . . . unless you are a fool yourself . . . The man who commits these crimes is normal when the fit has passed. So you'll have no warning. You may meet him tonight. If you do, he'll be the biggest surprise of your life. And the last.'

As she listened Helen's heart gave a sharp double knock, and her head swam, while Nurse Barker appeared to shoot up until she towered above her like a white pillar. She felt that she was losing her grip upon actuality. Everything was changing before her eyes in a hideous transformation. She did not know whom to trust – what to believe. In the confusion, friends masqueraded as enemies – humanity lost the common touch.

What really worried her was the fact that Dr Parry had spoken to her in the same horrible language. She had a vision of his face changing before her gaze – his smile stiffening to a grimace – the red touch of murder glowing behind his eyes.

The mist cleared from her vision as Nurse Barker lit a cigarette. All her unwholesome dream was burned away, like withered membrane, as one fear was killed by another. For the flame which reddened Nurse Barker's face revealed the shaven lip of a man.

CHAPTER 21

CLEARING THE WAY

The shock had the effect of steadying Helen's nerves. She had something definite to fight, instead of groping in a shifting horror of a nightmare. She had a problem for her brain to bite on, before she could decide on any course of action. Slipping through the darkened blue room, she went down to the hall.

Although the shaking of its one window, set high in the wall, reminded her of a storm at sea, it was less exposed than the sitting-rooms. It was also a point of vantage, where she could watch the staircase and the rest of the house. Moreover, she had the satisfaction of knowing that both the Professor and Miss Warren were within call.

Sitting on the lowest stair – her chin cupped in her hands – she took stock of the situation. To begin with, she knew that Nurse Barker was not the maniac, since her alibi, at the time of the murder, was established. At the worst, she was an impostor, who was in league with the criminal.

In that case, she must be kept under observation until they had sufficient evidence to ring up the police. Helen felt that four able-bodied persons

214

should be able to cope with her – or him. The real difficulty would be to convince the Warrens.

It was Mrs Oates who had started the hare of Nurse Barker's doubtful sex. Probably the idea was of alcoholic birth, for Helen was more inclined to regard her as a harsh jealous woman, handicapped by Nature with an unfortunate appearance. The fact that she shaved could be discounted, as a downy lip was not an uncommon feminine trait.

On the other hand, if Mrs Oates' suspicion was founded on fact, it opened up a range of ugly possibilities. It established a definite plot, for the genuine nurse must have been got out of the way. If the maniac had marked down herself as his next victim, he would not be stopped, by any obstacle, from reaching his objective.

His choice of herself was as inexplicable as the history of his crimes. With scores of girls in the town on whom to wreak his mania, he had undertaken a perilous climb in order to reach the governess's bedroom.

But, while in the cases of the countryside murders, he might have attacked the girls, when the itch for slaughter had suddenly awakened, this was different. It was the more horrible, because it was a patient, cold-blooded pursuit. She imagined him making enquiries, finding out her address, tracking her down.

What appalled her most was the way in which his path was being smoothed. No one could have foreseen such a chapter of accidents. Although he could not have planned them, they could not be coincidence, since each event had happened in its logical sequence.

'Why should he pick on me? I'm nobody. I don't look like a film star.'

As she cast the net of her thoughts over the past, she captured a memory. On her way to the Summit she had remained at the railway station for about an hour, while she waited for Oates' arrival with the ancient car. As her head ached from her journey down from London she took off her hat.

The bench on which she sat was under a lamp, which shone down on her bright mane of hair – the colour of pale flame. She remembered that a man had turned to stare at her, but his cap was pulled down over his eyes, so that she could not see his face.

'It was my hair,' she thought. 'But I'm an idiot. It's only Nurse Barker's idea. He's not after me. She's trying to frighten me.'

It all boiled down to the old question – who was Nurse Barker? Closing her eyes, she rocked to and fro. It was long past her bed time, and she had passed through a strenuous day. Worn out with strain, she felt herself growing drowsy. She began to glide over the surface of a tranquil river, shallow and crystal clear.

Suddenly it ended in a drop over a bottomless hole. Her heart gave a leap, and she opened her eyes with a violent start. To her surprise she was not alone. While she dozed the Professor had come out of his study, and was bending over her.

'Sleeping on the stairs, Miss Capel?' he asked. 'Why don't you go to bed?'

His formal voice and appearance restored her confidence. Crimes don't happen in well-conducted houses, where gentlemen dress for dinner.

'Very unwise,' he remarked, when she confided her proposed vigil. He passed her, and went up the stairs, holding on to the rail for support. She called after him.

'Professor, may I say something?'

He waited while she ran up to the landing.

'Mrs Oates wants the inside dope about that new nurse,' she said. 'I mean – she wants to know if she really comes from the Home.'

'Then why not find out?' enquired the Professor. 'There is the telephone.'

In spite of his aloofness, the Professor did not affect Helen with the hopeless feeling of fighting the air. She remembered that when she had been stunned by the thunderclap of the murder, he, alone had remained unshaken.

Stimulated with contact with him, she did not want to cut the wires.

'Are you going up to bed?' she asked boldly.

'Yes,' he replied. 'It is nearly eleven.'

'Then, I hope you'll get some sleep. But, if something crops up – something I can't cope with – may I knock you up?'

217

'Not unless it is urgent.'

Cheered by the grudging permission, Helen ran down to the hall, and consulted the telephone directory. Her habit of listening to scraps of conversation had yielded the address of the Nursing Home, which was fortunate, since there appeared to be a good crop of them. Presently, the Exchange put her through to the Secretary.

'Will you please tell me if Nurse Barker is at the Home?' asked Helen.

'No,' replied the Secretary. 'Who's speaking?'

'The Summit.'

'But she's at the Summit.'

'I know. Will you please describe her?'

There was silence, as though the Secretary wondered whether she was talking to an idiot.

'I don't understand,' she said. 'She's tall and dark, and one of our best nurses. Have you any complaint to make?'

'No. Has she a very refined voice?'

'Naturally. All our nurses are ladies.'

'Oh, yes. Did you see her get into the car from the Summit?'

'No,' replied the Secretary, after a pause. 'It was late, so she waited in the hall. When she heard a hoot, she went outside, carrying her bag.'

Helen rang off with the feeling, that, on the whole, the interview was satisfactory.

'I'd better check up, now, on Mrs Oates,' she decided.

Mrs Oates was sunken lower in her basket-chair.

She looked the picture of misery as she stared at the bottle of brandy on top of the dresser.

'You gave me the works,' she said reproachfully. 'You and your cawfee. I've not even got merry.'

'Tomorrow,' promised Helen. 'I've been ringing up the Nursing Home. Nurse Barker seems an awful brute, but otherwise I think she's all right.'

Mrs Oates would not give up her original idea.

'All wrong to me,' she grunted. 'I've a tin with a lid what 'as tightened up. Oates can't shift it. I'll ask her to open it, and see if she falls into my trap.'

'It would only prove she had strong fingers,' said Helen. 'She need not be a man. What's the time?' She glanced at the inaccurate clock. 'Five to eleven. That's near enough. When will your husband be back?'

Mrs Oates worked out the sum on her fingers.

'Say, one and a half hours to go, and two to get back. The old car's bound to take a rest up some of them hills. And Oates will play about, doing his business. Say five hours, at the outside, and maybe sooner.'

Helen felt a rush of new hope.

'He left about eight-thirty,' she said. 'So we've only another two hours, or so, to wait. I shall sleep like a top, once I know he's back. Will you bring your sheets down to the spare room, so that I shall know you're on the other side of the wall?'

'I don't mind,' promised Mrs Oates. 'It'll be safer there, than on top, with all the chimbleys.'

Suddenly Helen groaned.

'I'd forgotten. The Professor said we were not to let your husband in.'

'That's all right,' said Mrs Oates. 'The master gave his orders for you to obey. But he wasn't giving them to himself. Didn't he pack off Mr Newton after his missus? Of course, he means to let Oates in.'

Helen was astonished by the woman's shrewdness.

'You mean it was pose – to show he was master of the house?' she asked. 'If he was so keen to get the oxygen, he wouldn't let it sit in the garage all night. Directly we hear a knock I'll rush up and tell the Professor.'

'Oates will be inside the door by then,' prophesied Mrs Oates. 'D'you think I'd let my old man wait outside on the mat, with Welcome?'

Helen sprang to her feet, her face eager.

'I'll soon be back,' she said. 'I want to change into my dressing-gown. Then we'll make tea and be comfortable.'

When she was outside in the basement hall, she paused in indecision. It was quicker to use the back-way. But as she gazed up the dimly-lit spiral of narrow stairs, she shrank back, feeling that nothing would induce her to go up them.

There were too many twists on the way – too many corners. Anything – or anyone – might be lurking around the next bend – waiting to spring out upon her.

Although she knew her fear was absurd, she went up the front staircase. On the first landing she paused, arrested by a glimpse of the Professor's bedroom, through his partially opened door. He had not begun to undress, but was sitting in a low chair before his fireless grate.

As she lingered, she started at the sound of a muffled cry from the blue room. She waited for it to be repeated, but heard nothing.

'I wish I knew what to do,' she thought.

There was something about the noise which caught her imagination – a smothered note, as though a heavy hand were placed over someone's lips.

Presently she decided that she was the victim of her fancy. Lady Warren had called out in a nightmare, or else the nurse was trying to check her snores.

But as she climbed the next flight of stairs she discovered to her dismay, that she dreaded reaching the second floor. All the bedrooms, with the exception of her own, were now empty. There were too many hiding-places for anyone who might have crept up the back-stairs, as she mounted the front.

When she tried to open her door she thought, at first, that somebody was inside, shutting her out, so strong was the pressure of the draught. But as she snapped on the light, she saw only the rise and fall of the carpet, like the well of the sea.

She looked around the loaded room, at the painted mirror, the wall-packet to hold a duster, the photograph of Lady Warren the First, the numerous tiny shelves of the toilet-table, each with its lace mat.

'I suppose that governess-girl's room looked very much like mine,' she thought.

There seemed to be some septic aura hanging around Nurse Barker which had the property of arousing fear. She had stood for only a few minutes outside the blue room, yet her serenity had fled. It was of no use reminding herself that Oates was probably on his homeward journey; he might be as near as the front gate, and still be too late.

Up on the second floor, the full force of the gale was evident. A crack on the window made Helen look round nervously. It sounded as though someone were forcing his way inside.

Although she knew that it was impossible, she crossed to the casement and drew aside the curtain. Instantly, the black shape which had terrified her before, swung across, apparently touching the glass.

It was an unpleasant illusion, as though the tree was animated by some persistent purpose. Helen re-drew the curtain and sprang to the middle of the room, where she stared around her, in momentary panic. She felt that she was on the point of being attacked – like the other girl. At any moment, a window might burst open, or a curtain bulge.

Although she did not know it, somewhere on the floor below, a door was opened stealthily. A head looked around the landing – its eyes slanting to right and left. Someone stole across to the stairs, leading up to the second floor.

Suddenly Helen's glance fell upon the Cross which hung over her bed. In spite of the derision with which it had been assailed during dinner, it held actual virtue to heal her terror. She reminded herself that its Power was too enduring to be a fable or a myth. It would not fail her, in her need.

Without a thought of the ill-fated governess, she drew her green dress over her head. Shaking it out, she braved the menace of the wardrobe. No one was hiding behind the hanging garments.

She felt more comfortable when she had put on her short blue woollen dressing-gown, and heel-less slippers, which made her appear smaller than ever. Stealing noiselessly down the stairs, she stopped, to listen again at the door of the blue room.

Suddenly the silence was broken by the whimper of an old woman.

'Nurse. *Don't.*'

Helen could not recognize the coarse voice which shouted back,

'Shut up – or I'll give you what for.'

Helen's fingers clenched into fists and her face grew red with rage. Lady Warren might be the scourge of the household, but she was old – and she was in the power of an ill-tempered woman.

But she had learned the penalty of personal interference. This time she determined that she would appeal to the Professor.

The door of his room was still ajar, while he sat

in his original posture. His head was turned away from her, but she could see his hand upon the arm of his chair. It struck her that it was rather curious that he should not have moved during her absence.

'If he's dropped off,' she wondered, 'ought I to wake him up?'

She crossed the carpet noiselessly, but when she came closer to the chair she was gripped by a terrible dread. The Professor's face looked like a mask of yellowed wax, and his lids were clay-hued over his closed eyes.

On the table, by his side, was a small bottle and an empty glass. Seized with panic, she shook his arm.

'Professor,' she cried. '*Professor.*'

She was no longer afraid of disturbing him. What she dreaded was not being able to awaken him.

CHAPTER 22

ACCIDENT

Although Helen called him again and again, the Professor did not stir. Driven to boldness, she gripped his shoulders and shook him violently. But he only fell back limply against the side of his chair, like a corpse galvanized to momentary life.

Smitten with panic, Helen dashed out of the room and rushed downstairs into the study. As she burst in, Miss Warren raised her eyes from her book.

'The Professor,' gasped Helen. 'Come up to him. Quick. I think he's – dead.'

Her speech had the effect of rousing Miss Warren. She led the way, covering the stairs in long strides. When Helen panted after her, into the bedroom, she was bending over the inanimate figure in the chair.

'Really, Miss Capel.' Her voice held annoyance. 'I wish you would think twice before you frighten me unnecessarily.'

'But isn't he terribly ill?' asked Helen, looking fearfully at the corpse-like figure.

'Of course not. He has merely taken rather too much of a sleeping-draught.'

She picked up the bottle of quadronex, and studied it.

'I do not credit my brother with the folly of taking too stiff a dose. He would not make such a brainless mistake. Probably he may not have calculated its effect on his own devitalized condition.'

She felt his pulse, and then turned away.

'He is all right,' she said. 'We can do nothing, but leave him in perfect quiet.'

Helen stayed, as though rooted to the carpet, staring down at the motionless figure. It seemed the peak of ironic fate that the Professor had slipped away from them when she most appreciated his help.

Miss Warren crossed to the bed, picked up an eider-down, and laid it across her brother's knees.

'Come, Miss Capel,' she said.

'No,' said Helen. 'I – I'm afraid.'

'Afraid of what?'

'I don't know. But our very last man is gone.'

Miss Warren appeared struck by the remark.

'There has been a curiously thorough clearance,' she said. 'But I cannot see why you should be alarmed.'

'There's been a murder,' whispered Helen. 'There's a maniac somewhere. And everyone's going, one by one. I'm expecting things to happen now. It won't stop here. I may be left, all alone. Or you.'

'If you're nervous, why don't you stay with Nurse Barker?'

Helen shrank back as she recalled a recent incident.

'But I'm frightened of her, too,' she confessed. 'She's bullying Lady Warren. I heard her just now.'

Miss Warren opened her lips in indecision. It was not her habit to offer explanation, or confidence, to any employee. Some impulse, however, led her to break her rule.

'I do not usually discuss family matters with anyone outside the family,' she said stiffly. 'But I suppose you heard what happened to the last nurse?'

'Yes. Lady Warren threw something at her.'

'Exactly. It has happened before. Lady Warren is of an age and temperament when she cannot restrain her actions. Purely physical, you understand.'

Helen nodded, to show her comprehension of an evil temper allied to a lady with a title.

'Unfortunately,' went on Miss Warren, 'the matron of the Nursing Home has told me that her staff is unwilling to come to the Summit. So I've had to request her to send a nurse who is used to restraining her patients. Someone kind, but also *firm*.'

'I don't call her kind,' declared Helen. 'Won't you go in, and see how Lady Warren is for yourself?'

'Very well. We will leave on the light here.'

As they crossed the landing to the blue room, Miss Warren frowned at an object lying on the carpet.

'What is that?' she asked, peering short-sightedly.

'A chisel,' replied Helen, brightening at the sight of it. 'I wondered where it was. I was going to try to screw up your door-handle, but I forgot.'

As she stooped to pick it up, Miss Warren took it from her, and placed it on a chair inside her own room.

'It looked very untidy,' she said. 'Have you ever heard of the lines:

> "Sow an act, reap a habit.
> Sow a habit, reap character.
> Sow character, reap Destiny"?'

Helen did not reply, as she realized that the question was only a reproof in disguise. She followed Miss Warren into the blue room. As no snores sounded from the dim white fleecy mound on the bed, Helen concluded that Lady Warren was really asleep.

'I hope she's not doped,' she thought uneasily.

The air smelt a trifle more sour, with its odours of rotten apples and rugs. It caused Miss Warren to shudder with distaste.

'A repulsive atmosphere for anyone who is not trained,' she said. 'I've had to endure it all day. It has affected my head. That is why *I* value Nurse Barker's services, even if you are unable to do so.'

Helen understood the hint.

'She means she'll back up the nurse, and I shall go to the wall,' she decided.

She was struck by the mildness of Miss Warren's

manner when she tapped at the dressing-room door.

'May we come in?' she asked.

Nurse Barker gave them permission. She was sitting, with her feet stretched across a chair, smoking a cigarette, which she laid down on the ash-tray, while she rose, in grudging respect to her employer.

'I'm sorry to disturb you,' apologized Miss Warren. 'I only wanted to know if you'd had any trouble with Lady Warren?'

'She was rather naughty about her sedative,' replied Nurse Barker, 'but I soon persuaded her to take it.'

'Then I hope you will get a good night.'

'In this wind? What a hope. I'm staying up, like everyone else.'

'Who do you mean?' asked Miss Warren. 'I am going to bed. And the Professor will certainly sleep until morning. He has taken a slight overdose of a sleeping-draught.'

Nurse Barker clicked contemptuously.

'Why didn't he ask me to measure out the right quantity?' she asked.

'The Professor would hardly ask a woman to do what he could do better himself,' said Miss Warren stiffly. 'He might have been aware of what he was doing when he insured some sleep. He knows the importance of conserving his strength, with so many dependent on him.'

Nurse Barker was not listening to the hint of the

source of her own wages. A phosphorescent gleam – half of alarm, half of satisfaction – lit up her deep-set eyes.

'Odd,' she gloated. 'It looks as if someone was clearing the way for himself.'

Helen saw panic leap into Miss Warren's eyes.

'How is that possible?' she asked. 'There is a good reason for all that has happened. Take one instance alone. Mr Rice, and my nephew and his wife all left this house because I turned out that dog.'

'No, you must go back a bit further,' declared Nurse Barker. 'Did Rice know you hated dogs?'

'Yes.'

'*Ah*. Then, do you know who first told him about a dog for sale?'

Helen listened with a chill at her heart. Did the sequence of events appear harmless because she saw only the trivial links? How far back did the chain really stretch? To what dark brain did it lead?

It was a relief when Miss Warren spoke impatiently.

'Of course you could conjecture endlessly, but it is entirely futile. What sinister agency was at work when *I* forgot to screw the cap of the cylinder?'

Helen was on the point of giving the true explanation of the incident, when she remembered that she must not betray Mrs Oates' confidence. She listened, unhappily, while Nurse Barker turned the knife again.

'Now there are only three women in the house,' she said.

'Four,' corrected Helen proudly. 'I saw Mrs Oates was only confused. So I pulled her round. She's sober now.'

Miss Warren and the nurse stared at Helen. 'It seems to me,' said Miss Warren reflectively, 'that you are capable of looking after yourself.'

'I've done it all my life,' Helen assured her.

'I'm sure you're equal to an emergency, Miss Capel,' she said. 'All the same, if you do not intend to go to bed, I should feel easier in my mind if I knew you were with Mrs Oates.'

Helen, who was beginning to crumble under the combined excitement and strain, began to gulp at this unexpected sign of consideration.

Mrs Oates was still slumped down in her chair when she returned to the kitchen; but she had climbed out of her slough of depression. Some of her old jovial humour beamed from her eyes as she shook her finger at Helen.

'Stealing about on rubber heels?' she asked. 'Trying to put salt on my tail, are you. You'll find I'm too old a bird to be caught that way.'

'The plot thickens,' Helen said dramatically. 'Exit the Professor.'

Mrs Oates listened to her story of the Professor's mishap with little concern.

'He's no loss,' she said. 'He does nothing but set in his study, and think.'

'That's my point exactly,' explained Helen. 'Without him, we're a body without a head.'

Apparently, the same thought had occurred to

Nurse Barker, for, a little later, she entered the kitchen with the dignity of a queen who had temporarily laid down her sceptre.

'I thought we had better have an agreement,' she said. 'In the Professor's absence, who is to assume authority?'

'The mistress, of course,' replied Mrs Oates.

'She's not competent,' declared Nurse Barker. 'She is definitely a neurotic type. You must allow me to know my own subject.'

'*I* shall continue to take my orders from her,' said Helen. 'She engaged me, and she pays my salary.'

'Hear, hear.' Mrs Oates clapped her hands. 'Listen to the doctor's young lady, telling you off.'

'I didn't know you were engaged to Dr Parry,' said Nurse Barker.

Her thin lips were sucked together in a thin line while her sunken eyes gleamed with jealousy.

'I'm not,' said Helen hastily.

Although the subject was obviously tender Nurse Barker seemed unable to discard it.

'I suppose it's your size,' she said. 'Rum how men always choose short women. It's a sign of their own mental inferiority. They know that your brain corresponds with your size, and they feel unable to cope with their intellectual equals.'

The speech made Helen see red, for she was sensitive on the score of her defective education.

'Perhaps they find us more attractive,' she said.

Nurse Barker lit a cigarette with fingers which shook with passion.

'You mean to insult me deliberately,' she said huskily. 'Isn't that rather unwise? Very soon you'll be left alone with me.'

'Mrs Oates will be here, too,' Helen reminded her.

'Will she?' Nurse Barker gave a meaning laugh. 'If I were you I wouldn't bank upon that.'

Puffing fiercely at her cigarette, she tramped out into the hall.

'What did she mean?' asked Helen uneasily.

'Bilge,' commented Mrs Oates. 'All the same,' she added gloomily, 'we didn't ought to do it. She came down here for a crack and we turned her sour. I begun it, and you finished it.'

'She shouldn't leave poor old Lady Warren so much,' said Helen defensively.

'Now, don't go and be sorry for her,' advised Mrs Oates. 'She can take care of herself. Locking up them two is like shutting in a lion with a tiger. You wonder which will walk out in the morning.'

'I wish I could be sure that Lady Warren can defend herself,' Helen said. 'I've got a real fear of that nurse.'

'Don't let her know it,' advised Mrs Oates.

'No.' Helen glanced at the clock. 'I wish I knew exactly whereabouts on the road Mr Oates is at this minute,' she said. 'The time seems to crawl. If only I can last out, till he comes.'

'Why shouldn't you?'

'I've a terror of one thing which may happen to me,' confessed Helen.

'Don't tell me,' urged Mrs Oates. 'You never know who may be listening to you.'

Helen opened the kitchen door and looked into the deserted basement hall.

'This is what I'm scared of,' she said. 'Supposing I heard a child crying outside. I believe I should *have* to go out. Just in case, you know.'

'Now, don't you go and be a fool,' implored Mrs Oates. 'In all the time I've been here there's never been a baby parked on the doorstep. Miss Warren's not the sort to come home with a bundle in her arms.'

Helen laughed as she sprang to her feet.

'I feel so guilty,' she said. 'She'll be wanting to go to bed soon, and the handle of her door is not screwed up.'

Grateful for a job, she ran upstairs, to the first floor. Everything seemed especially safe and normal as she passed through the hall. When she reached the first floor landing she noticed that the light was shining through the transom above Miss Warren's bedroom door.

'I hope she's not going to bed,' she thought, as she tapped at the door.

'Yes,' called Miss Warren's voice.

'Oh, Miss Warren,' said Helen, 'I'm terribly sorry to disturb you. But could you hand me out the tools you put on your chair?'

'Certainly, Miss Capel, only don't leave them outside again.'

Helen heard Miss Warren's step crossing the

polished boards and then the handle revolved in an impotent whirl. She watched it, in slight surprise.

'Can't you open the door?' she asked.

'No,' was the reply. 'The handle keeps turning round in my hand.'

CHAPTER 23

WHAT SHALL WE DO WITH
A DRUNKEN SAILOR?

Although vaguely disturbed, Helen felt mistress of the situation.

'It's all right,' she called. 'I'll open it, this side.'

Full of confidence, she gripped the handle, only to feel it slip round in her fingers, as though it were oiled.

'It seems to have gone completely,' she cried. 'You have the tools. Do you think you could manage to put it right?'

'No, the screw is missing,' was the reply. 'It doesn't matter. Oates will repair it early tomorrow.'

'But, Miss Warren,' persisted Helen, 'it's not right you should be locked in. Suppose – suppose there's a fire?'

'Why should we suppose it? Please go, Miss Capel. I have important work to finish.'

'Is the key your side?' Helen asked.

'No. The lock is broken, so I had a bolt put instead . . . Now, please leave me in peace.'

Helen turned forlornly away. As she passed the

blue room, Nurse Barker, who had been attracted by the noise, poked her head around the door.

'What's the matter now?' she asked.

When Helen explained the situation she gave a disagreeable laugh.

'What did I tell you? She locked herself in, on purpose.'

'I can't believe it,' declared Helen. 'Why should she do that?'

'Funk. Oh, *I've* seen it coming on . . . *And* – I've seen something else, which is due before very long. Your troubles are not over yet, my girl.'

Helen was impressed by the woman's perspicacity.

'Nurse,' she cried impulsively, 'I want to apologize to you. If I've hurt your feelings, it was unintentional.'

'Rather late in the day to eat humble-pie,' sneered Nurse Barker. 'The harm's done.'

'But can't I do something to make up?'

'You can pledge yourself to obedience.'

Helen hesitated to give her promise, as her thoughts flew to Dr Parry. She knew that Nurse Barker would do everything in her power to block his interference. On the other hand, he was not likely to rush over to the Summit, while the woman was a formidable obstacle to any move on the part of the maniac; she had extraordinary physical strength and a mind which bit like a ferret.

She gave a military salute.

'I promise, Sergeant,' she said.

'This is no joke,' frowned Nurse Barker. 'I'm not sure I can trust you. In all my experience, I've never been so grossly insulted as by an intoxicated char and a raw, untrained girl.'

'Oh, Nurse,' she said, '*I* never thought it.'

Nurse Barker clocked back to the listen-in incident.

'Yes, *she* said it,' she remarked. 'But you were licking up her words.'

'No, I had to humour her, because she was a trifle cockeyed. I never thought what she did.'

'*What* did she think?'

Helen understood the alleged hypnotic power of a serpent, as Nurse Barker held her with a glittering eye.

'She thought you were a man,' she admitted.

Nurse Barker swallowed convulsively.

'She'll pay for that,' she muttered, as she turned back to the blue room.

Helen reviewed as much of the past as she could remember, on her way downstairs. She wished that her conscience was entirely clear on the score of Nurse Barker, as she hated to feel a hypocrite.

On the whole, she felt tolerably comfortable. She had discounted the razor incident, and had mentioned it to no one. When Mrs Oates had boasted of her conquests, she had disclaimed them. Her dislike of the nurse was her own affair.

The sight of the telephone reminded her of the latest casualties, which she had almost forgotten.

One fear had again driven out another; and, for the present, she stood chiefly in dread of Nurse Barker.

'I think I'll ring up Dr Parry,' she thought, 'and tell him what's happened.'

It was a long time before she got through to him, and when, at last, she heard Dr Parry's voice, it sounded gruff and sleepy.

'What's up?' he asked.

'The Professor's doped,' replied Helen, 'and Miss Warren's locked in her bedroom.'

As Dr Parry made no comment, Helen hastened to excuse her action.

'I suppose I shouldn't have bothered you. But it does seem queer the way they're all disappearing, one by one . . . What do *you* think?'

'Blowed if I know,' was the reply. 'It *seems* in order. I think Miss Warren is the wisest. Why don't you follow her good example?'

'Because – you won't believe me, after all the fuss I made about sleeping in her room – but I don't like to leave old Lady Warren alone with that nurse.'

'D'you think the nurse rough-handles her?'

'I don't know. But I do know she has a horrible temper.'

'Then I'll give you a tip. If it should come to a scrap between those two, put your shirt on the old one.'

Although Mrs Oates had given her the same warning, Helen was not convinced.

'Thank you for your advice,' she said. 'I'm sorry I bothered you, but you encouraged me to be a nuisance.'

'Here – don't ring off,' urged the doctor. 'I'm wondering what to do about the Professor. Ought I to come over?'

'He looks *awful*,' declared Helen, making the most of her chance.

'He would. What did Miss Warren do?'

'Felt his pulse, and covered him up.'

'Good.' Helen could hear his sigh of relief. 'That sounds all right. She's a clever woman. Now, we'll leave it at this. If I should change my mind regarding the situation I'll bike over at once. In fact, you've only to say one word, and I'll start now.'

'You'd come for me?' asked Helen.

'For you, only.'

In spite of her exhaustion and loneliness – in spite of the menace of the night – Helen became suddenly surcharged with glorious life.

'Now I know that,' she said, 'I don't want you to come. I feel gorgeous. I—'

She rang off at the sound of a footstep on the landing. Nurse Barker was leaning over the balustrade, looking down at her.

'Who was that?' she asked.

'The doctor,' replied Helen. 'I rang him up, to tell him about the Professor, but he decided that it was not necessary for him to come over.'

'He would prefer to take us by surprise,' prophesied Nurse Barker. 'I don't trust that young man

'. . . And hadn't you better go to your alcoholic patient? You're giving her more rope than I should.'

Filled with sudden misgiving, Helen hurried across the hall. As she opened the door leading to the basement, she kicked in front of her some hard object, which bumped from step to step with an appalling clatter. Running downstairs after it, she picked up, from the mat at the bottom, a small pint milk-can.

'Mrs Oates,' she cried, as she entered the kitchen, 'who put this at the top of the stairs?'

'I don't know,' replied Mrs Oates.

In sudden suspicion, Helen looked up at the dresser. To her relief, the bottle was still on the top, and, apparently, untouched.

In spite of this proof of her innocence, Helen fancied she detected a deterioration in Mrs Oates. The maudlin grin, which robbed her face of its underhung tenacity, hovered around her lips, imparting a muddled expression. As Helen watched her, the lines of a sea-shanty swam into her head.

'What shall we do with a drunken sailor?'

'After tonight, I could write a book on this subject,' she thought, with the glib assurance of one who only wrote a letter, as a penance.

It was evident that Mrs Oates was making stupendous efforts to concentrate on Helen's tale of Miss Warren's door-handle, for she kept repeating every point, in the form of a question.

'Oates will want some supper,' was her only comment.

Helen took the hint, and picked up a tray.

'I'll help you get it,' she said. 'Get up.'

Placing her hands under Mrs Oates' armpits, she gave a strong hoist. But the woman only slipped back again.

'You must let me take it easy for a bit longer,' she advised. 'Remember, I've a half-bottle inside me. I'll soon be all right.'

'All right,' said Helen. 'I'll carry on, alone.'

It struck her that it might be a valuable test of her own will-power, to go, alone, into the larder. As she opened the scullery door, and snapped on the switch, every corner of its clean bareness was revealed by the yellow glow. Outside, in the passage, she could hear the loose window banging against its shutter.

The sound was distinctly nerve-racking, for it gave the impression that someone was determined to force an entry. The passage, too, looked a gloomy tunnel, in the dim light. Around the bend, stretched the dark labyrinth of Murder Lane.

Helen knew that she must keep her imagination strictly controlled. She must not think of the horror which had actually taken place within these walls, or wonder if the girl still lingered somewhere in the atmosphere, the dust, or the stones.

Reminding herself that she had policed this stretch herself, and searched thoroughly every potential hiding-place, she entered the larder.

Besides a side of bacon and string of onions, its shelves held so many tins and bottles that Helen's curiosity took charge of the situation. The Summit laid in a heavy store of preserved provisions, so that it was difficult to make a choice.

Her eye was greedier than her stomach, as she piled her tray with tongue, sardines, dainties in aspic, and pots of savoury paste.

Balancing it on her hip, she switched off the light at the same time as she kicked open the scullery door. Instantly, there was a loud rattle, as a tin tray crashed down on the stone flags.

Helen frowned thoughtfully, for she did not like the repetition of the trick. Suddenly she was rent with a suspicion which was vaguely alarming. Mrs Oates could not hear her when she walked sound-lessly in bedroom shoes, so she had placed these tins in order to have some warning of her approach.

If it were true, she had something to hide. She was not playing the game. In spite of her load, Helen crashed recklessly into the kitchen.

Mrs Oates was still in her chair, her back turned towards Helen, while Nurse Barker stood over her, with folded arms.

'Where have you been?' she asked.

'Larder,' explained Helen. 'Getting some supper for Mr Oates. We thought we could all do with a snack, just to pass the time. Could you?'

Nurse Barker nodded, while a peculiar smile flickered round her lips, causing Helen to rush into nervous explanations.

'I thought Mrs Oates and I would have ours, down here, and I'd carry up yours into your dressing-room. Will that suit you? And what kind of sandwiches would you like?'

'Ask Mrs Oates which she would prefer,' said Nurse Barker. 'I thought you undertook her responsibility.'

Filled with foreboding, Helen slammed down her tray, and rushed around to Mrs Oates. But, before she could reach her, the woman stretched her arms upon the table, and laid her head on them.

'What's the matter?' cried Helen. 'Are you ill?'

Mrs Oates opened one eye, with difficulty.

'I'm that sleepy,' she said, 'I – I—'

As her voice died away, Helen shook her shoulder.

'Wake up,' she cried. 'Don't leave me. You *promised*.'

A gleam of smothered recollection fought with the guilt in Mrs Oates' eyes, and then died out.

'Someone's – got – me,' she said. 'I'm doped.'

Dropping her head again on her arms, she closed her lids and began to breathe heavily.

With a horrible sense of helplessness, Helen watched her sink into stupefied slumber. Nurse Barker stood by, licking her lips, as though savouring the humour of the situation. Presently Helen broke the silence.

'Can we do anything?'

'Why not offer her a drink?' asked Nurse Barker derisively. 'Stimulant might revive her.'

Helen recognized the advice for a jeer. There was no doubt in her mind as to the cause of the catastrophe. Just as burglars drug a watch-dog, as prelude to robbery, someone had taken advantage of her absence to tamper with Mrs Oates.

Afraid to tax Nurse Barker with the offence – even while she was sure of her guilt – she tried to keep her suspicion from her face and voice.

'What's the matter with her?'

Nurse Barker gave a scornful bark.

'Don't be a fool,' she said. 'It's obvious. She's drunk as a lord.'

CHAPTER 24

A SUPPER-PARTY

In spite of her shock, Nurse Barker's words were almost a relief to Helen. Like an explosion inside her head, they shot away the foul cobwebs of suspicion.

No treachery had been at work. There was only a landslide of Mrs Oates' good intentions before the pressure of temptation.

'How could she get at the brandy?' she asked. 'I'm sure she was not in a condition to climb on the dresser.'

Nurse Barker kicked forward a substantial footstool, mounted it, stretched out her arm, and removed the bottle from the top shelf.

'You forget everyone is not a midget like yourself,' she said. 'Mrs Oates is not so tall as I am, but she has a reach like a gorilla.'

Helen bit her lip as she realized how easily she had been duped.

'You must think me a gull,' she said. 'But I counted on her promise. All the same, she's not touched the brandy. The bottle's still half full.'

Sniffing scornfully, Nurse Barker uncorked the

bottle, smelt the cork, and then shook out a few drops on the back of her hand.

'Water,' she remarked.

Helen looked reproachfully down at Mrs Oates, sunken deep in hot and steamy sleep.

'What shall we do with her?' she asked helplessly.

'Leave her where she is.'

'But can't I put a bandage soaked in vinegar-and-water round her head?' persisted Helen. 'She seems so hot and uncomfortable.'

'You'll do nothing of the sort,' snapped Nurse Barker. 'She has let us down, and we've no time for her. She's nothing but lumber. Get supper. I've had no dinner, and I'm sinking. Bring the tray up to my room. We'll have it there.'

Although the words promised a new partnership, Helen felt like a fag to a new bully.

'What would you like?' she asked eagerly.

'Cold meat, potatoes, pickles, cheese. Don't stop to cut sandwiches. Make a strong pot of tea. Remember – we've got to keep awake.'

'You don't really think there's any danger?' asked Helen apprehensively.

Nurse Barker looked at her fixedly.

'I'm in luck to be saddled with *you*. You're a fool – and a fool is twice as dangerous as a knave. Can you do elementary arithmetic?'

'Of course.'

'Well, then, there were nine persons in this house

at dinner-time. Now there are only two. How many have gone?'

'Seven,' gasped Helen, horrified by the shrinkage.

Nurse Barker licked her lips with gloomy relish.

'And do you realize what it means?' she asked. 'It means he's getting very close to *you*.'

Although Helen was sure that Nurse Barker was playing on her fear, her heart sank as the woman went out of the room. In spite of her malevolent nature, she was some sort of company.

One catastrophe after another had so weakened her resistance that she felt terrified at being alone in the basement. Every bang on the passage window was duplicated by a knock at her heart. Although, down below, the roar of the storm was muted, the garden was nearer. She remembered how the bushes had writhed, like knotted fingers tapping the glass, and how the tentacles of the undergrowth had swayed in mimicry of subaqueous life.

'It's trying to get in,' she thought. 'Suppose there is some secret entrance I overlooked. Anyone could hide between the two staircases and in all the empty rooms.'

Her one wish was to get upstairs as soon as possible. Although she had time to cut her sandwiches, while she waited for the kettle to boil, her appetite for dainties had deserted her.

She hastily prepared her supper-tray, and then returned to her sitting-room to watch the kettle. As she did so, her thoughts jerked disconnectedly, like the limping music of an old barrel-organ.

'I believe Miss Warren was grateful to be locked in . . . The accident couldn't have happened if I hadn't been so careless. She quoted that bit about actions and character, just to tell me it was my fault . . . So, between us, we're responsible for that part of it . . . And no *one* else.'

Although she was comforted by her logic, she shied at the question it raised. Was there some unseen link in the chain, which had precipitated – or influenced – this interplay of character?

She, with her impulsive carelessness – Miss Warren, with her selfishness – and Mrs Oates, with her craving – had each acted as an independent agent – true to its own type. Yet the board was rearranged as though they had been pawns, used in someone's game; whatever the impulse of their moves, they were now placed to suit the unseen player.

The kettle coughed out a gust of steam and the lid rose, with a spill of water. Helen made the tea hurriedly and crabbed up the stairs, shooting nervous glances over her shoulder. At the top she kicked the door behind her.

There were no snores from the bed when she passed through the dim blue room, doing her utmost to subdue the rattle of the china. Inside the dressing-room Nurse Barker was lighting a new cigarette from her old stub. She broke into a complaint as Helen put down the tray.

'I've nearly broken my fingers trying to turn that key.' She nodded towards the second door.

'Disgusting, putting me in a room next to a man's bedroom, with a connecting door.'

'It used to be a dressing-room,' explained Helen. 'Besides, the Professor is not like that. He won't pay you a visit tonight.'

She turned away to hide her grin. Besides amusing her, the incident had raised her spirits, for it had laid Mrs Oates' hare as dead as stone. The last vestige of her suspicion faded, as she realized that Nurse Barker's fingers lacked the requisite strength of a thug.

'Shall we open the door, so that you can hear Lady Warren call you?' she asked.

'She won't,' grunted Nurse Barker. 'I've fixed her.'

'D'you mean you've doped her, like – like babies?'

'Well, why not? That's all she is – an old baby.'

'But – it seems rather drastic.'

Nurse Barker merely grunted, as she poured out a cup of tea, to which she added several drops of brandy. Helen watched her, in astonishment, as she piled her plate with cold potatoes and thick slices of cold meat, smothered with pickles.

'Enough for a man,' she thought, as she followed the clearance of the meal with wide-eyed interest.

The spirit improved Nurse Barker's temper for she held out the bottle, in invitation.

'Like a drop in your tea?'

'No, thank you.'

'You'll need it before you're much older. That

guy has tasted blood. You saw how Mrs Oates couldn't keep off the bottle after she'd cracked it. She had to finish. He's the same – only he's a famished tiger, with dripping chops.'

Helen put down the bit of cheese she was nibbling.

'Nurse,' she asked, 'why do you dislike me?'

'Because you remind me of someone I hate,' replied Nurse Barker. 'She was the spit of you – a little skinny thing, all legs and giggles, with frizzed-out hair, like a doll. Only, she was a blonde.'

'Why did you hate the horrid little blonde?' Helen asked, with a spurt of her native curiosity.

'Because of a man,' Nurse Barker replied. 'It was when I was a probationer. He was a doctor, and very clever. But he was so small, I could have lain him across my knee and spanked him.'

'That's the attraction of contrast,' said Helen. 'Were you engaged?'

Her interest was not assumed, because Nurse Barker's strange confidence had stirred up the sweetness of her own romance.

'Odd,' she thought, with a flicker of her submerged sense of drama. 'Here we are – the long and the short of it – coming together over a cup of tea, because we are both in love.'

'Not engaged,' replied Nurse Barker. 'Just leading up. It would have happened. But the blonde took him away from me, curse her.'

'What a shame,' said Helen, with real sympathy.

'Shame?' Nurse Barker laughed bitterly. 'It was

251

my life. That was my only man. There's never been another – never will be.'

'Were they married?' asked Helen.

'No, she threw him over. She only wanted to take him from me. But there was only the husk of him left. Nothing for me . . . That's why I hate women like her. If a man wanted to twist their throats, I'd say good luck to him.'

As Nurse Barker glared at Helen the girl shrank into her shell. Her desire to talk about her own hope was slain; she only sought for some way to avert the penalty of an unlucky resemblance.

'Do you know,' she said, 'you and I have a lot in common. We're in the same boat. Men have always ignored me – because I am *small.*'

The greedy glitter in Nurse Barker's eyes told her that she had swallowed the bait.

'Isn't the doctor your fancy-man?' she asked.

'Of course not. That was only Mrs Oates' fairy-tale. I've never had a real affair. I've always had to earn my own living, and I've never had money to buy clothes.'

'Are you speaking the truth?' insisted Nurse Barker.

Helen nodded, as she remembered the humiliation and neglect which had marked her girlhood. And Nurse Barker believed her, in spite of her likeness to the blonde, as she stared at her with penetrating eyes.

At that moment Helen appeared an ill-developed scrap – superfluous, unskilled labour – nobody's woman. If she were murdered, she would not be missed, or mourned, and one more job would be released.

But, although she felt only contempt for the weakling, she no longer bore her a grudge.

As she took up the bottle of brandy Helen gave a cry of protest.

'Please don't.'

'D'you think I'm going to pass out on a toothful of brandy?' sneered Nurse Barker.

'It's not that. But after what's happened, I'm terrified. Suppose that brandy is doped.'

'If it is, you'll be left all alone. I'll risk it.' She raised the cup to her lips and drained it. 'It might be the best thing that could happen to me,' she continued. 'When he comes, he'll go for you. If I interfere, he'll turn on me, too.'

'But I'd stick to you,' cried Helen. 'There's only two of us left. If anything happened to you, I think I should go mad with terror.'

'It all depends on you,' said Nurse Barker spitefully. 'You are the weak spot. You'd double-cross me to save your own skin.'

It seemed useless to argue further. Unable to eat, Helen sat and watched Nurse Barker finish her supper. It was a protracted process, for she smoked between every mouthful.

The small room was hazed with smoke, so that Nurse Barker's gigantic white figure loomed through a fog. Sometimes Helen's vision played her a trick, and she appeared to spread out like a cloud. The atmosphere, too, was close and torrid as a jungle.

'I must keep awake,' she thought desperately. 'If I take my eyes off her, she will disappear.'

Yet, even as she strove to concentrate on her surroundings, at the back of her mind was a desperate conviction that she was trying to grip something, which, even then, was slipping through her fingers. Mrs Oates had failed her, and Nurse Barker would fail her too.

But, at least, the night was passing. Apparently the same thought struck Nurse Barker, for she glanced at her little travelling-clock upon the mantelpiece.

'We may expect him now, any minute,' she said. 'I wonder what his first move will be.'

Helen checked her shudder, as she realized that the bully was merely tormenting the new fag, in order to make her squeak. With a flicker of her old spirit, she made a sudden counter-attack.

'Don't forget this,' she said. 'No one seems to trouble much about me, alive – but I'd be mighty important if I was dead. If anything happened to me, here, tonight, there'd be an inquiry, and lots of publicity. And they'd hold *you* responsible.'

Nurse Barker's eyes drew together, for she had overlooked this contingency. She had to depend on her profession for a living, and her reputation might be damaged if she had to undergo a gruelling examination at an inquest, and could not disprove a charge of cowardice.

'Don't be a fool,' she said. 'We hang together – What is that noise?'

Helen heard it, too – a low, muffled thud, from somewhere downstairs.

'It sounds like knocking,' she said.

'Don't go to find out,' Nurse Barker warned her. 'It may be a trick.'

'But I *must*. It might be Oates.'

Before Nurse Barker could stop her, she had opened the door, and was running noiselessly through the blue room. When she reached the landing, the sound was clear and imperative – a loud tattoo on the front door, followed by the pealing of the bell.

Helen stopped dead and gripped the balustrade – her brain paralysed by the poison of Nurse Barker's warning. The person who waited outside *might* be Oates, who had returned sooner than she had dared to hope. Yet – for that very reason – she dared not stir.

Suddenly a new idea sprang to birth. Instinctively she knew that Dr Parry was knocking at the door. In spite of his reassuring words, he had not been satisfied with the situation at the Summit.

Her eyes shining with welcome, she dashed down the stairs, just as Nurse Barker reached the landing.

'Stop,' she shouted. 'Don't open the door.'

'I must,' panted Helen, calling over her shoulder. 'It's the doctor. He promised to come. I *must*.'

She heard Nurse Barker's heavy footsteps thudding in pursuit, and she tried to run faster. In spite of her efforts, however, just as she reached the swing doors leading to the lobby, she felt herself held in strong arms.

'Hush, you little fool,' whispered Nurse Barker hoarsely, as she laid her hand over Helen's lips. 'He's outside.'

CHAPTER 25

THE WATCHER

In spite of the conviction in Nurse Barker's voice, Helen continued to struggle. She was positive that Dr Parry was outside the door. It was torture to feel he was so near to her and yet she could not break through to him.

From the first she knew she was beaten, for Nurse Barker had her pinioned inside one arm, while she pressed her hand heavily over her face. The strength of her grip was amazing, and Helen could only kick – feebly, but frantically – with soft felt soles.

The knocking and ringing seemed to go on for an eternity. When it ceased, Nurse Barker did not relax her grasp, but waited, until she heard a distant hammering from another part of the house.

'He's gone round to the back-door,' she said grimly. 'He's persistent. And so am I.'

Helen could only writhe weakly, for her sufferings had become physical as well as mental. She felt on the point of suffocation, from the iron pressure around her ribs and over her mouth. When, after a second pause, the assault was

257

renewed on the front door, she had reached the limit of endurance.

'Go away, dear. It's no good. For my sake. Go away. It's no good.'

As though he actually heard her voiceless entreaties, which raced, in a circle, round her brain, the knocking was succeeded by so prolonged a silence that Nurse Barker released her.

'*Oh*,' gasped Helen, stroking her neck tenderly. 'You've nearly choked me.'

Nurse Barker gave a short, grating laugh.

'So that's the thanks I get. Pity I didn't let him in. He'd have cured you of sore throats for a long time to come . . . You are not worth the saving.'

'You didn't save me,' Helen said. 'That was Dr Parry.'

'How do you know?'

'Because he promised he would come to me.'

Nurse Barker drew her bushy brows together.

'You told me he was not your lover.'

Helen felt too low-spirited to protest.

'What does it matter – now?' she asked wearily. 'You've sent him away.'

'Only this. It means you lied to me, just now. You tried to trade on my sympathy. And all the time you were laughing at me, in your sleeve.'

As Helen looked at the livid face, she remembered Stephen Rice's remark that her personal safety depended largely on the character of her companions.

She could tell by the congestion of Nurse

Barker's colour that she had plunged herself into a hell of jealousy. Suddenly she felt so sorry for the vindictive, unattractive woman that she lost her dislike.

'I told you the truth,' she said gently. 'It only happened tonight.'

'*What* happened?'

'Nothing.' Helen gave a little low laugh. 'But – it's everything, all the same . . . There's something in him that draws out something in me. So, he must feel the same, or he couldn't call to me. *You* understand, don't you? It happened to you, too.'

In her eagerness to forge a link between them, she caught Nurse Barker's hand. But the woman pushed her away with such force that she fell on her knees.

'Yes,' she said, 'I know exactly how it begins. I know the end, too. A hollow cheat, with frizzy hair, like yours.'

'But it's not fair to punish me for someone else's fault,' protested Helen. 'I've done you no harm.'

'And you've done me no good. You've been pert and insolent about my personal appearance. Because I'm tall, and my face shows character, you dared to compare me with a man.'

'I never did. Oh, do be friendly, if only for tonight. We oughtn't to be fighting like this.'

'Oh, yes, I get your angle. Men find small women more attractive, don't they? But small women need protection. You'll miss me when I'm gone, and you are left alone.'

The words struck a chill to Helen's heart.

'If that happened,' she said, 'I think I should die of fear. But I won't.'

'It may.' The woman looked down her nose, while a fugitive smile darkened her lips. 'We have assumed that the Professor is drugged, and the cook is drunk. But how do we know that they've not been doped?'

It was a horrible possibility which appalled Helen, as she remembered Mrs Oates' mumbled excuse.

'Who could dope them?' she cried.

'Someone might have crept in by the basement,' suggested Nurse Barker. 'Things have been most peculiar all the night, just as if someone was working the trick from inside.' She added, with sinister meaning, 'We shall know, if I pass out. I took brandy in my tea. I wonder if it's that which makes me feel so dizzy?'

As she spoke, she staggered slightly, and passed her hand over her brow. Helen stared at her, speechless with horror. In spite of the woman's venom, she clung to her as desperately as a drowning person clings to his rescuer.

Although her common sense reminded her that Nurse Barker was plugging at her alarmist policy in order to terrify her, events over which she had no control seemed to indicate some subterranean direction of the general withdrawal.

One after another her companions had left her. They slept, while she remained, to watch. In the end, she would be alone.

Determined that Nurse Barker should not have the satisfaction of knowing that she had drawn blood, she kept her head high and her lips steady. But Nurse Barker looked at her eyes and noticed how the pupils had swamped the iris.

Helen saw her smile, and was suddenly inflamed to reprisal.

'I can't understand why you should grudge me my first chance of happiness,' she said. 'It's mean. When I was hungry, it didn't help me to know others were hungry, too. In fact, it was worse, for I always had bread, and I could guess what it meant to those who had nothing at all.'

'Oh? So you've starved?' asked Nurse Barker.

'Not exactly. But I've gone very short, in between jobs.'

'That only proves you're of no use. There's a glut of unskilled labour. You'd never be missed.'

Again Helen glimpsed the blue star of daylight shining at the end of the tunnel.

'I wish it was tomorrow,' she sighed. 'Oh, nurse, help me to come safely through the night.'

'Why? You wouldn't put yourself out for me.'

'I do wish I could prove it was genuine,' Helen said eagerly. 'I was a horrible little beast. But you've grown on me. I think I understand, now, how your doctor felt.'

Nurse Barker listened in silence, her expression enigmatic. In the pause the telephone-bell rang, with startling shrillness. The sound was music to Helen's ears, with the reminder that the Summit was still resistant to the Hollywood tradition of the cut wires.

She rushed across the hall, her pale face suddenly vivid with colour and glow.

'You were right, as usual,' she panted. 'Dr Parry wasn't outside, for he's ringing me now.'

She was so sure of hearing his voice, when she took up the receiver, that her disappointment was acute at the sound of mincing feminine accents.

'Is thet the Summet?'

'Summit speaking,' replied Helen dully.

The next minute, she spoke to Nurse Barker.

'The call's for you.'

Nurse Barker arose with an air of importance.

'Who is ringing me?' she asked.

'I don't know.'

Unconscious of impending disaster, Helen watched Nurse Barker with none of her usual interest.

'Nurse Barker speaking. Who is it? . . . Oh, is it you, dear?'

The Secretary of the Nursing-Home explained the position.

'How nice to hear your voice, dear. I'm still on duty. We've a rush op., and I'm trying to get Blake. He's on holiday, and I'm chasing him all over England. So, while I'm waiting I thought I'd ring you up, just in case you hadn't gone to bed.'

'Not much chance of that,' said Nurse Barker.

'That doesn't sound too bright. Isn't the case comfortable?'

'Most *un*comfortable. In fact, it's all most unpleasant and very peculiar.'

'I'm not surprised, dear. I think you ought to know that someone rang me up and asked me the most extraordinary questions about *you*.'

'About me?'

Helen caught the inflection of Nurse Barker's voice. With a sinking heart, she listened to half of the dialogue.

'Please repeat that . . . Indeed. Anything else? . . . *What*? The insolence . . . *Who* rang you up? . . . You are sure it was a girl's voice? . . . When? Please try to remember, because I mean to trace this back to its source . . . Are you sure it was that time? . . . Then I know *which* girl it was, for the other had left the house . . . Not at all. You are quite right to let me know. Good-bye.'

Nurse Barker rang off, and looked at Helen.

'You wanted to prove yourself?' she asked. 'Well, you've done it. Completely. You're a liar and a sneak. If I could save your neck by lifting my little finger, I wouldn't do it.'

Helen opened her lips dumbly, in an effort to explain. But her mind felt as incapable of coagulation as a lightly-boiled egg. She could only realize that she had alienated the defence, and that a man was prowling outside, in the streaming darkness.

The man was still there, encircling the house. Lashed by the gale, twigs flogged his face, like wire whips, as he stooped over the sodden ground to examine each small basement window.

Once he thought he had found a vulnerable spot, for a casement shook before his pressure. Inserting his pen-knife inside the frame, he hacked away a make-shift fastening of a peg and some string, but only to meet the resistance of an inner shutter.

The house was armed to its teeth. It was blind and impregnable as an armoured car.

Dr Parry should have been pleased by this evidence of obedience to his orders. He had advised the most stringent precautions. Yet, as he looked upwards at the blank walls, seeking in vain a gleam of light from some upper window, he felt a chill.

He had always disliked the tree-muffled isolation of the Summit, although he was a lover of solitude.

Endowed with swift intuitions – swayed by violent likes and dislikes, he recognized – and fought – a streak of superstition in his nature. At that moment he distrusted the exterior of the Victorian house, whose tall chimneys seemed to bore the ragged clouds.

Suddenly he thought of a simple way of getting into communication with Helen. Snapping on his lighter, he searched in his pockets to find a scrap of paper. When he had discovered an old envelope, he managed, with difficulty, to scrawl a message upon it. Then he slipped it into the letter-box and gave the postman's traditional double-knock.

'That'll bring her down, quicker than a stick of

dynamite,' he thought, as he withdrew to a position on the gravel drive which commanded a view of the house.

As the minutes passed, however, and no signal-light gleamed from any of the upper windows, he grew apprehensive. The lack of response was not typical of Helen's curious nature. With a memory of her sensational scampers up the stairs, he knew that it would not take her long to reach the second floor, even if she had followed his advice to sleep in the basement.

Presently he grew tired of standing in the rain, as though he were planted with the trees. It was evident that the Summit – following her character of respectable widow – was not at home to stray knocks, after dark.

He was on the point of turning away, when a light glowed in a bedroom on the second floor. The window was closed, but not shuttered, and screened by a light curtain of turquoise-blue.

At the sight his face lit up with welcome. Not until he was on the point of hearing her voice again, did he realize the strength of his feeling for Helen. The glow in his heart rose to his lips and flamed into a smile. His lover's rapture made the subsequent disappointment the keener. With a shock of positive horror, he saw – thrown upon the light screen of the curtain – a furtive, crouching shadow. It was the head and shoulders of a man.

CHAPTER 26

SAILOR'S SENSE

Outside the Summit was elemental fury; inside, the clash of human passions. Terrified by Nurse Barker's dark, swollen face, Helen grew almost frantic in her efforts to conciliate her.

'Oh, can't you understand?' she implored. 'It was after the murder. We were all worked up and jumpy. Honestly, I thought it would clear the air if I made certain we'd got the right nurse. You see, Mrs Oates was sure you were an impostor.'

Her explanation only fed Nurse Barker's anger. Encased in the frame of a giantess was a dwarfed nature, which made her morbidly sensitive of the impression she created on strangers.

'You tried to worm yourself into my confidence,' she declared vehemently. 'You led me on to talk of – sacred things. And then, directly after, you rang up the Home. A dirty trick.'

'No,' protested Helen. 'All this happened before our talk. I've been loyal to you, ever since my promise.'

'That's a lie. I caught you at the telephone.'

'I know. But I was ringing up Dr Parry.'

Nurse Barker only sucked her lips together in a crooked line. She knew that silence was the best punishment she could administer, since it kept the girl on the prongs of suspense.

As Helen waited, fearfully expectant of the next attack, she started at the sound of a low thud.

Her thoughts flew to the Professor. In her ignorance of the effects of drugs, she still clung to the hope that he would become conscious in time to control the situation.

But Nurse Barker shattered her illusion, as she broke her silence, to bark out a command.

'See if the old woman's fallen out of bed.'

Glad to be of service, Helen obeyed – rushing up the staircase. When she reached the landing, she checked her headlong flight, and stole cautiously into the blue room.

Lady Warren lay huddled up in the big bed, fast asleep. Her mouth was open and her snores were of genuine origin.

Helen looked around her, noticing that the fire was burning low. As she carefully piled on some of the snowball coals, she was too engrossed to hear Dr Parry's double knock on the front-door.

Nurse Barker, however, started up, at the sound. Peering suspiciously to right and left, she pushed open the swing-door, and went into the lobby.

Her first glance showed her a white object, gleaming through the glass of the letter-box. Pulling it out, she examined the note with contracted eyes. It was scrawled on the back of an envelope, which was addressed to 'Dr Parry,' and was signed with the initials, 'D. P.'

Her heart was wrung with a spasm of jealousy at this proof that Helen's instincts had been true. While they struggled together, Dr Parry had actually been outside the door, insistent and eager.

'She knew,' she muttered. 'How?'

The girl's familiarity with the windings of love's labyrinth was a mystery to the thwarted woman, who, all her life, had hungered for a clue to help her to thread the tangle. Only once had she ventured a little way into the maze, but had never reached its heart.

But Helen knew how to draw the heart out of a man, and how to call to him, so that – at the end of a hard day – he lost his sleep, for her sake.

Nurse Barker could appreciate the extent of the sacrifice on the part of a general practitioner. Her eyes were like flints as she read the note, which was obviously meant for Helen.

'Have biked over, to see how things are, for myself. Been knocking like mad, but no luck. When you get this, open your bedroom window, and I'll shout up to you, so that you'll know it really is I, and not some trick. But, for Heaven's sake, let me in. I'll explain everything to the Professor, afterwards.'

From the moment she had first set eyes on Helen, Nurse Barker had been frantically envious of her. She was just the type which she, herself, would have chosen to be – quick as a needle and

268

smart as paint. While she was able to help herself, she was of fairy fragility, which appealed to the protective instincts of men.

She swallowed convulsively, as she tore the paper into tiny fragments and dropped them inside the drain-pipe umbrella-stand.

'Dead Letter Office,' she murmured grimly.

Meanwhile, Helen was busy in the blue room, unconscious of the destruction of her vital mail. She straightened disarranged furniture, shook up cushions, and put away articles of clothing; presently she came out on the landing laden with a big basin of soapy water and an armful of crumpled towels.

As she did so, she was vaguely aware of some stir in the atmosphere, as though someone had come that way, a few seconds before her. The door leading to the back-stairs quivered faintly, as though it would swing open, at a touch.

Her small white face swam up in the dim depths of the mirror in the old familiar way; but, as she drew nearer, she noticed something which was both mysterious and disturbing. A faint mist blurred the glass, about the height of a man's mouth.

'Someone stood here, a few seconds ago,' she thought fearfully, as she watched the patch become bright again.

Gripping her basin with stiff fingers, she stared at the closed doors. She was afraid to take her eyes off them, lest one should open – afraid to move, lest she precipitated the attack.

Suddenly her nerve crashed. Putting her basin

down on the carpet, she turned, and hurled herself down the stairs.

Nurse Barker watched her as she sank down, panting, on the lowest step.

'Well?' she asked with cool unconcern.

Ashamed of her unfounded terror, Helen rapidly became composed.

'Lady Warren is asleep,' she said. 'We didn't hear *her*.'

'Then where have you been all this time?'

'Tidying the room.'

'You've not been up in your own room?' Nurse Barker asked.

'No.'

'Well, I wouldn't, if I was you. It's a long way up, in case you met someone.'

Again the dull thud banged in the distance.

'There it is again,' said Nurse Barker. 'I wish it would stop. It gets on my nerves.'

As she listened, Helen suddenly located the sound.

'It's down in the basement. It must be the window I tied up. It's blown open again.'

She hastened to add quickly, 'It's all right. There's a shutter up, so no one can get in.'

'It's criminal carelessness, all the same,' declared Nurse Barker, with an elaborate yawn.

'Are you sleepy?' asked Helen sharply.

'My eyes are just dropping,' declared Nurse Barker, with another yawn. 'It's all I can do to keep them open. I came straight off night-duty. I ought to have had a night in bed, between my cases.'

With a chill at her heart, Helen recognized the too familiar signals of the landslide. While she had been afraid of Nurse Barker succumbing to some treacherously-administered drug, she was, in reality, nearly overpowered by natural sleep.

As she watched her, Helen realized that her failure to stay awake was inevitable. Nurse Barker was due for a good night's rest. She had made a journey in an open car; since then she had eaten and smoked heavily, and had taken a fair quantity of brandy. The air of the shuttered house, too, was close.

There seemed no connection between this latest example of cause and effect, and the mysterious conspiracy which threatened Helen's safety; yet her fear of being left alone, to watch, was real, because the incident was timed with such horrible accuracy.

Suddenly, Nurse Barker's head dropped forward with a jerk, which awakened her. She staggered as she rose slowly to her feet.

'Where are you going?' asked Helen anxiously.

'Bed.'

'Where?'

'Patient's room.'

'But you can't do that. You can't leave me here, alone.'

'The house is locked up,' Nurse Barker said. 'You're safe, as long as you remember not to open the door. If you forget again it's your own funeral.'

'But it's worse than that,' wailed Helen. 'I wouldn't tell you before, because I wasn't sure.'

'Sure of *what?*' repeated Nurse Barker.

'I've a terrible fear that someone is in the house, locked in with us.'

Nurse Barker listened sceptically to the story of the rustle on the back stairs and the blur of breath on the mirror.

'Wind,' she said. 'Or mice. I'm going to bed. You can come up too, if you're going to throw a fit.'

Helen hesitated, swayed by temptation to accept the offer. If they locked the Professor's door, as well as the blue room, they would be secured in an inner citadel, together with the vulnerable members of the household.

But Mrs Oates would be left outside, in the trenches. In spite of the special Providence which was supposedly detailed, to guard her, Helen felt she could not risk leaving her there.

'Could we possibly get Mrs Oates up to the blue room?' she asked.

'Drag a drunken log up two flights of stairs?' Nurse Barker shook her head. 'I'm not taking any.'

'But we can't leave her there. Remember, *we* should be held responsible, tomorrow morning.'

Fortunately Helen struck the right note, for Nurse Barker was caught by the argument.

'Oh, well, I'll have to make do with a lay-down in the drawing-room.'

Helen followed her into the big tasteless room, which still blazed with electric light. It held traces of its last tenants – the careless, bored youngsters

– whose pose of modern indifference had been so fatally shattered by the split-atom of passion.

Coffee-cups, with sodden cigarette-ends inside, were scattered about, together with stray sheets of newspapers, open magazines, choked ash-trays. Nurse Barker collected a couple of satin cushions, which lay on the carpet; tucking them under her head, she stretched herself out on the vast blue settee.

Closing her eyes, she fell, almost instantly, to sleep.

'Now, I'm alone,' thought Helen. 'But I can wake her up, if anything happens.'

As she kept vigil, she looked around her with strained eyes, dilated to black pools. There was no danger of her being soothed, insensibly, to unconsciousness, by the rhythm of Nurse Barker's heavy regular breathing. Her brain was excited to a pitch when it became a storehouse of jumbled impressions.

But, through the chaos and confusion, she knew that she was chasing a memory.

Suddenly she remembered. The basement window.

It had been left open, for minutes at a stretch, while the bar of its shutter lay uselessly on the kitchen table, and she and Stephen Rice had gloated over Mrs Oates' ancient history.

Her heart gave a leap, but she tried to reason herself out of her panic. It was the hundredth chance that the criminal, with acres of lonely country-side for shelter, would rush into a house, filled with people – the thousandth chance, that he would find the one point of entry.

'But, if he *did*,' thought Helen, 'he could hide in any of the dark cellars. And then, when the coast was clear, he could make a dash through the scullery and kitchen, for the back-stairs.'

There was only one way of safeguarding Mrs Oates. She would have to make a thorough search of the basement. When she had satisfied herself that it was empty, she must lock the kitchen door, and take away the key.

Nurse Barker did not hear her, as she went out of the room. The woman was sleeping too heavily to be aware of the noise of the gale, which shook the long windows, with its fury.

Presently she awoke with a start, and sat up rubbing her eyes. Refreshed and alert, she looked around for Helen, who had kept vigil, by her side.

But the girl had disappeared.

Dr Parry, too, no longer stood, like a sentinel, in the garden. Almost directly after the head and shoulders had been shadowed on the curtain, the light in Helen's bedroom went out.

As he waited for something else to happen, he did his best to master his uneasiness. Although he knew that Helen's bush of hair could not assume the silhouette of the clean outline of a man, Miss Warren, or the nurse – minus her veil – might have passed across the blind.

Presently he turned away. Conscious that he had let his personal feeling for a girl work himself up into an unreasonable panic, he was anxious to get a second opinion on the situation.

Cutting across the plantation, he soon reached Captain Bean's whitewashed cottage.

The blind was undrawn, so that he could see into the lamp-lit sitting-room. Captain Bean, in his shirt-sleeves, sat at a paper-strewn table – a tea-pot beside him. It was evident that he was sitting up late, to write one of his articles on travel.

In spite of the interruption to his work, he came, at once, to the door, at the sound of Dr Parry's knock. His clean-shaven face was a muddle of small indeterminate features, and his original blond colouring had been scalded by tropic suns.

'You'll wonder why I'm knocking you up, this time of the night,' said Dr Parry. 'But I'm a bit puzzled about things up at the Summit.'

'Come in,' invited Captain Bean.

Dr Parry was rather astonished by the gravity with which he listened to his story.

'The fact is,' he admitted, 'there's a girl in that house that I'm not quite easy about. She's such a scrap. And she's very frightened.'

'She's reason to be,' snapped the Captain, 'after that girl I found in my garden this evening.'

Dr Parry, who wanted the reassurance of scepticism, stared at him with anxious eyes. He looked haggard and unkempt, while the stubble of his chin smudged his face, as though with grime.

However, the Captain gave a comforting hint of personal bias in his next sentence.

'I never cottoned to that house. And I never cottoned to the family. I'll walk over with you and have a look round.'

'N. d. g.' said Dr Parry hopelessly. 'The place is like a fortress. And you can ring till you pull the wire out.'

'Police?'

'I've thought of them. But I don't know what grounds I can give them for forcing an entry. It's all in order. And I'm chiefly to blame for that – curse it.'

Dr Parry got up from his chair, to pace the room excitedly.

'It's that shadow that gets me,' he said. 'In her room. It didn't look the shape of any woman.'

'Still, there are young men about the house,' remarked the Captain.

'No, they've all left. There's only the Professor – assuming he's shaken off the effect of quadronex.'

Captain Bean grunted as he rammed fresh tobacco into his pipe.

'I want the entire log,' he said. 'I've knocked about all over the Globe and seen all the ugliest sights. But that girl's body, in my own garden, gave me a turn. Since then, I've been thinking of all sorts of things.'

He listened, with close attention, to the story, but made no comment. When it was finished, he rose and drew on his Wellington boots.

'Where are you going?' asked Dr Parry.

'Bull. To 'phone the Police-Station.'

'Why?'

'There's some things can't be said. You've got to prove them, by compass . . . But I never like it when the rats leave the ship.'

'Hell. Stop hinting, man. Say what you mean.' The Captain shook his head.

'You can't call a spade, a spade, when it might turn out to be a ruddy fork,' he said. 'I'll only tell you this. I wouldn't risk a daughter of mine in that house, tonight, for a million pounds.'

CHAPTER 27

'SECURITY IS MORTAL'S CHIEFEST ENEMY'

At first, Nurse Barker could not credit the fact that Helen was gone. She looked around her, searching, in vain, for a small blue figure amid the crowded confusion of settees and chairs. Only the ginger cat – aroused by her noisy movements – jumped off an old-fashioned Prince of Wales divan, and stalked from the room.

Thoroughly aroused, she followed him into the hall, where she raised her voice in a shout.

'Miss Ca-pel.'

There was no reply – no soft scurry of felt shoes. She drew her brows together, in displeasure, while her eyes glowed green with jealousy.

She had no fear of misfortune to Helen. In her opinion the Summit was impregnable. She had been playing on the girl's fear, from a double motive – to urge her to super caution, and also, in revenge for fancied insult.

She told herself that Dr Parry had managed to get in touch with Helen in spite of his intercepted note.

'She's let him in,' she thought. 'Well, it's none of my business.'

With professional caution, she always avoided contact with scandal. If there was suspicion of irregular conduct in any house where she nursed, she knew nothing about it. When, on the following morning, the Professor or Miss Warren questioned her about Dr Parry's presence at the Summit, she would be able to assure them that she had kept to her proper place – the patient's room.

With a twisted virtuous smile, she went upstairs to the blue room. As she entered Lady Warren stirred in bed.

'Girl,' she called.

'Now, that's not the way to speak to your nurse,' remarked Nurse Barker.

Lady Warren struggled to a sitting posture.

'Go away,' she said. 'I want the girl.'

'Shut your eyes and go to sleep. It's very late.'

Lady Warren, however, looked wakeful as an owl, as she stared at Nurse Barker.

'It's very quiet,' she said. 'Where's everybody?'

'Everybody's in bed, and asleep.'

'Tell the Professor I want him. You can go through the dressing-room.'

The remark reminded Nurse Barker of a grievance.

'Do you know the connecting-door won't lock?' she asked.

'You needn't worry.' The old woman chuckled. 'He won't come in after you. Your day's over.'

Nurse Barker disdained to notice the insult. She had no warning of the peril which actually would steal through that door, or the shock of unseen attack – the grip of choking fingers around her throat – the roar of a sea in her ears – the rush of darkness . . .

In her security, all she wanted was to settle down for the night. She was growing sleepy again.

As she had no intention of explaining the sleeping draught fiasco to Lady Warren, she made a pretense of awakening the Professor. Passing through the dressing room, she entered his bedroom.

His chair was placed directly under the high light, so that a pool of shadow was thrown over his face, which looked unnatural, as though composed of yellow wax. To increase the resemblance, his seated figure had the rigid fixity of a mechanical chess-player.

'Is the Professor coming?' asked Lady Warren eagerly, as Nurse Barker returned to the blue room.

'No, he's fast asleep.'

Lady Warren watched her as she crossed the room and locked the door.

'That'll keep her out,' she thought with a smile of grim satisfaction.

'Why did you do that?' asked Lady Warren.

'I always lock my door in a strange house,' replied Nurse Barker.

'I always kept mine open, so that I could get out

quicker. When you lock out, you never know what you're locking in.'

'Now, I don't want to hear anything more from you,' said Nurse Barker, kicking off her shoes. 'I'm going to lie down.'

But before she dropped down upon the small bed, she crossed to the other door, which led into his dressing-room, and turned the key, as though for extra security.

In spite of the precaution, she did not go to sleep. Her thoughts circled enviously around Helen and her lover. She wondered where they were – what they did.

At that moment, Dr Parry was suffering solitary torment, while Helen endured her self-imposed ordeal – alone. Down in the basement, a flickering candle in her hand, she groped amid the mice, the spiders, and the shadows.

These shadows held possession of the passage – tenants of the night. They shifted before her, sliding along the pale-washed wall, as though to lead the way. Whenever she entered an office, they crouched on the other side of the door, waiting for her.

She was nerved up to meet an attack which did not come, but which lurked just around the corner. It was perpetual postponement, which drew her on, deeper and deeper, into the labyrinth.

Footsteps dogged her all the way; they stopped after she halted, with the perfect mimicry of an echo. Whenever she slanted a startled glance behind her, she could see no one; yet she could not be assured that she was alone.

Just as she turned round the bend of the passage and entered the pitchy alley of Murder Lane, someone blew out her candle.

She was left in the darkness, trapped between the window and the place where a girl had met with death. In that moment of horror, she heard the window burst open and the pelt of leaping footsteps.

Suddenly, fingers stole around her throat and tightened to a grip. A heavy breathing gasped through the air, like a broken pump. She felt the frantic hammering of her heart as she was swept away on a tidal-wave of horror.

Presently, the pressure on her neck lessened, as her petrified muscles relaxed to elastic tissue. In sudden realization of her own involuntary action, she released her throat from the clutch of her hand.

The draught which had blown out her candle, still beat on her cheek and neck. Yet, even while she knew that she was the victim of imagination, her nerve had crashed completely. Breaking free from the spell which paralysed her legs, she rushed along the passage, through the kitchen, where Mrs Oates snored in her chair, up the stairs, and back to the dining-room.

The ginger cat occupied Nurse Barker's vacant place on the settee, his head resting upon the satin cushion. As she stared at him, he jumped down and followed her up to the first landing.

Still quivering with panic, Helen turned the handle of the door desperately. When she realized that Nurse Barker had locked her out of the blue room, she was filled with a healing glow of indignation.

Nurse Barker took no notice of her knocks, until they grew so frantic that she was forced to get off her bed.

'Go away,' she called. 'You're disturbing the patient.'

'Let me in,' cried Helen.

Nurse Barker unlocked the door, but did not open it.

'Go back to your doctor,' she said.

'My – what? I'm alone.'

'Alone, now, maybe. But you've been talking to Dr Parry.'

'I don't know what you mean.'

When Nurse Barker suddenly threw open the door, Helen had a shock of wonder at her altered appearance. She had removed her veil, as well as her shoes. Instead of the cropped head of Helen's imagination, her masculine features were crowned with permanently waved hair.

'Where have you been?' she asked.

'Down in the basement,' Helen gulped guiltily. 'I – I remembered that I'd left a window open. So I went down to see if anyone had got in.'

The girl looked so confused that Nurse Barker realized that her suspicions had been baseless. She turned back to the blue room.

'I'm going to rest,' she said, 'even if I can't sleep.'

'May I come in with you?' pleaded Helen.

'No. Go to bed, or lie down in the drawing-room.'

Her advice seemed sound, yet Helen still clung to company.

'But I ought to stay with you,' she said, using Nurse Barker's own argument. 'You see, if anyone's after me, he'll have to dispose of you, first.'

'Who's after you?' asked Nurse Barker scornfully, whirling round, like a weather-cock in a gale.

'The maniac, according to you.'

'Don't be a fool. How could he get in, through locked doors?'

Helen felt as though she were standing on solid ground, after struggling for foothold in a quicksand.

'Then why have you been frightening me?' she asked reproachfully. 'It's cruel.'

'For your own good. I've had pros, like you, their heads filled with nothing but men, men, men. I had to teach you not to open the door to the first Dick, Tom, or Harry . . . Now, I'm going to bed, and you are *not* to disturb me again. Understand?'

She was turning away, when Helen caught her sleeve.

'Wait. Why did you think I was with Dr Parry?' she asked.

'Because he was outside, just now. But he's gone, for good.'

In spite of the triumphant gleam in her eyes, as she slammed the door, Helen felt suddenly revived. For the first time for many hours, she was free from fear. After the creepy gloom of the basement, the hall, glowing in the midst of lighted rooms, seemed the civilized family mansion of any auctioneer's catalogue. She realized that she had just received a valuable object-lesson in the destructive property of uncurbed imagination.

'Everything that happened was myself,' she thought. 'It's like frightening yourself, by making faces in the glass, when you're a child.'

She called to the ginger cat, who was playing around the door which led to the back-stairs. But, although he preserved his character for civility, by purring and arching his back, he explained that he wished to go down to the kitchen.

Helen dutifully opened the door, when he changed his mind. Instead of descending to the basement, he pounced on a small object on the coconut-matting strip, at the foot of the flight.

Helen left him to his game of pretending he had found a mouse. Had she the curiosity to examine what he was throwing in the air, her new-born confidence would have been shattered.

It was a small tassel of larch, from the plantation. Someone had brought it into the house, stuck on to the sole of a muddy shoe and had thoughtlessly scraped it off, on the mat.

She was the only one – on the day's official return – who had passed through the plantation.

And she had reached her bedroom by way of the front stairs.

Happily unconscious that the ginger cat had turned detective, and discovered a valuable clue, she went down to the drawing-room. The divan invited her to rest, but she was too excited to follow Nurse Barker's advice. She forgot her anger over the woman's interference, in happiness at the knowledge that Dr Parry had made a second journey through the storm, for her sake.

'I've got a lover, at last,' she thought triumphantly, as she crossed to the piano. She could only play by ear, but she managed to pick out a fairly accurate reproduction of the Wedding March.

Up in the blue room Lady Warren sat up in bed.

'Who's playing the "Wedding March"?' she asked.

'No one,' said Nurse Barker, not opening her eyes. 'Shut up.'

'No,' muttered the old woman maliciously, 'you didn't hear it. And you never will.'

She listened again, but the music had ceased. Helen had realized that her performance might disturb the remnant of the household. She closed the piano, and opened a novel, only to discover that she could not concentrate on what she read.

She found that she was listening to the noises of the night, as though she expected to hear some unfamiliar sound.

Presently she got up and turned on the Wireless, in the vain hope of hearing the announcer's voice.

But the London Stations had closed down, and all she got, from the air, was an explosion of atmospherics.

They reminded her of amateur stage effects, and the only time she had ever appeared in a dramatic performance. It had been a modest business, at the Prize-giving of the Belgian Convent, where she had received most of her brief education.

The English pupils had played the Witches' Scene from *Macbeth*, and she had been unhappily cast as Hecate. Not only was she inaudible, through stage-fright, but she forgot the end of her speech, and rushed from the stage.

The lines swam back, now, to her memory, as an unpleasant and ill-timed warning.

> 'And, you all know, security
> Is mortal's chiefest enemy.'

Helen started, as though the great voice in the chimney were actually roaring the words. She looked at the old-fashioned comfort of the room – the white skin rug, the pleated pink silk lampshade – which were mute witnesses, against the violence of murder.

'Of course, I feel safe,' she thought. 'I'm not left alone. Nurse Barker is my ally, even if she's got a temper. I haven't got to sleep in the blue room. Oates will soon be back. And – nothing's happened.'

Yet, in spite of the reassurance of her review, she

realized that she was keyed up to a pitch of unnatural expectancy. She was listening so intently that she believed she could almost catch the high squeak of a bat.

Something had twanged on her ear, like the vibration of a drawn wire. She heard it again – slightly louder – faint and wailing as the mew of a sea-gull.

It was a cry in the night.

CHAPTER 28

THE LION – OR THE TIGER?

Helen raised her head to listen – a great fear at her heart. What she most dreaded had actually happened – the need to make a perilous decision.

Yet, the very fact that it had occurred aroused her suspicions. Someone with a knowledge of her character was playing a trick on her, in order to draw her away from the security of the house.

This theatrical element made her tighten her lips in resolution. She had spoken, in pity, of a child crying out in the darkness and storm. And here was the child – delivered, according to schedule.

But, as the thin cry was repeated, Helen's lips parted, in suspense. Although it was difficult to locate the sound, because of the shrieking of the wind, it seemed to come from somewhere within the house. A new dread knocking at her heart, she slowly mounted the stairs.

As she did so, the crying grew more distinct, and like the weak sobbing of someone very young, or very old. And it came from the direction of the blue room.

Once again the natural element was shaping the

drama – yet the result would be the same. She was being tempted to abandon her last line of defence.

Nurse Barker was the only person left to keep her company. Helen clung to her, as a child, terrified of the dark, will hang on to a bad-tempered nurse. She had aroused her antagonism too often to risk another quarrel.

Next time, Nurse Barker might carry out her threat to leave her alone. Helen grew cold at the mere thought of desertion. She had been used to plenty of company; too much of it, in fact, so that she sometimes craved for solitude.

At this crisis, her early training left her especially susceptible to the menace of loneliness and her own imagination. She knew that she would experience all the heralds of a nervous crash; shadows would flicker over the wall – footsteps creak up the stairs.

'I *must* keep my head,' she resolved desperately.

She reminded herself that Lady Warren was not some gentle old soul, at the mercy of a brute. At her best, she was a cantankerous old bully; at her worst, she might be a murderess. When she was younger, she had killed hundreds of small, defenceless creatures, merely for her own amusement.

Although Helen was careful to paint Lady Warren's portrait in darkest hues, she was drawn, imperceptibly, up the staircase, until she stood outside the blue room.

Presently she heard smothered, hopeless sobbing.

It was not assumed for effect, because it was so low that she could not have known anyone was crying if she had not strained her ears.

She flinched, as though she had been struck herself, at the sound of a rough voice.

'Stop that row.'

The sobbing ceased immediately. After a pause, Lady Warren spoke appealingly.

'Nurse. *Please*, come to me.'

Helen heard heavy footsteps crossing the room, and Nurse Barker's voice raised in a shout.

'If I come to you, I'll give you what for.'

Helen felt herself grow hot, as she rapped impulsively on the door.

'Is anything the matter?' she called.

'No,' replied Nurse Barker.

'But wouldn't you like me to sit with Lady Warren for a short time?' persisted Helen.

'No.'

Helen turned away, wiping her face.

'That was a near shave,' she murmured.

At the top of the stairs she was arrested by the sound of a high scream of mingled pain and rage.

Hot with indignation, she burst into the blue room. Nurse Barker stood over the bed, shaking Lady Warren furiously. As Helen entered, she threw her away from her, so that she lay on her face, in a heaving crumpled heap.

'You great coward,' cried Helen. 'Get out of here.'

Like David threatening Goliath, Helen looked up at the towering figure.

'The old devil went for me,' said Nurse Barker.

'You're a thoroughly bad-tempered woman,' she declared. 'You are not fit to have control of anyone.'

Nurse Barker's face grew dark as a storm-cloud.

'Say that again,' she shouted, 'and I'll go out of this room – and not come back.'

'You'll certainly go, and you *won't* come back,' said Helen, carried away on a wave of power.

Nurse Barker shrugged her shoulders as she turned away.

'I wish you joy of your bargain,' she sneered. 'When you are alone, with her, remember you *asked* for it.'

Helen felt the first chill of reaction as the door slammed behind the woman. There was something ominously definite about the sound.

With a rush of pity, she turned towards the bed. Instead of the prostrate form, Lady Warren was leaning back against her pillows, a complacent smile on her lips.

Helen experienced the sensation of having walked into a trap.

'You'd better lie down,' she said, anxious to justify her championship. 'Do you feel weak after that awful shaking?'

'What she gave me was nothing to what I gave her,' remarked Lady Warren.

Helen stared at her – the dawn of an incredulous horror in her eyes, as she ran her finger over her lower denture.

'I grudged the money for these teeth,' she said. 'But they're very good teeth. I bit her thumb almost to the bone.'

Helen gave a mirthless laugh.

'Someone told me to bet on you,' she said. 'But I didn't believe him. I wonder – are you the lion – or the tiger?'

Lady Warren stared at her as though she were an idiot.

'Cigarette,' she snapped. 'I want to get the taste of her out of my mouth. Quick . . . Haven't you got any?'

'No.'

'Say, 'No, my lady.' Go down to the library and get a box of my nephew's.'

Helen was only too glad of the excuse to leave the room. Too late, she realized that she had been tricked, and she wanted to make her peace with Nurse Barker.

As she reached the door, the familiar bass bellow recalled her.

'I feel sleepy, girl. That nurse held my nose and poured a filthy draught down my throat. Don't disturb me, if I drop off.'

When Helen reached the landing, the light shone through the transom above the bathroom door, while the sound of running water indicated that Nurse Barker was bathing her thumb.

'Nurse,' she called. 'I'm terribly sorry.'

There was no reply. Helen waited, listening to the splashing of water. After making a second attempt, with no better luck, she went downstairs to the library.

When she returned, with a box of cigarettes, the blue room was dimly revealed in the faint glow of the lamp. Lady Warren had switched off her bed-light, and had composed herself to sleep.

Helen sat down wearily by the fire. It was burning low, for the stock of snowballs in the scuttle was running out. Every now and again a twig tapped the window, like a bony finger giving a signal. The clock ticked, like a leaking tap, and the wind blew down the funnel of the chimney.

'Here I am again,' she said, with a hopeless sense of finality. All the evening she had been fighting Fate, only to beat the air.

There was one comfort – the night was wearing away. Oates too, would be on his return journey. But the reminder now brought no prospect of relief. Nurse Barker would refuse him admission, just as she had shut out Dr Parry – or whoever had knocked at the door.

For the first time, Helen realized the possible value of the precaution. Since she had been tricked by Lady Warren, she felt that she was groping amid a network of wires and snares.

With newly-awakened suspicion, she glanced at the dim white form on the bed. It suddenly struck her that Lady Warren was unnaturally still. There was no sound of breathing, and not the slightest stir of movement.

She remembered that the old woman had been

shaken violently and that her heart was danger-ously weak. Smitten with sudden dread, she rushed over to the bed.

'She'll be the next,' she thought. 'I shall find her dead.'

Her foreboding was fulfilled in a curious manner. Lady Warren was gone, indeed, while nothing could have been less animate than the pile of pillows, covered with the fleecy bed-jacket, which occupied her place in the bed.

Helen stared at the dummy with the stupefaction of Macbeth when he beheld the forest marching against him. The incredible fable was true, and Lady Warren could walk.

As she stood, she became aware of a strong odour of drugs. Turning over one of the pillows, she noticed that it was sopping wet, and stained a yellowish-brown.

'She tricked the nurse, too,' thought Helen.

She had a mental picture of the struggling Lady Warren, turning her head, between every mouthful of the sleeping-draught, and letting it trickle out from the corner of her mouth. With a new respect for the old woman's cunning, she made a brief search of the room, although she was sure it was but waste of time. As the dressing-room, too, was empty, she rushed out on to the landing.

The light still shone through the bathroom transom, although the splashing of water had ceased. In her fright, Helen hammered on the door.

'Nurse,' she shouted, 'Lady Warren's gone.'

The door opened, and Nurse Barker stood looking down at her with unfriendly eyes.

'What's that to do with me?' she asked. 'I've thrown up the case.'

'You're not really going?' gasped Helen.

'Directly I've packed my case. Miss Warren will hear, in the morning, that I was dismissed by the domestic help.'

'But you can't do that,' cried Helen, in a panic. 'I'll apologize. I – I'll do anything.'

'Shut up. I'm through with *your* promises. I'm going – and I'm going now. That's my last word.'

'But – where will you go?'

'That's my business. I'll find a place for the night. It is not so late, and I'm not afraid of the dark, or a spot of rain.'

Nurse Barker paused, before she added maliciously, 'Once I'm out of this house, I'll feel *safe*.'

She was taking her revenge, as she drove home the horror which Helen had almost forgotten. The girl gazed at her with imploring eyes while she gave a parting thrust.

'Keep your weather-eye open. She's up to no good.' She glanced at her bandaged thumb. 'And while she's out of the way you had better look for her gun.'

Helen bit her lip as the bathroom door was shut in her face.

'She can't really mean to go out in this awful storm,' she decided.

Besides feeling vaguely frightened, she was utterly

perplexed, and worried with a sense of her own responsibility. As it was impossible to guess what purpose had drawn Lady Warren from her bed, it seemed hopeless to try and find her. She might play hide-and-seek indefinitely in that house.

She might even be bent on committing suicide. Not only was she old, but her life held that dark unexplored corner. Remorse might drive her to kill herself.

Helen shuddered at the thought of finding her body hanging in the cellar. Not knowing where to go first, she went back to the blue room.

Her first glance at the bed told her that the dummy had acquired a more definite shape; and, when she drew nearer, she saw Lady Warren peeping at her with black slitted eyes.

'Oh, where have you been?' asked Helen.

'In the Land of Nod,' was the innocent reply.

Her inscrutable stare dared the girl to disbelieve her statement. Feeling that it was hopeless to persist, Helen returned to her chair.

'Has the nurse gone?' asked Lady Warren.

'Tomorrow,' replied Helen.

'Quick work. I soon clear them out. I hate them. Always washing your face . . . Don't move, girl. I want to keep my eye on you.'

Helen thought involuntarily of the hidden revolver; and, with her characteristic urge for information, she had to refer to the subject.

'Mrs Oates tells me you used to shoot a lot,' she said.

Lady Warren threw her a sharp glance before she replied.

'Yes, I used to pot game. D'you shoot?'

'No. I think it is cruel.'

'Yet you eat meat. If everyone had to kill their own meat, nine-tenths of the population would turn vegetarian within a week . . . I did my job properly. I didn't wound. I killed.'

'But you took life.'

'Yes, I took life. But I never gave life. Thank God . . . Get out of my room.'

Helen started, and then turned her head in the direction of Lady Warren's pointing finger. Nurse Barker had entered the room. Without speaking, she marched to the dressing-room, where her belongings were stored, and shut the door.

As Helen strained her ears, she could hear her moving about, opening and shutting drawers. Apparently she was making good her threat, and packing her suitcase. As she sat in the oppressive room she was the victim of a morbid suspicion, bred of the close atmosphere.

Long ago, two girls had died unnatural deaths in this house. But no one knew the actual truth about the tragedies. It was smothered in conjectures, and buried in a vague Coroner's verdict.

'She's queer,' thought Helen, glancing uneasily towards the bed. 'Suppose she killed them – and her husband knew. Suppose – she shot him, so that he couldn't tell.'

Presently, she realized that the sounds from the

adjoining room had ceased. With a rush of hope, she remembered that there was a divan in the dressing-room. The probability was that Nurse Barker had decided to put off her departure until the morning, and was going to bed.

The fact that she was so near inspired Helen with confidence. As she reviewed the events of the evening, she saw her present position as the logical result of her own folly. Nurse Barker had been specially selected, by the Matron of the Nursing Home, to look after a tiresome patient, with whom she herself could not cope.

Helen felt overwhelmed with humiliation.

'If she's not asleep, I'll go in and tell her I've been a horrible little brute,' she decided. 'I'll ask her to wipe her boots on me.'

Creeping across the carpet to the dressing-room, she cautiously opened the door – now unlocked. Then she gave a little cry of dismay.

Nurse Barker had gone.

CHAPTER 29

ALONE

Helen stared around her with startled eyes. The disorder of the room pointed to a hurried departure. Drawers had been pulled out, while a suitcase and umbrella lay upon the table.

'She's not gone yet,' thought Helen.

But a moment's reflection robbed her of that hope. Nurse Barker would naturally leave her heavy luggage behind, to be forwarded to the Home. An umbrella, too, would be useless in the gale.

Feeling sick with suspense, Helen opened the wardrobe. Nurse Barker's out-door uniform no longer hung upon the peg. A hurried search through the chest, showed all the drawers to be empty. All that remained was a collection of cigarette ends and ash.

It was a planned desertion. With deliberate mental cruelty, Nurse Barker had left the girl alone – reaching the landing through the Professor's room.

Helen felt almost overwhelmed by this last blow. Throughout the evening she had noticed the steady march of events towards some inevitable climax. While she dimly felt its objective was her own isolation, she had played into the hands of destiny by goading on Nurse Barker to take her revenge.

Yet, even so, she had been forced to make her moves, as if she were a puppet controlled by another will.

'I'm all alone,' she thought fearfully.

It was true that others were still in the house; but hers was the only active brain – hers, the only quick body. The others were shackled by fetters of flesh.

With a desperate need of company, she opened the second door, and entered the Professor's room.

But there was no comfort here – only an increase in loneliness. The Professor – still holding his rigid posture, as though carven in stone – was too much like a corpse awaiting burial.

She wanted to leave him, yet she dreaded returning to the blue room. The old woman lacked the human quality, for which she hungered. At this crisis she would have welcomed the harshest abuse from Nurse Barker, could she have drawn her back.

The longing to hear another voice grew so acute that she went out on the landing and beat frantically upon Miss Warren's door.

'Miss Warren,' she screamed. 'Help.'

But there was no response. She might have been appealing to a sealed tomb. Only the wind shrieked, as though a flock of witches sailed overhead, racing the moon, which spun through the torn clouds like a silver cannonball, shot into Space.

'She's cruel,' whispered Helen, turning away.

But Miss Warren was too soundly asleep to hear her cries. Contact with others always gave her the impression that her nerves were drawn through her skin, and exposed to the open air. Tonight, after all the accidents and alarms, she felt as though each fibre were actually bruised.

She had the natural craving of a recluse for her own locked study. But she had been picked out of her shell – made to endure hours of enforced companionship with an unpleasant old woman, in a lethal atmosphere.

The storm, too, had played havoc with her nervous system. The accident to her door-handle, which had imprisoned her, therefore, came as a welcome release from responsibility. She made no effort to free herself, but slipped her bolt, and shut out the World.

With plugs of cotton-wool in her ears, and blankets piled over her head, to deaden the noise of the gale, she was soon submerged in the slumber-sea of utter exhaustion.

Although Helen felt perilously near to collapse, her will still functioned – telling her that she must not yield to panic. She reminded herself that all the wires were not cut. She was still linked up with civilization.

But, as she went downstairs, she realized how hopelessly she had become entangled in the snare of fear. She could not ask anyone to come to the house because she dared not draw the bolts.

The Professor had laid down the command that the door must not be opened; and the order had been dictated by a cool brain, which prepared for every contingency. His policy had been framed in the interest of the general safety.

Since then, Nurse Barker had warned her against any disobedience; and Helen had learned – through bitter experience – that, in the case of Lady Warren, at least – she had been right.

If she – herself – were the ultimate aim of some dark Desire, then this steady withdrawal of defence was planned to plunge her into such panic, that, if she heard a knock, she would rush to open the door.

Someone wanted to draw her outside the safety of the Summit.

'If I arranged a signal-knock,' she thought, 'it wouldn't be safe. Someone might be listening-in. No. It's hopeless.'

Yet she knew that the mere act of talking to another person would act as a tonic to her flabby nerves. She did not know whether Dr Parry had returned; her mind was too confused to calculate time or distance. But, if he were still absent, she could ring up someone else.

'The Nursing Home,' she decided. 'I'll tell them about Nurse Barker, and ask them to send out another nurse.'

The fact of having a definite message to send

steadied her. Once more, she was Miss Capel, whose name was only too familiar to the Employment Bureau and not a stranded nonentity. With a touch of her former assurance, she took off the receiver.

To her dismay, there was no responsive tinkle; no humming along the wire told her that she was linked up with the Exchange; no voice inquired her Number.

The telephone was dead.

She looked around the hall with frightened eyes. She knew that there was a natural explanation of the silence. The country lanes must be blocked with poles and wires, wrecked by the fury of the gale. This was no human plot – it was an Act of God.

But Helen would not admit it. This faithful accompaniment to the thrill-drama – the cut telephone-wire – had arrived with too-perfect timing.

'It's not accident,' she told herself. 'Things don't happen all together, like this.'

She did not know where to feel safe, so great was her fear of the house. Yet she dared not rush into the storm, lest she should make the very move which had been planned, by the anonymous player, at the beginning of the game.

'I'd better go back to Lady Warren,' she thought. 'After all, I took her on. She cannot be left.'

She went through the Professor's room, in a wild hope that he might yet awaken from his drugged sleep. With his cool brain to take control, she felt she would face any danger. But he still lay back in his chair – withdrawn face and clay-coloured lids – as rigid as a mummy in its case.

When she lingered in the dressing-room, she heard a scuffle and rapid footsteps, on the other side of the wall.

'She's got out of bed again,' she thought dully.

If her suspicion were correct, Lady Warren did not lack the strength for a rapid scramble; for she lay composedly covered with her old-lady white fleece, when Helen entered.

'Why did you leave me, girl?' she demanded. 'You're paid to look after me.'

Helen lacked the spirit to lie.

'I went to telephone,' she said. 'But – the line has been blown down. I couldn't get through.'

As she spoke, Helen became aware of Lady Warren's uneasy glances around the room. The fact that she had power to be an unwelcome obstacle to some plan, braced her up to come to grips with the old lady.

'Why did you get out of bed?' she asked.

'I didn't. I can't. Don't be a fool.'

'I'm certainly not such a fool as you think. Besides, there is nothing to hide. You're not officially paralysed or bed-ridden. People have got the impression that you are helpless – that's all. Why shouldn't you get out of bed if you want to?'

Instead of being furious, Lady Warren pondered the speech.

'Never tell the whole,' she said. 'Always keep

305

something up your sleeve when you're old, and at the mercy of other people. I like to get about, when no one's looking.

'Of course, you do,' agreed Helen. 'I'll tell no one, I promise.'

And then her deathless curiosity prompted another question.

'What were you looking for?'

'My charm. It's a lucky green elephant, with its trunk up. I wanted it, because I was afraid.'

As Helen looked at her, in surprise, because she thought that age outlived the emotions, she suddenly remembered the cross which hung above her bed.

'I've something far better than any green elephant,' she said eagerly. 'I'm going to fetch it. And then nothing can hurt you – or me.'

It was not until she was outside the room that she wondered whether Lady Warren had wanted to send her away. But, even if she had played into her hands, she did not care, so strong was her wish to hold her Cross.

'I needn't have been afraid,' she thought. 'While I forgot about it, all the time, it was there – keeping me safe from all evil.'

Although the wind was howling in the empty rooms on the second floor, and anyone might keep step with her, on the back-stairs, while she mounted the front, she felt raised above fear. Fighting the fierce pressure of the draught, she snapped on the light in her bedroom.

The first thing she saw was the bare wall above her bed.

The Cross had disappeared.

She caught at the door for support, as the ground seemed to collapse under her feet. An enemy was inside the house. He had robbed her of the symbol of protection. Anything might happen to her. Nothing was safe or sure.

At that moment she felt she had reached the dividing-line between sanity and madness. At any moment a cell might snap in her brain. She felt poised on the lip of a bottomless drop.

And then her mind suddenly cleared of its mist, and she believed she had found a solution of the mystery.

The disappearance of the Cross was a trick played on her by Nurse Barker. The woman was hiding somewhere in the house.

Rushing downstairs, to the lobby, she found that her intuition had not played her false. The front door was still bolted, and the chain in its place.

'Unless she went out by the back-door, which is most unlikely, she's still here,' thought Helen.

Although she was vaguely worried by her loss, the relief was overwhelming. What she now feared far more than danger outside, was the threat of peril from within.

The disorder of the bed told her that, in her absence, Lady Warren had been engaged in her mysterious search. A drawer protruded from a chest, which stood in an alcove, showing that the old woman had been disturbed in her labours.

As she was out of sight of the bed, Helen went up to it, and tried to close it – to be prevented by some object stuffed at the back. Getting hold of one corner, she managed to pull it out.

It was a white scarf.

CHAPTER 30

THE WALLS FALL DOWN

Helen turned over the scarf, in fingers which had grown suddenly cold. It was of good-quality silk, machine-knitted, and was quite new. There was a smear of mud on one side, and pine-needles were entangled in the mesh of its fabric.

Conscious of overwhelming horror in store, she shook it out – revealing a gap in the fringe, at one end – a jagged, irregular tear, as though it had been bitten.

With a strangled cry, she threw it from her. This was the scarf that Ceridwen's teeth had closed over in her death-agony. It was horrible, unclean. It had encircled the throat of a murderer.

Like a rocket, shooting up through the darkness of her mind, and breaking into a cluster of stars, a host of questions splashed and spattered her brain. How did the scarf get inside Lady Warren's drawer? Was she hiding it? What connection had she with the crime? Or had someone else put it there? Was the murderer actually inside the house?

At the thought, she felt already dead. Every cell

seemed atrophied, every fibre withered. She stood locked in temporary paralysis, muscle-bound, with rigid spine, and blasted faculties.

Yet while she could not see the room, or hear the sound of the wind, or feel the table under her fingers, she seemed to be looking inwards at a mental picture.

The Summit was breaking up. The walls had cracked in every direction. Those thin lines, like the veining of a flash of lightning, were splintering into fissures. All around her was a tearing and a rending, as the branches widened, leaving her defenceless to the night.

Suddenly she heard the sound of a sob, and realized that it was her own voice. In the glass she saw a girl's face – pinched and pallid – staring at her, from dilated eyes, black with fear. By the aureole of crisping light-red hair, she knew that girl was herself.

At the sight, a memory stirred in her mind.

'"Ginger for pluck",' she whispered.

She was lying down, waiting for the attack, instead of standing, with her back to the wall. Nerving herself to examine the scarf, she noticed that it was only slightly damp.

'It would have been soaked, if it had been lying out in the rain,' she thought. 'It must have been brought inside directly after the murder.'

The deduction opened up fresh avenues of horror. No one knew the exact time when Ceridwen was strangled, except that it was round about twilight. As everyone – except Oates – was at the Summit, any person could have slipped outside, for a few minutes, unnoticed. From the Professor downwards, all were under suspicion.

Dr Parry had warned her that the crime might have been committed by someone she knew and trusted. The Professor worked at high mental pressure, while both his son and Rice were periodically moody. Even Dr Parry had the same opportunities, and he had visited the blue room.

This wholesale suspicion might even include old Lady Warren. Miss Warren had dozed in her chair, that evening, at twilight. How had she used her half-hour of liberty?

'I'm mad,' thought Helen. 'It can't be everybody. It's nobody here. It's someone, who got in, from outside.'

She shuddered, because, at the back of her mind, persisted that horrible memory of an open window.

'Girl,' called Lady Warren, 'what are you doing there?'

'Getting you a clean handkerchief.'

Helen was astonished by the coolness of her voice. Under the influence of fear, she seemed to be a dual personality. A self-possessed stranger had taken command and was carrying on for her, while the real Helen was staked amid the ruins of the shattered fortress – bait for a human tiger.

'Have you found – anything?' asked Lady Warren.

Helen purposely misunderstood her.

'Yes, a pile,' she said, as she hurriedly replaced the scarf. With a handkerchief in her hand, she approached the bed.

Lady Warren snatched it from her, and threw it on the floor.

'Girl,' she whispered hoarsely, 'I want you to do something.'

'Yes. What is it?'

'Get under the bed.'

Helen's eyes fell on the ebony stick, by the bed, with a flash of understanding. The old woman was wandering again, and she wanted to play her favourite game of stalking housemaids.

'When I crawl out, will you crack me over the head?' she asked.

'You mustn't come out. You must hide.'

The new Helen, who had taken command, thought she grasped the significance of this move. It was a ruse to hold her in such a position that she could see practically nothing of the room.

'It's too dusty under the bed,' she objected, as she moved cautiously towards the door.

She had realized the importance of the scarf, as evidence. The Police should have it in their possession, without delay. She could not telephone to them, because of the damage – accidental, or otherwise – to the line; but she could run over to Captain Bean's cottage, and ask him to take the necessary steps.

Lady Warren began to whimper, like a terrified child.

'Don't leave me, girl. The nurse will come. She's only waiting for you to go.'

Helen hesitated, although she remembered that, in their last encounter, Lady Warren had triumphed. Yet the balance of power did not remain equal, even in a jungle fight; today it might be the tiger's turn, but, tomorrow, the lion's.

She had not yet solved the mystery of Nurse Barker's disappearance. If she were actually hiding in the house, she might take her revenge.

'I wish I knew the right thing to do,' she thought.

'If you leave me,' threatened Lady Warren, 'I'll scream. And then, *he'll* come.'

Like the flash of a fer-de-lance, Helen whipped round.

'He?' she asked. '*Who*?'

'I said, "She'll come".'

It was obvious that Lady Warren realized her slip, for she bit her lip and glowered at Helen, like an angry idol.

Helen felt as though she was trying to find the path which threaded a maze. The old woman knew something which she would not reveal.

It was curious how she remained shackled by ordinary conventions and considerations, even while one-half of her was pulped with elementary terror. But, throughout the evening, no single event had been abnormal, so that, unconsciously, she responded to the laws of civilized life.

The actual murder had taken place outside the Summit, which reduced it to the level of a newspaper

313

paragraph. The maniac was a kind of legendary figure, invented by the Press. The most shocking occurrence was the fact that the housekeeper had got drunk.

It was true that both Nurse Barker and Lady Warren were most unpleasant types; but, in the course of her experience, Helen had met others who were even more peculiar. She knew that her own fear was responsible for the grotesque fancies and suspicions, which shifted through her mind.

Tomorrow would come. She held on to that. She reminded herself that she had a new job to hold down. If she failed, at a pinch she might find herself out of work again.

She must not let Lady Warren scream. If the Professor was startled in his drugged sleep, there might be danger of shock to his brain. It would be cruel, too, to alarm Miss Warren, while she was imprisoned.

Besides – the whisper stirred, like a snake, in her brain – it might attract *someone else.*

As she lingered, Lady Warren's mind apparently wandered.

'There's a storm blowing up,' she said. 'It's growing dark.'

With a sharp pang of alarm, Helen realized that the room seemed to have become actually dimmer. She rubbed her eyes, but the illusion did not vanish. The electric-light was gleaming murkily, as through a slight fog.

Her lips grew stiff, as she wondered if this were a prelude to complete darkness.

One more feature of the thrill-drama had arrived, with the same suggestion of cumulative effect.

'It's getting nearer,' she thought fearfully.

In spite of her resolution, she shared her doubt with her companion.

'Someone's tampered with the fuses,' she whispered.

Lady Warren snorted.

'The batteries are running out, idiot,' she snapped.

Helen gratefully grasped at the commonplace explanation. Oates was responsible for the power-plant, and he was notoriously idle. In her nervous dread of being alone in the darkness, she had recklessly switched on nearly every light, without a thought of possible shortage.

'I'd better snap off most of the lights,' she said.

'Yes,' nodded Lady Warren. 'Fetch candles, too. We can't be left in the dark.'

Helen looked around her for candles, only to realize that these were used exclusively for domestic purposes, in the basement. She remembered seeing bundles in the storeroom, which was next to the larder.

'Do you mind being left?' she asked. 'I must go now, before—'

Unable to contemplate a complete extinction, she rushed out of the room and down the stairs. The hall seemed to flicker, as she passed through, as though the house were sighing. It was warning her not to delay; in a panic, lest she should have to grope her way through darkness, she leaped down the kitchen stairs, like a scared antelope.

Mrs Oates still slept in her chair, apparently peaceful as a good child. As she passed, Helen touched her cheek, and found that it was warm.

'Thank Heaven, there's a special Providence to look after children and drunks,' she thought.

In the passage, a spiral of red wire gleamed through the pear-shaped hanging bulb, and the light was so dim that Helen held her breath. As she dashed into the storeroom, she expected, every minute, to be plunged in darkness, and the horror of Murder Lane.

Snatching the candles, she rushed back, laying a black trail, as she snapped off each light. When she reached the hall, she repeated the operation, in each reception-room. But, while she knew that she was doing the only sensible thing, she vaguely felt that she was in the grip of a horrible fatalism, which ordained that she should deliberately blind the house.

Even as the thought crossed her mind, the oasis of light in which she lingered was suddenly swallowed up by the surrounding shadows.

The eclipse was but momentary. With the next second, the hall flickered back again; but the work of demoralization was done.

The house had given a signal to the night. So intense was her fear of it, that Helen felt a mad temptation to rush out into the night, and take her chance in the open.

Captain Bean would give her shelter; his cottage was only a short distance away, if she cut through the plantation. The trees no longer held any terror, while she welcomed the thought of the wind and the rain dashing in her face. The savage landscape had become sanctuary, because the real menace was inside – hidden somewhere in the house.

She was on the point of unbolting the front door, when she remembered the helpless inmates of the Summit. Lady Warren, the Professor, and Mrs Oates were unable to protect themselves. When the maniac found his prey had escaped, he might wreak his disappointed fury upon them.

With the feeling that she was going to her doom, she returned to the landing. After a pause, to recover her nerve, she pushed open the door of the blue room.

Nothing appeared to have happened in her absence. Lady Warren sat humped up, in bed, almost swamped in ultramarine shadows.

'You've been gone a long time, girl,' she grumbled. 'Light the candles.'

There were no candle-sticks, so Helen dropped melted wax upon a marble mantel-shelf, and fixed two candles in position, before the mirror.

'They look like corpse-candles,' remarked Lady Warren. 'I want more. All of them.'

'No, we must keep some in reserve,' Helen told her.

'They'll last our time.'

Although the finality of the old woman's voice

sounded ominous, Helen was aware of a change in her. Her eyes were opened wider, and they gleamed with satisfaction, as she held up one bony hand.

'Look,' she cried. 'It doesn't shake. Feel how strong my fingers are.'

As Helen crossed to the bed, she forgot her invitation.

'I'm going to sleep,' she said. 'Don't leave me, girl.'

She closed her lids, and very soon her chest rose and fell with the regularity of a machine, while her breathing was quiet and regular. It was an extraordinary example of concentration and will-power, for Helen was sure that she had actually lost consciousness.

'I wonder if I shall see her awake again,' she thought.

She felt as though the last link of connection with the finite world had snapped. In the course of the night, she had witnessed the temporary flight of so many spirits, each slipping away, where she could not follow them.

Although her own lids seemed weighted with lead, she, alone, was awake in a sleep-bound world. She had to watch.

Suddenly she sprang to her feet, her heart leaping with terror. Someone was moving in the dressing-room. She distinctly heard the sound of footsteps, and stealthy movements.

Stealing across the carpet, she opened the door

an inch, revealing a crack of light, blocked by the dark figure of a man.

Even as criminals give themselves up to justice, she knew she could bear no longer the torture of suspense. Screwed up to a pitch of desperate courage, she flung open the door.

To her joy and surprise, she saw the Professor standing at the small bureau. At the sight of the familiar formal figure, everything grew safe and normal again. The house ceased to sway and gape, as the walls closed together, in the security of a fortress.

She fought to keep back her tears, for the relief of having rational company again was almost overpowering. But the Professor's glacial eye checked her hysteria.

'Oh, Professor,' she cried. 'I'm so glad you're all right again.'

'I am unaware that anything was wrong.' The Professor spoke coldly. 'I merely procured some necessary sleep.'

Something had annoyed him, for he frowned as he opened another empty drawer.

'Where is the nurse?' he asked.

'Gone,' replied Helen, feeling incapable of lucid explanation.

'Where has she gone?'

'I don't know. Perhaps, she's hiding in the house.'

'She – or someone else – has taken something of mine which I am anxious to find. But it doesn't matter, for the present.'

As though struck by some recollection, he turned round and faced Helen.

'How did you get back to the house?' he inquired.

She did not understand the question.

'When?' she asked.

'When you were coming through the plantation. I heard your footsteps. I waited . . . But you never came.'

At the words, suddenly – Helen knew.

'*You*,' she said.

CHAPTER 31

GOOD HUNTING

Helen *knew* . . .

The acid of terror cleared the scum from her mind, so that she felt a rush of mental activity. Every cell in her brain seemed to be on fire, as – in a succession of films, reeling through her mind – she saw the whole story, in one ghastly moment of realization.

Professor Warren had strangled those five girls, even as his father, before him, had murdered two servants. Only Lady Warren knew of the crimes and had fulfilled the Law. After the death of the second maid, she had shot her husband.

But, since then, she had grown old, and her brain had greened, so that she babbled of trees. She believed it to be her repulsive duty to shoot the son – but she kept putting it off. After each murder, she told herself that it was the last; and, still, there had been another one.

But with the arrival of a new girl at the house she had smelt danger. Her suspicions were aroused, and she tried to protect Helen. She wanted to keep her in her room, where she would be safe.

When she had asked the Professor to light her

321

cigarette, she had looked into his eyes, and seen the too-familiar glow, which warned her that he had committed another crime. Yet, in spite of this, she wished to save him from the Police. She had got up, secretly, and searched his room, for any incriminating object.

Then – she had found the scarf.

Helen felt a rush of gratitude towards the old woman, even though nothing mattered now.

'I'm glad I took her part against the nurse,' she thought.

Yet Nurse Barker, too, was revealed in a new light – as deserving of pity, rather than suspicion. The spirit of an intensely feminine woman – craving admiration – had been encased in an unattractive envelope. Her natural instincts had been thwarted, and she had soured into a bully.

Helen wondered uneasily what had become of her. At this crisis, she longed for the aid of the masculine strength and brutality from which she had shrunk.

She looked at the Professor with incredulous eyes. Outwardly, she saw no change in him. He appeared grey, bleak, and intellectual – a civilized product, used to dressing-gongs and finger-bowls. His formal evening-dress completed the illusion, while his voice had preserved its frigid academic accent.

She could not fear him – as he was. What she dreaded, in every fibre and bone, was the transformation to come. She remembered how Dr Parry had told her that, in between his fits of mania, the criminal was normal.

She did her best to hold him in this familiar guise.

'What were you looking for?' she asked, forcing her voice to sound casual.

'A white silk scarf.'

The reply drained the blood from her heart.

'I saw it in Lady Warren's drawer,' she said quickly. 'I'll get it for you.'

For a second a mad hope flared up that she might yet make a dash into the open. It died instantly, as the Professor shook his head.

'Don't go. Where are the others?'

'Mrs Oates is drunk, and Miss Warren is locked in her room,' replied Helen.

A faint smile of satisfaction flickered around his lips.

'Good,' he said. 'At last I have you, alone.'

His voice was still so detached and self-controlled that Helen did her best to keep him interested.

'Did *you* plan this?' she asked.

'Yes,' replied the Professor, 'and no. I merely touched the spring which set the machinery in motion. It has been rather amusing to sit still and watch others clearing the way for me.'

Helen remembered the drift of the conversation at dinner. The Professor had proved his theory that a clever man could direct the actions of his fellows. He had set himself up above God.

'What do you mean?' she asked, only anxious to stave off the horror which might lurk behind the next second.

'This,' replied the Professor, as though he were demonstrating a thesis. 'I could have got rid of – interference – by exercising my ingenuity. It presented quite a pretty mental problem. But my knowledge of human nature prompted a subtler – and simpler – method . . . To begin with, I tipped Rice of a dog for sale. When he brought it home, I knew I had several members of the household tied to the same string.'

'Go on, do,' gasped Helen, thinking only of the passage of time.

'Need I explain?' The Professor was impatient with her stupidity. 'You saw how it worked out, according to plan. I counted on my sister's cowardice and aversion to animals, also on each dominant passion asserting itself.'

'It sounds very clever.' Helen licked her dry lips as she strove to think of another question. 'And – and I suppose you left the key in the cellar door, on purpose?'

Again the Professor frowned, in irritation.

'That explains itself,' he said. 'It is obvious that Mrs Oates would find a way to get rid of her husband.'

'Yes, of course . . . Did you count, too, on Nurse Barker running away?'

The Professor made a wry face.

'Ah, there, I confess my plan broke down,' he said. 'I calculated that you, in your impulsive folly, would clear her from the board. You let me down. I had to do my own preliminary work.'

He spoke almost like a schoolmaster rebuking an idle pupil.

Helen knew that there was one word she must not mention; yet in her anxiety to know Nurse Barker's fate, she risked its implication.

'How?' she asked. 'Did you hurt her?'

To her relief, the Professor began his explanation calmly.

'Only temporarily. She is gagged and bound, under her bed. She must remain, as a witness, to testify that she was attacked from behind, by some unseen assailant, and that I was unconscious, during, during—'

His tone blurred, and his mind seemed to lose grip. To Helen's horror, she saw that his fingers were beginning to twitch.

'Why did you turn the Police away?' she asked with the desperate feeling that she was trying to feed a furnace with flimsy sheets of tissue-paper.

'Because they will pay me a visit, tomorrow.' Again the Professor's fingers curled. 'Their time will be wasted. Yet no clever man underrates the intelligence of others. During two visits to the same house, they might notice some trifle which I have overlooked . . . But we are wasting time.'

Helen knew that the moment had come. It could be staved off no longer. The house was locked, so that she had no hope of rescue. Yet she asked another question.

'Why do you want to kill me?'

Perhaps, in some unconscious way, the Professor's

theory was being demonstrated, in that tense interlude. Just as it was in Helen's nature, to explore, his own instinct was to satisfy any wish for knowledge.

'I consider it is my duty,' he told her. 'I have a scientist's dread of an ever-increasing population and a shrinking food supply. Superfluous women should be suppressed.'

Helen did not know what she was waiting for, when the end was so certain.

'Why am I superfluous?' she asked wildly.

'Because you have neither beauty, nor brains, nor any positively useful quality, to pass on to posterity. You are refuse. Unskilled labour, in an over-crowded market. One extra mouth to feed. So – I am going to kill you.'

'How?' whispered Helen. 'Like the others?'

'Yes. It won't hurt you, if you don't resist.'

'But you hurt Ceridwen.'

'Ceridwen?' He frowned at the recollection. 'I was disappointed. I was waiting for you . . . She gave me trouble, for I had to carry her over to Bean. I did not want the Police coming here. All unnecessary fatigue.'

Helen stood her ground, as the Professor advanced a pace. She had the feeling that any sudden action might touch the spring, which unloosed that ghastly transformation.

He, for his part, seemed in no hurry to begin. He looked around him, with an air of satisfaction.

'We are quiet here,' he said. 'I am glad I waited

. . . I was on the point of doing it, three times, this evening. In the plantation – when you were asleep, on the stairs – and when you were alone in your room. But I remembered that there might be interference.'

He rubbed his fingers reflectively, as though massaging them.

'This is hereditary,' he explained. 'When I was a boy I saw my father cut a girl's throat, with a dinner knife. At the time I was sick, and filled with actual horror. But, years later, the seed bore fruit.'

A green light was glowing behind his eyes. His face was melting into unfamiliar lines – changing before her eyes. Yet Helen recognized it! Before her floated the seared face of evil desire.

'Besides,' he added, 'I like to *kill*.'

They stood, facing each other, only divided by a few yards. Then, frantic with terror, Helen turned and rushed into his bedroom.

He followed her, his features working and his fingers hooked into claws.

'You can't escape me,' he said. 'The door is locked.'

Filled with the panic of a coursed creature, Helen broke away from him. She did not know who she was – or where she was – or what she did. All around her, and within, was noise and confusion – a reeling red mist – a sound like the crack of a whip.

Suddenly she realized that the end had really come. She was penned in a corner, while the Professor closed her in. He was so near that she could almost see her reflection mirrored in his eyes.

But, before he could touch her, his body sagged, as though some vital spring had snapped, and he crashed heavily down upon the carpet, and lay still.

Looking up, Helen saw Lady Warren standing in the doorway, holding a revolver in her hand. She wore the white fleecy jacket of a nice old lady, decorated with rose ribbons. One gay pink bow dangled at the end of a spike of grey hair.

As the girl reached her, she collapsed in her arms. The effort of her shot had been too great. Yet she smiled with the grim satisfaction of a sportsman who had exterminated vermin, although her last words expressed a certain regret.

'I've done it . . . But – fifty years too late.'